CW01217662

SALMON MOON
RIVER OF NO RETURN

A NELLIE BURNS AND MOONSHINE MYSTERY

Novels by Julie Weston

NELLIE BURNS AND MOONSHINE MYSTERY SERIES:

Moonshadows

Basque Moon

Moonscape

Miners' Moon

Moon Bones

Salmon Moon

SALMON MOON
RIVER OF NO RETURN

A NELLIE BURNS AND MOONSHINE MYSTERY

JULIE WESTON

Encircle Publications,
Farmington, Maine, U.S.A.

SALMON MOON Copyright © 2024 Julie Weston

Paperback ISBN-13: 978-1-64599-581-4
Hardcover ISBN-13: 978-1-64599-582-1
Ebook ISBN-13: 978-1-64599-583-8

Library of Congress Control Number: 2024948887

ALL RIGHTS RESERVED. In accordance with the U.S. Copyright Act of 1976, no part of this publication may be reproduced, distributed, or transmitted in any form or by any means, or stored in a database or retrieval system, without prior written permission of the publisher, Encircle Publications, Farmington, ME.

This book is a work of fiction. All names, characters, places and events are either products of the author's imagination or are used fictitiously.

Cover and book design by Deirdre Wait
Cover image: painting by Marie Haasch Whitesel

Author photograph by Gerry Morrison

Published by:

Encircle Publications
PO Box 187
Farmington, ME 04938

info@encirclepub.com
http://encirclepub.com

*For love of Idaho rivers and
the Frank Church River of No Return Wilderness*

Chapter 1

FRANKIE KNEW STEPPING OUT WITH two men might be riskier than she wanted. So far, neither knew about the other. Norman thought she lived in Twin Falls and worked in a dress shop, sewing. She met him when he picked up a hat for his mother. She wasn't sure what he did for a living, but he seemed to have money enough to treat her nice. James, good-looking with slicked back hair, dark eyes, strong arms, and an arrogant walk, suspected she operated as an informant for the police, and she was as dishonest as he was—out for herself and any money she could make telling on others. How James and Norman ended up in 1924 Idaho as two members in a gang of thieves, she didn't know.

And then she was stuck on a leaking wooden scow, chasing water and rapids down a frightening river. She could see why it was called the River of No Return. The scow was a short boat with a big paddle called a sweep on a long pole at each end. The paddles rested in the water and James used the pole to steer the boat from the back and keep it in line in the front. He ran both sweeps, dodging back and forth in the boat as she curled up on a bench and held on as tight as she could. She didn't have a life preserver, dry pants, or regular boots. She shook like an aspen leaf in a strong breeze. James seemed to know what he was doing, but water sloshed over the sides and in heavy water, came in the front.

When James proposed taking her downriver to meet up with his gang at an abandoned ranch on the Salmon River, she had agreed and then acted the way she thought a gun moll would—a little sassy, smart-mouthed, and knowledgeable. Everybody had read about Al Capone and his henchmen and girls. Instead of a confining dress, she wore men's Levi's and cowboy boots. A warm wool jacket and a flannel shirt completed her river outfit, along with a knit hat and mittens. The mittens struck an odd note, but she wore them anyway. Halfway there, Frankie regretted ever getting involved with James. He really was a criminal, if even a quarter of his stories about moonshine and Canadian liquor were true.

"We'll pick up Norm and head down to Corn Creek. We're gonna meet up with a few more men and round up a herd of cattle waiting in a hidden meadow. Piece of cake!" James, his voice as deep as the wretched river, sounded jubilant. "And I'll have a woman with me. No one else will!" He made it sound like she was the Queen of Sheba.

Frankie knew the Norm he mentioned was her man-friend from her quiet life. James had described him, told her earlier they were meeting Norm, a tall, lanky man with not much hair on top and long arms and big hands. That was Norm to a tee.

James used his whole body, not a small one, to move a sweep and the scow headed for the right side of the river. "Get out!" he yelled. "Pull it in!" Another shout.

Frankie stared at James. Get out? Into the river? She could see it was deep, even as the wooden boat neared the shore. She would sink and maybe never come up. "I can't! It's too deep."

James pushed harder on the sweep. It hit a rock and cracked. "Get out! Catch the boat!"

Frankie didn't let go of her death grip on a wood strut and bench. The boat tilted and water rushed in on the side opposite the shore. She'd have to get out. "James, help me!"

The man leaped from the scow and landed in hip-deep green water. "C'mon! Jump! I'll catch you!" He held his arms out.

Water pouring in would drown her. The deep water by James would drown her. She'd have to trust him to catch her. Frankie climbed up on the tipped edge of the scow. Her left foot slipped but she fell forward, not back. James stepped sideways and let her fling herself into the water. She sank. Even as water covered her head, she knew the river poured into her boots and pulled her down. She tried to lift her head and push against the ground with her feet, which had found a rounded stone.

Before she could bend her legs and shove up, a hand grabbed her jacket and pulled her head into the air. She spewed water and choked. James had saved her, laughing heartily, as if her drowning had been a joke. She wanted to kick him, but her boots wouldn't move because of the river water in them.

James shoved her toward shore while he tried to catch the scow. He was too late. While Frankie tried to get her footing on the rocks along the shore, she saw the current drag the scow back into the river. "Damn it! This is all your fault!" The man frowned and tried to sweep water toward Frankie. By then, she had found her footing and moved onto the shore. She wanted to scream back at him, but she was still choking from the water that had filled her mouth and throat. She crawled on her hands and knees to rough-cut stairs and sat. When she could move, she dumped water out of her boots and wrung her knit hat as dry as she could. Her mittens, water-logged, might as well have been two dead fish.

"Look what you done!" A new voice joined the shouting. Norman. "The boat's gone for good, you idiot!"

Frankie ducked her head. She tucked her hair back into the wet hat. How was she going to explain this to Norm? Or James, for that matter.

By then, James had reached shore and emptied water out of his boots, too. "Aw, cram it. There's a dory in one of them sheds up there. We can go down the river in it. Easier to maneuver, anyway."

"Who's this?" Norm asked. "You didn't say you was gonna bring anyone else to the ranch."

"Frankie. I think you know her. She wanted a little adventure." He chuckled. "Guess she found it. She's not one of those old ladies you hustle for a living."

Frankie had no choice but to look up. "Hi, Norman." She could feel her face flush—an old lady she was not. Had he hustled her? "I thought I'd come along for the ride. I didn't think he would try to drown me." She turned her head to look at the water. "I never saw the Salmon River before."

"You! Frankie! How do you know this law-breaker?" He stepped down the stairs and lifted her up to hold her at arm's length. "You look like a drowned rat." He took her hand. "C'mon up to the house, and I'll get you warm." He glared at James. "Pretty clear, he doesn't give a damn." He helped her along, his arm around her back. He called back to James. "You won't believe what I found up here. We won't need those cattle!"

Frankie had a bad feeling about the two of them—a thief and a hustler?—and about being at the sagging and desolate ranch across the field. She wished she were home sewing someone's dress and putting together a straw hat for a summer party.

"Frankie can get warm on her own," James said. "Help me get the dory down here. I can't do it alone." He ignored Frankie and headed toward a shed. "What did you find?" he called back.

Frankie held onto Norm's hands. "Help me," she pleaded. He shook her loose.

"I'll show you our prize in a bit," he said. Then he followed James.

When Frankie entered the derelict cabin, she could hardly believe the mess. Norm must have searched the whole place, pulled stuffing from cushions, emptied cupboards, flung newspapers around. She removed her boots and wrung the socks out. The cabin was warm, so she curled up on the ruined couch. She wasn't a sissy. Her mother taught her sewing before she left for good. Frankie's father had taught her to ride and hunt on their farm near Twin Falls before he went broke. He had warned her about bad men. She half-dozed until she heard the men's voices.

"You didn't need to bang Bull on the head." Voices came closer. That was James. "He was a friend of mine."

"Oh yes, I did," Norm answered. "Didn't you see the stack of gold I found? He tried to stab me, so I stopped him with a shovel. He'll come 'round. And if he doesn't, who cares? Nobody ever comes to this wreck of a ranch." The voices stopped as they reached the doorway. "We just need to tie him up. Make sure he doesn't tell anyone about us."

Frankie pretended to be asleep. Gold, she thought. Maybe the whole trip was worth it after all.

"You only gave me a peek. Where's the rest?" James asked. "I want to see this treasure. It might be fool's gold, knowing Bull as I do. He's quite a joker."

The men entered the door, their boots stomping. One squished. That was James.

"What'd you do? Tear the place apart?"

"Once I found the gold in that shed, I decided there might be more treasure hidden—cash or hooch or whatever."

"Find anything else?"

"You could let a girl get some rest," Frankie said. She wanted to be part of the conversation, so she gave up her pretend sleep. "What's this bull guy? He wasn't very clean."

Norman left the room and came back with a box. The box looked old and worn and cattywampus. "Here," he said, pulling off the lid. James and Frankie both stood up to peer in. It was filled with paper. Frankie recognized it before James did—money. Norman pulled out a sheaf and tossed it up. "See what I mean?"

James almost cackled. "Don't spill it! How much? Is it real?" He grabbed at the papers and stuffed what he could in his pocket.

Frankie wanted a handful for herself. Through the open door, though, she heard men's shouts. She rushed to the door. "Pick it up," she called. "There's a long boat out there, coming in. Looks like a big guy jumping off."

James joined her. "I know him. Trouble. Frankie, you sneak out the back and down to the horses. Norman, where's the gold? We need to hide it and play dumb about Bull."

"In the horse shed in a pack in the straw. I hit Bull with a shovel, Frankie. See if he's still out and hit him again if he's not. Then cover him up."

James pulled a revolver from the back waistband of his pants. Frankie wondered where that came from. She looked at Norm. He motioned for her to go, so she did. Norm followed her out and watched. She slipped around to the shed. As she entered, she heard gunshots. She ducked and hid in a hay stall, briefly. Then she found three horses in another shed.

She recognized Norm's horse. So that was how he got there. She looked around and found his blanket and saddle. After she slung both onto the horse, a man stumbled into the stall. She could see where blood had run down and over his neck. He was a big man, and he pointed a shotgun at her.

"You're a girl." He lowered the gun, and she grabbed it. She heard a shout outside. A horseman had ridden in. James, Norman, a rider, a second boat—Frankie felt overwhelmed. She swung around and aimed the gun out the window of the shed. The man behind her grabbed it. They wrestled, Frankie pulling and the man jerking back, and it went off. The man fell back as if he had been shot. She leaned over and pushed at him. He didn't move. The shovel hit must have been harder than Norm thought. She piled handfuls of straw over him, as he appeared unlikely to get up. After casting a glance out the window again, she hid the gun under a load of hay. Then she led the horse toward the door. The gold.

Frankie poked through the rest of the straw and found a dirty pack. It was filled with rocks, nuggets, and small leather bags. Empty saddlebags hung from a hook with other horse tack. A cupboard with no door held horse medications, liniment, and brushes in heaps, as chaotic as the cabin had been.

Two more shots rang out. James dashed into the shed, leaving the door standing open.

"That Bull man came in from there," Frankie said and pointed to his legs. "Where is Norman?"

"The man from the boat killed Norm. I shot him." James acted like shooting a man happened every day. "C'mon. We gotta get outta here. Find the gold?" He grabbed the pack that Frankie held. She had fastened the flap on top.

"That's it." The saddlebags sat beside her in the straw. "That's Norm's horse. I'm not getting on that water again." She turned to James. "Norman? Dead? He was keeping watch." Poor Norman, or maybe he was as bad as James. Frankie sagged against the horse. She gestured toward the straw heaped over the fallen man. "You tie him up. I don't want to touch him. I'm going on the horse. I can meet you in Challis. Wait for me there. Please."

Chapter 2

A FRUMPY AUTOMOBILE PULLED UP TO the open Last Chance Ranch gate, and a man jumped out. He strode rapidly up the lavender field to the ranch, puffing as he arrived at the front porch. Nellie Burns had been trying out her new camera, perched on a tripod and aimed at aspen trees beside the house, their leaves fluttering in a slight breeze. She put aside her black cloth that she used to cover her head and focus.

"Hello," she said. "Can I help you?" Strangers didn't often arrive at Last Chance, not since she and Charlie had moved in when they returned from their sojourn at Lava Hot Springs after their wedding. She had relished the quiet, not missing the bustle of either Ketchum or Hailey.

"Is Nellie Burns here?" The man's voice was loud, as if she were hard of hearing. He stared at her. His livery clothes looked dated and mussed. He calmed down somewhat but still had the look of a man in a hurry. "I got a message for her. Are you Miss Burns?"

"Yes, I am." Nellie had decided to keep and use her own name. Charlie had supported her, although several people had been upset—Goldie, her previous landlady, for one. "What can I do for you?" The warm fall seemed to be never ending. "Would you like a glass of lemonade?"

"No need for lemonade. I'm kinda in a hurry." The man gawked and wiped his mouth. He pulled out a large blue handkerchief and wiped his forehead.

Nellie looked around. The yellow and orange aspen leaves quaked and a few scattered clouds crossed the sun, bringing a spate of cold air. She shivered.

"The sheriff is hurt. If you want to see him, you gotta go up to Stanley and get on the river. That's the fastest way. The road north is closed down 'cause of that fire that started this summer and won't seem to let go." The man glanced north as if he could see smoke. "Sam the barkeep called the hotel in Ketchum, and they sent me to find you. I'm supposed to take you to Stanley, and Sam will take you to a riverboat. He rounded up a nurse to go with."

"But, but…" Charlie hurt! He couldn't be. They just got married. "How was he hurt?" No sense in telling the messenger her situation, alone and taking care of Rosy Kipling's place. Then she realized—she must go! "What will I need? How far and which river?"

"The Salmon, of course. Dress warm. It'll be darned cold on the river." He glanced at her split skirt. "I'd pack some pants and boots if you have any. Sweater. Hat. Scarf." He shook his head, as if he were guessing at what a woman might need on a river. He wiped his neck and stuffed the handkerchief back in his pants pocket.

Wringing her hands, Nellie knew she needed to be quick and calm. "Bring your auto down the road to the front porch. I'll get ready as fast as I can. Should I pack some food?"

The man had already turned away and headed to the gate. Nellie packed her camera and tripod. She'd take it, but maybe leave it with the barkeep if the riverboat was too open and it would get wet. She wished she still had her smaller Premo, the one smashed up at the ghost town of Vienna in the summer. As much as she loved her new camera, it was awkward to carry.

Nellie dashed into the house, hurried up the stairs off the living room and grabbed a bag to put in a few items of clothes. She glanced at the bed. She hadn't even made it after Charlie had left for town early the day before. And now he was hurt in some godforsaken place along the Salmon River! But he must be alive, or the barkeep would have said differently, wouldn't he? She choked and sniffed back tears. Since Rosy Kipling, her friend the retired miner, his sister, and the boys had moved back to town for school and work, she and Charlie had been staying at the ranch for a few weeks.

Moonie, her black Lab dog, almost tripped her as she ran back down the stairs with her bag. "Moonshine! You need to come with me!" She grabbed a leash from the kitchen and stuffed it in a canvas bag along with jerky, biscuits, a half loaf of bread, a hunk of ham, and two bottles of seltzer. A canteen—she would need that, too. Nell rushed to a back shed and pulled out a canteen, two blankets, two towels, her boots, a flashlight, her revolver, some bullets, a coat and scarf, and a knit hat. A lot of good that would do on the river. Her new-to-her auto was parked at the back of the ranch. She should drive that instead of riding with the messenger. She'd feel better with her own transportation.

The messenger stood beside his black car, a DeSoto, Nell could see. Maybe 1920 or thereabouts. "I will drive my own automobile. I know where the barkeep is. You don't need to take me. You can go back to the hotel."

"That barkeep said to bring ya. That deputy in town said the same thing."

"Rosy? He knows about this? Why didn't he come to get me?"

"And you can't take that dog in this auto. It ain't mine. It belongs to the hotel. No animals."

"You go back to that hotel. Call Sam the barkeep and tell him I'll drive to the sal— uh, the café and meet him there. You tell Rosy he can come with me or not. It depends on what's going on in Ketchum and Hailey, but I'd like him with me, if he can. Tell Rosy I am leaving the ranch, and he needs to lock it up."

The man sputtered. He shrugged his shoulders. "Women!" he muttered and climbed back into his DeSoto, turned it in a circle, and left.

Nellie carried her gear to her own auto, whistled for Moonshine, and he climbed in. "Keep a good thought for Charlie," she said to her dog and hugged him.

* * * * *

Nellie had rarely driven the auto Gwynn Campbell, the sheep rancher, gave to her. It was a different model than the automobiles she knew—Rosy Kipling's and Henry the miner's. Henry lived at the boarding house where she had lived until she and Charlie married. Even so, she wanted her own means of locomotion and a way to bring Charlie home if he was in bad shape. It wasn't long since he recovered from the beating he'd taken that summer.

Focusing on packing the gear helped her avoid breaking down at yet another emergency that came in this wild state of central Idaho. Charlie, her husband now and the sheriff of Blaine County, insisted she keep the gasoline tank full, so she didn't have that worry. It was a good rule to follow while they lived at Rosy's Last Chance Ranch, six miles out of Ketchum.

The auto started up right away when Nellie pressed the

starter—no cranking, thank goodness. She headed out the road and turned north at the end of the driveway. "Hang on, honey. I'm coming." Her drive up to Galena Lodge passed quickly with no other autos and no animals. She stopped at the store to tell Lulu about her mission.

"Lulu," Nell called, as she climbed down from her seat.

The Galena store proprietor stepped out onto the porch. She had a western look—split skirt, leather vest, and a denim blue shirt. Her hair was pulled back from her face.

"I'm on my way to Stanley. Charlie's been hurt down river. I'm going to catch a boat, I think. What will I need? Moonie is with me, too."

"Do you have your revolver?" Lulu was always no nonsense.

"Yes, but maybe I need more ammo. Do you have any?"

"Yep. Come on in." Lulu turned on her heel and re-entered the store. "Do you know if the boatman has life preservers for you and your dog? The river will be low and travel by boat a little risky. How far are you going?"

"I don't know. I got word from a driver for the hotel—maybe Guyer Hot Springs in Ketchum. He said he'd take me, but I wanted my own automobile."

Lulu stepped behind the counter and unlocked a metal box. She pulled out a dozen bullets wrapped in a paper sleeve. "Here you go." Then she opened the door of a storage closet. "I got two preservers you can take. If you don't need 'em, just bring 'em back. I won't charge you." She sorted out two cloth covered cork pieces with straps. "You'll need an extra strap or two for Moonshine. He won't like it, but it'll keep him from sinking. If you end up in the water, keep your feet down river and this cork piece behind your head." Lulu demonstrated the life preservers.

Nell knew how to swim. The cork preservers looked awkward and seemed heavy to her. "I don't think we'll need these."

"You will if you get conked on a rock or swept off with a branch. Take 'em." She piled the preservers on the counter. "Got a flashlight? First aid kit? Warm hat and gloves? Extra socks?"

Nell nodded with each question. "Not a first aid kit, but the driver said a nurse would be coming, too. Is your telephone working? I'm going to try Rosy. I left a message with the hotel driver, but who knows if he's reliable."

With Lulu's nod, Nell stepped over to the telephone on the back wall and clicked for the operator. She asked for the sheriff's office in Ketchum and then Hailey. No answer at either place. "Operator, this is Nellie Burns. Keep trying for Rosy Kipling please. Tell him I'm on my way to Stanley in my own automobile, and tell him to try to telephone Sam the barkeep at the café, or Lulu here at Galena to get my message. Thanks."

Lulu helped carry the life preservers and ammo to Nell's auto. "I'll get you a canvas bag for your revolver to keep it dry." She ran back in and returned with a bag.

"I hope I don't need it, Lulu, but it's a good idea to take the bag, just in case."

"Have you thought about how you'll get the sheriff back upriver if he's hurt?"

"No. I'm hoping Rosy can come to Stanley and take the road down river. It's faster than the river itself is what I understand and maybe closed because of fires." Nell climbed behind the steering wheel, patted Moonie, and waved to Lulu. "Thanks for your help, Lulu. I hope to see you in a day or two."

Nell headed for the steep pass, glad it was a clear fall day. From the top, she let the auto go fast, but then had to slow to take the curves. The aspens had lost most of their leaves and the bare branches reached like white bones. The few leaves left fluttered brown or black on a light wind, denoting cold days and nights. Moonshine slept in the passenger seat. He raised his head when Nellie drove up to the saloon/café.

Sam the barkeep strode out the door. "Glad you finally made it, Miss Burns, er, Miss Nell. Took your time."

"I got here as soon as I could, Sam. Maybe the hotel messenger took his time." She had stepped out of the auto. "I didn't think he could get here any faster than I could. Tell me what you know and where I should be going, please."

"Come in and wet your whistle. No one's around this time of day."

The saloon looked the same as usual, except empty. The wood floor was scraped with cowboy boots and spurs and maybe a few miners' boots, too. It felt lonely without any cowboys at the bar. She glanced toward the room to the side where she had sat with her Chinese friend, Sammy Ah Kee, and Joe High Sing in the summer. It, too, was empty. Sun splashed through the front door and front windows, revealing dust.

"Water or beer?"

"Water, please. Could I fill my canteen as well and a jar for my dog?"

"Sure." Sam pushed through the swinging doors into the kitchen and came back with a glass of water for her and a beer for himself. He sat at the bar. Nellie stood.

"A cowboy came in all dusty and wore out. He said he'd ridden up from Challis and that Sheriff Azgo had been in a tussle at one of the ranches down that way. He said the sheriff was hurt and so was another man. A second man took a horse and left. A third man grabbed a small dory and paddled his way down the river and disappeared. This was yesterday and last night."

"Did he say why the sheriff was there? I understood Charlie was coming up to Stanley to deal with some horse thieves or maybe cattle thieves. He wasn't too clear when he stopped by on his way from Ketchum to Stanley yesterday afternoon, but he said he might be away one night. He didn't say anything about going down river. It was supposed to be around the Yankee Fork Dredge." She sipped her water, worried. She should have gone with him. "Did you see him?"

"I saw him as he came through in his official automobile. That was what I thought, too. He said he was going to Custer. Hoped he'd be back in a few hours' time but wasn't clear on what the problem was. That road is pretty bad, though. Just drivin' it would take some time. And there was a flood back that way this spring, so it mighta been broken up completely."

"So where did the cowboy say Charlie was?"

"There's an old rancher down the river a ways. He pretty much runs a few cattle and sheep, has a house of sorts and some outbuildings. Who knows? Maybe he pans for gold now and then and gets a little dust. The cowboy wasn't clear about what happened. Said someone's gotta take the riverboat down and pick up the two men before they bleed to death."

Nellie shuddered. This sounded too familiar. "Isn't there anyone else at whatever ranch it is to take care of wounded men?" She placed the empty glass on the bar. "And why didn't the cowboy help out?"

"Sounded like he was hell-bent on gettin' out of there. He didn't stay long here, either. Headed into the hills to one of those dude places."

"Can you tell me how to get to the riverboat? Is it near Custer? Isn't that just a fork and I have to go to the main river somewhere?"

"There's Mormon Landing past Lower Stanley, past Sunbeam Dam—the one the fishermen want to blow up—and past the hot springs. I think someone is waiting for you to arrive. Don't know about your dog, though. The river rats mostly use flat-bottomed boats to go down river. You know it's called the River of No Return."

"Yes, I know. Gwynn said that was because the boats couldn't get back up it."

Sam raised his eyebrows. "Well, that, too."

Nellie filled her canteen and took the jar for Moonshine.

"I think Mormon Landing might be too close. Just keep drivin' until you see a wooden scow pulled in at a beach. It might be as far as Basin Point. You'll have to leave your automobile there." Sam stopped talking and leaned toward Nellie. "Say, I better go with you and bring it back here. No telling what could happen along that road—fires and such."

Indecision made Nellie freeze. Could she trust Sam the barkeep? He'd been helpful in dealing with her mother in the summer, even helped her with trapping a bad man who might have hurt both her mother and her. "All right," she said. She really had no choice. Leaving her auto along a lonely road above the river was not the right thing to do. "Thank you for offering, Sam. I hadn't thought of the danger to my new automobile." She turned to head for the door. "Let's go. I hope the riverboat has waited for me. Does it know I'm coming?"

"No, it just waits for passengers and mail to be loaded up. Scheduled to leave late afternoon, so it'll get to Challis for the night. That's after you get off wherever Charlie is and load him on.

And maybe the other guy."

"But how will I get Charlie back here?"

"I dunno. Just hope he's ready to get on the scow. The trip from there to Challis goes through a canyon. Unless he can ride a horse. Then you two can come the way the cowboy did—rough riding." Sam followed her out the door and locked it. "No new scow for another month, if then. It's gettin' late in the year."

Uh-oh, Nellie thought. She had a bad feeling about this rescue mission. If only she could get to Charlie in time.

"There's a nurse going to go with you," Sam said. "She already left for the scow after the cowboy told me about the tussle. I sent him to tell her to get on her way. So, even if we don't get there in time, she will."

"A nurse? There isn't even a doctor around here. I remember that from this summer when we needed a doctor for Joe High Sing's leg. Why didn't you tell me then?" Nellie opened the door of her auto and climbed in. Sam kept surprising her with new information. What hadn't he told her about the nurse before?

Sam settled in the passenger seat and Moonshine moved to the rear. "I can't take care of no dog."

"Moonshine is coming with me." Nellie would not argue with anyone about that. She would just bring Moonie and ignore any more remonstrances about dogs.

"Janie doesn't stay around here much. She has a place not far from the Middle Fork of the Salmon and only comes in for provisions and a glass of beer from time to time. She kind of rides circuit to the few ranches up that way and fixes up people's wounds and stuff."

"Wounds?" Nellie shifted into gear and drove back to the road going east, through Lower Stanley and beyond. The pavement ended right past the roadhouse where she had stayed the summer before, taking photographs of the heart-stopping views of the Sawtooth Mountains and the River of No Return. She hoped she and Charlie would both return.

* * * * *

Nellie and Sam passed a body of water, a reservoir behind Sunbeam Dam, and found the river scow at a takeout eddy along the river, not far from the road. The boatman still waited. Sam helped her carry her gear down a rocky path to a long flat boat. Two long poles rested, one on either end. "Those're poles with sweeps, uh, big paddles on the ends. The boat ain't all that maneuverable, but the boatmen always seem to know what to do."

The front and back of the scow sported blunt ends. Along the sides, a fence of sorts, made of double sheets of plywood with spacers in between, held onto the goods and passengers. As Nellie neared, she could see the bottom slats and sighed a little relief. Maybe her boots wouldn't get wet. Moonie on his leash kept close to her legs, as if he knew he couldn't escape. Nellie doubted he would like riding in a scow. She wasn't too sure about it, either. Stacks of goods sat mostly in the middle in front of a bench and along the sides.

"Howdy there, little lady. I heard you was comin'. Glad you made it in time." A man helped her climb aboard from one blunt end pulled up on the beach. "I'm Ace, your coach driver." He chuckled into a full mustache and beard. His grin showed one tooth gone, and his pale blue eyes twinkled at her. He motioned to another passenger who sat on the wooden bench fastened to the slats. "This here's Janie. She's used to riding scows, so she can help you get settled. We gotta take off in a few minutes." He said no word about Moonshine.

"Thank you, uh, Ace. I'm Nellie Burns, and this is Moonshine." She stepped hesitatingly to the middle of the boat as it moved up and down with the river water pushing against its sides. "Do you have life preservers? Lulu at the Galena store told me I had to wear one—my dog, too." She eyed the stack of her gear as Sam loaded it over one side.

"Nope. But you go ahead. Janie asked me the same thing. 'Course, she's ridden with me lots of times and never fallen out. I try to be a mite careful when I got passengers, especially women. The men can take care of themselves. I lost one or two of them along the way." He chuckled again, a low melodious sound for a man.

"I'm Janie," said the woman on the bench. She had turned to Nellie. Her hair was white as a swan's and her face as un-wrinkled as a new apple's, her cheeks almost as red. Dark eyes flashed from under a bonnet on her head. "Miss Burns, isn't it? You follow Lulu's advice and put on that cork thing. I just naturally float." She spread her arms to reveal a comfortably plump figure. "You look a little skinny to be floating in this river."

Nellie donned the life preserver, then fitted the other one to Moonie and wrapped the extra strap around him. He didn't fidget, as if he knew this would help him at some point in the boat ride. "All right, I'm ready."

Ace and Sam pushed the scow off the sand and Ace leaped in. He stood by the pole and moved the sweep to get the scow into the current of the river. Nell waved to Sam as he climbed back to her automobile. She hoped she and Charlie would return to it.

Nell rode in the scow as if she were on a horse for the first time;

she hung on wherever she could—the seat, the edge. No pommel. She would have grabbed Janie or Ace if she could without shame. She must reach Charlie lying hurt downriver. She was on the Salmon River, the River of No Return. She hoped that wasn't prescient. The water looked a deep green except when it tumbled over white-topped waves. They curled toward them, and the scow rode stiffly across. Sometimes, the water sloshed across the front and appeared to almost drown Ace, but he kept the boat heading forward in a steady bumpy ride.

Hurry, hurry, she wanted to scream to Ace, the water, the breeze, the air. *Charlie is hurt!*

Along a quiet non-rushing stretch where the water turned dark and deep, Janie stared up a cliff. "Hear that, Miss Burns?"

Beyond the sheets of smooth, glassy water, up and up the gray and silver rocks, Nellie heard a sweet song of descending notes. "Is someone up there?" Who would have climbed those heights?

"It's a bird, a canyon wren." Janie whistled the same dropping cadence.

At one curve of the river, just past a maelstrom of white water when Nellie was certain the scow would sink, Janie pointed to the shore. "Three bears, see? A mother and two cubs. My, they're certainly a blond color, but I think they're black bears. Not many grizzlies around here."

At first, Nellie couldn't find them. Their colors merged with rocks and grasses along the shore. Once she spotted them, watching them cavort near the water calmed her from the fear she experienced in the waves. Ace knew what he was doing and used the sweeps to get the scow back and forth in the water. He swung on them with his whole weight in the rough times.

Except for the stretches of white water where waves and wind brought sheets of river over the front blunt end of the scow, Nell watched the territory they floated through. Steep slopes rose directly from the river. The river must have carved its own path through the landscape. Trees hugged some of the shoreline, and branches from those tilting toward the water could indeed brush a passenger off who didn't watch and duck. Janie warned Nell more than once to lean forward and down. Nell hung onto Moonshine, so he wouldn't land in the water and be lost.

During the rougher stretches, the roar of falling water, waves, and wind kept conversation to a minimum. During the quieter sections, Janie talked about her experiences on the river and at her own ranch near the Middle Fork. She raised a large garden and had brought produce with her so it wouldn't spoil from any killing frosts that showed up while she was gone. After her tuneful canyon wren's song, Janie pointed out other birds and a few small animals drinking from the river. She also showed Nellie the high trail that followed the river for horseback riders and pack trains. "Some of those people won't give up on the gold. The only gold here in this canyon is the scenery—trees, mountains, animals, and such."

Nellie nodded her head. If she had thought the Big Wood River running from Galena down to south of Bellevue was beautiful, this canyon had it beat. The low river was much wider, and there were many wild and scenic portions. Janie told of people trying to dam it and hoped they would not be successful. "That awful Sunbeam Dam has already stopped the salmon and steelhead from swimming to where they want to have babies." She leaned close to Nellie's ear and kept an eye on Ace. "One of these days, they'll set some dynamite and then *kaboom!*" She grinned from ear to ear. "The salmon run is mostly over for the year, but you can still see some of the red Chinook in the water, if you look down into it."

Ace rarely spoke, just warning of rapids ahead or tree branches. He moved from front to back or back to front to push the poles and dodge tree roots from fallen behemoths. As Sam the barkeep had said, this driver knew his job well. Janie whispered he was one of the best. The river channel rocks dried out from being above water. Between large boulders, white water coursed below high mountain slopes, some growing ponderosa with their yellow bark and alpine firs, green in the sunlight. Others swept up to rocky scarfs with golden grasses. On each side of the river, rocks and brush lined up, almost forming a fence.

The smells of river, pine needles and sap, and dried grasses waving in the breezes intoxicated Nellie. Her head swiveled back and forth trying to see everything. Her hands ached from hanging on so tightly. She opened and closed her fists to get the blood flowing again. She could ride like this forever, if not for her fear for Charlie and twinges in the falling water.

Finally, the driver pushed on a sweep and the scow pulled into a quiet gravelly cove, such a relief for Nellie from the rapids, booming water, and intense sky, although scraps of white and pewter clouds had begun to move above the canyon walls. Nell stripped off the cork preservers from herself and Moonshine and placed them with her gear. She was glad to have a warm coat and pulled it out of her bag to don. Janie did the same. A cool wind had begun to flow downriver with the water.

"Where is the sheriff? Where do we go?" She wanted to hustle off the scow and head up the riverbank.

"Slow up, ladies," Ace said. "We gotta pull the boat up. Take that leather bag and fill it with water. A hurt man needs water."

He gestured to a pack under the wooden bench.

"Do you know how he is hurt?" Janie asked. "I packed whatever I had handy on my horse, but no one said the cause of the hurt."

"Heard he shot a man, and the man shot back. Heard there was two men."

Someone had taken care to place stone steps from the river landing up a middling steep slope. Janie climbed first and then Nellie. She turned to confirm that Ace wasn't leaving. He puttered around the boat, re-securing loads, and seemed content to wait. At the top of the rough stairs, Nellie stopped to see where she and Janie were going. A low house with a mossy roof that sagged, matched by several outbuildings, lay back up against a group of trees. Behind the trees, mostly evergreen, overgrown fields in amber and beige extended several hundred feet. She remembered a horseman had left this place and ridden to Stanley.

The two women strode toward the house, picking their way through low shrubs, some sagebrush, and an outgrown, golden field of grass. The river behind them made the only sound, a combination of rushing and bubbling. Nellie and Janie looked at each other. The place seemed totally deserted. No smoke came from the chimney. A gray camp robber bird chattered from its perch on the roof of the low-cut house. The outbuildings had a similar profile and roof. Nothing stirred.

"May as well go in," Janie said. "Doesn't seem to be a soul around."

Chapter 3

"LET'S HOPE THE SHERIFF IS here." Nellie kept glancing at the buildings, hoping not to be surprised by a soul or anything else. She thought of the bears they had seen along the river. She wouldn't be surprised to see a mountain lion or wolf in this wild place. The house didn't appear lived in for some time.

"Let me go first, Janie. It is my husband we are seeking. I don't want anything to happen to you."

"Your husband! I thought it was a sheriff." Janie touched Nellie's shoulder.

"He is the sheriff. He gets called into all sorts of strange goings-on. I think the federal marshal sent him on this river chase." That may mean bootlegging but there was no evidence of a still or a stack of wood for a fire or anyone tending a fire. Charlie had been assigned to other bootlegging crimes in the Stanley Basin and in North Idaho.

Nellie walked up three steps to a front door. She knocked first, not expecting any response. The door opened just as she was going to knock again. There stood Charlie.

Sheriff Asteguigoiri stepped out to greet Nellie. He wore no hat, and his black hair stood in clumps around his head. He might have been sleeping.

"Charlie!" Nell threw her arms around him. "You aren't dead!" She couldn't stop a few tears from leaking but straightened as Janie joined them. "Janie, this is Sheriff Azgo from Ketchum and Hailey. His true last name is Asteguigoiri, Basque. Azgo is easier. He is also my husband." She tried to keep a note of pride out of her voice.

"How do you do, Sheriff?" Janie held out her hand, which Charlie took. "I'm Janie Altman. We understood you were hurt and in dire condition. Obviously, you are not." She shifted to look beyond the front door. "Is anyone else?" She put her hands on her hips. "Why was I called then?"

The sheriff smiled, first at Nell, and then at the nurse. "I *was* in dire condition, Miss Janie. However, I managed to take care of the wounds. Would you please look at me and see if I did anything wrong?"

"Where?" both women asked at once.

"My leg." He used his head to gesture inside the house. "The other person in dire condition no longer needs help." He grasped Nellie's hand. "My right shoulder might need tending, too."

Charlie let the two women go first through the door into a place that smelled of mold, ancient beer, spoiled meat, and dirty clothes. The smell had fouled the room into which they walked, stopped by the chaos of overturned furniture, animal horns, wrinkled newspaper pages, and detritus of undetermined origins. Nellie held her nose. Moonshine followed her and then began sniffing. He followed his nose around the room.

"Goodness," Janie said. "It looks as if a war took place in here." She turned one way and another. "And smells like it, too."

Charlie glanced around. "I tried to clean up some of the mess, but there was no end." He pulled a chair close so he could sit on it.

He lifted a pantleg to his knee. A bandage, slightly soiled, covered his whole lower leg. "A bullet went through the back side," he said. Moonie sat down in front of the sheriff.

"Is there any clean water in this… this house?" Janie stooped to study Charlie's leg.

"We have the water bag the scow driver had us bring up. I think it's for drinking, though. Are you thirsty, Charlie? I'll get it. I left it on the porch." Nellie made her way through the mess, stepped through the door, and retrieved the bag from the front steps. When she returned, she heard Charlie and Janie discussing a well in the side yard. Nellie held out the bag.

"Not really. We had well water in here for a while. The well is outside." He looked at the nurse. "You can use that bag of water to prime the pump, but there is a bucket beside the pump. Should have water in it."

"Where is the other person?" Nellie asked. "Should I take a photograph?"

"Do you have your camera here?"

"It's in the boat, wrapped in canvas. I can go get it."

The sheriff scratched his head. "Yes, I guess it would not hurt to have one. He has one bullet hole, from a gun other than mine, and looks like pellets from a shotgun in his back. The man who shot him escaped. Somehow, the body got dragged into one of the bedrooms."

"What did the cowboy have to do with all this?"

"He had been out hunting and heard the gunfire. Glad he came by, so I could get a message to you. I knew you would worry, but I did not think you would come."

Janie came back in carrying a pan of water. "Take off that bandage, please, or I can do it if you don't know how."

"You do it, Janie. If his hands have been in this mess, they are probably filthy." Nellie moved around to stand behind Charlie. She wanted to see the wound, see how bad it was. She had heard horror stories about gangrene. "How's your hand?" He had been beaten by two men seeking gold Charlie had taken into custody over the summer, gold that Sammy Ah Kee and Nellie had found in the ghost town of Vienna.

The sheriff's right hand went up. He curled his fingers into a fist. "It is fine, thanks to that sheepherder friend of yours."

With a gentle touch, Janie pulled the bandage away from the wound on the back of the sheriff's calf. The gauze had stuck to dried blood, but the wound itself appeared all right, just a dark hole in the back of his leg. Two holes, Nellie noted—one in and one out of Charlie's muscular calf. She wanted to stroke his leg, but that didn't seem appropriate right then. Janie had already pulled from her kit a flask and a bottle of red liquid. She brushed whiskey on the wound and then the red. Charlie cringed but said nothing. Then Janie folded new bandaging material. She dusted crushed oregano leaves on the white surface and wrapped the whole thing around the sheriff's leg. "Here, Nellie. Hold this in place while I tape it closed."

Nellie knelt. Working on the back of Charlie's leg was awkward, but between the two of them, they secured the new bandaging. He stood up. Nellie noted he was careful not to put too much weight on his left leg. Poor man. The life of a sheriff, she supposed, glad she took photos instead of serving as a deputy. She smiled to herself. Charlie had given her the choice a while ago. She had chosen wife and photographer.

"Now what about your shoulder?" Nellie glanced at Janie, who seemed competent at taking care of bullet wounds.

Charlie nodded and winced. "Yes, my shoulder. I do not know if the bullet is still there. Feels like it might be."

"Sit down again, Sheriff, so I can have a look," Janie said. Moonie had climbed beside the sheriff on the seedy couch and licked the man's arm.

"How is it?" Nell had noticed Charlie's bloody shirt. He took it off and a large welt on his right side looked tender to the touch. She raised her eyebrows at Janie.

Janie turned to Nellie. She lifted one hand and turned it back and forth. "I'll see what I can do."

Nellie wished she had Sammy Ah Kee and his Chinese bark salve to treat the wounds. Either that or Alphonso the sheepherder's greens. She hurried out to the well site. The pump arm helped her locate it right away. The overgrown field looked as if it hadn't been watered in some time. The grasses shone gold in the sunshine and smelled of fall, unlike the house. She was glad to be outside for a few moments. She poured water from a bucket into the pump top, fought to move the handle up and down, and within a few tries, water trickled and then poured out. Nell had found what looked to be an unused pan from the house and filled it. She re-filled the bucket and left it for the next priming.

Back in the living area, Janie worked around Charlie's shoulder. Nell pulled a rickety chair up to his legs and sat. "What happened here?"

Charlie grimaced as Janie cleaned the wound and poured more whiskey on it. "Three people. Part of a gang involved in poaching, cattle and sheep rustling, and—what else?—bootlegging. That was why the federal marshal called on me to take to the river." His words slowed when Janie pressed hard, and he winced.

"I came down the river with another boatman. He had been

sent word that they were holed up here. He left me off, and I found a nest of vipers." He stopped, cringing when Janie pressed the wound with a damp cloth. A dribble of blood came out, but that was all. Nell could hardly bear to watch.

"I know this hurts, Mr. Sheriff, but we need to stop any infection. It'll cool down in a bit. Want some laudanum?" Janie turned to her kit and brought out a brown bottle and held it up.

"No!" Charlie was emphatic.

"It'll help the pain," Janie said.

"I need to be alert," he said. "I know what that does." He looked at Nell with pleading in his eyes.

Nell knew what he meant. "Never mind, Janie. I'll find a clean stick outside, and he can chomp down on that." Again, she went outside and brought in a twig she had torn off a tree. She handed it to Charlie. "Where are the other men?"

The sheriff motioned with his good arm to the rest of the house. He removed the stick from his mouth. "One is dead. One took off in a wooden boat, a dory. The third one hid in one of the outbuildings. I think it might have been a woman. I only caught a glimpse. There are horses in a shed out there." He replaced the stick because Janie again pressed on his shoulder, rubbing salve into it.

"All right, Sheriff. Let's look at the back of that shoulder. Can you lean forward?" Janie waited for the man to struggle to shift forward. "It looks clean from this side. The back will tell us if the bullet is still in there or went out." She turned to Nell. "I've worked on another Basque or two near the Middle Fork with their sheep. Your husband's accent sounds like theirs."

"I can feel something moving around." Charlie put the stick back between his teeth.

Nellie also winced, knowing her husband was in deep pain. Janie leaned over to get a good look. "It might be a bone moving," she said. "There's an exit wound, almost as clean as the entry. I'll put bandages on both sides with some of my medicine. They should heal up all right." She probed around in her kit again. "Can you lift your arm?"

Charlie tried, but without success. His face crumpled.

"Well, it might be broken inside, or maybe just a muscle got torn. We'll know in a day or two. Hold still now. This is gonna hurt again." Janie brushed more of the whiskey and red liquid on the back of Charlie's shoulder. "If this had been the other side of your chest, you'd be dead by now." She hummed as she worked, unfolding bandages, dusting oregano, and spreading honey with a spoon on the wounds, getting out tape. "Here, missus, you hold onto the bandage, while I get it secured so it won't move around."

When Janie finished, Nellie helped Charlie sit up straight. "Should I find the other man?"

Charlie nodded and closed his eyes. Janie's treatments had worn him out. When Nell was sure he'd said what he had to say, she scooted toward the door. Janie settled in near Charles. "You go find the body," she whispered. Moonshine jumped down from the couch. He nosed Nellie's hand.

What if the other man was still alive? She wondered how Charlie knew he was dead. She guessed if there had been a shootout, it might have been obvious. The smell was so rank in the rest of the house, Nell held a hankie up to her nose. She pressed down a hallway and saw a closed door. Maybe it held another bedroom. She opened it, but the door hit against an obstacle, keeping it from opening all the way. There was enough space for her to see what caused the effort, a folded-up rug, it appeared. By looking down and a little sideways, she saw a man's bloodied shirt and torso splayed on the floor. This must be the dead man. Time to get her camera.

Back through the overgrown field Nellie went. At the scow, she woke up the driver who had relaxed on the bench with a pillow behind his head. "Mr. Ace, the sheriff is wounded but Janie has taken care of him. We need your help in bringing down another man. Er, he's… not alive." She poked under the bench and found her canvas-covered camera. "I need to take some photographs."

"Better hurry up. I got a schedule to keep, you know." Ace grumped around and then accompanied Nellie up to the house.

"My god, what happened here? This used to be a fine place!"

The sheriff sat upright on a bolster. He introduced himself to the boatman and said he would need help moving a dead man. When the two of them managed to drag the body to the living area, they left it on the floor. Enough sun came through undraped windows to lighten the scene for Nellie. She fixed her tripod and camera to take photographs. When she brought out the black cloth and put it over her head, she heard Ace say, "Just like the real thing." She took some umbrage but said nothing. She had a job to do. When she was finished, she said, "We need to get a blanket from one of those dreadful rooms and wrap him. Ace is in a hurry to get going." She motioned to Janie to help. Soon they returned, blanket in hand. Nell laid it out on the floor. Ace rolled the body into it.

"Are y'all comin' with me?" Ace took hold of the wrapping by the legs. He didn't look happy. "If so, it means I'm gettin' pretty loaded up with this here… man. I'll need to shuffle some stuff around."

"Not sure yet," Charlie said. He had sat again, clearly feeling the wounds and treatment. "I need information about whether there is a trail between here and downriver. Would a wooden boat be able to go the same places as your scow? The murderer took off in a dory." He stood to pick up the other end of the wrapped body. "I want to catch up with him, but I am not sure if it would be faster to go with you, or to ride downriver."

Ace motioned toward the river. "I'm supposed to be at Challis tonight. It's—" he said and screwed his mouth sideways— "I'd say another 2-3 hours of travel, but not quite so much white water." He thought again. "There's a sorta road from here to there. Don't know if it's closed because of the fire. It was." He leaned over and began to pull the body. "You take the legs."

Charlie aimed toward the man's legs. "Do you know him?" he asked.

Ace shook his head. "Nope. Never seen him before. He never rode my scow."

"Oh no you don't." Janie had gathered her kit together and returned to the group. "You'll tear them bandages and the bleeding will start up again." She turned to Nellie. "Don't let him carry that… that wrapping down to the boat."

Nellie looked from Janie to Charlie. Then she went to Ace. "I'll take a leg. You take the other. We'll drag him down and leave his head to follow. He won't care."

* * * * *

Nellie had asked Janie to check the sheds for horses. Ace turned down Nell's help and pulled the dead man across the overgrown field to the boat, the wrapping helping to ease his burden. He had hurried the women along. "I can't waste the whole afternoon here, ya know."

Before long, Janie came back to the ranch house. Nellie had packed up what she found of the sheriff's gear: Stetson, revolver, belt, canvas jacket, pack, boots, and socks. She would have to get those back on his feet. The afternoon sun shone through the clouded windows, so the bare floors had warmed. Charlie returned to the couch and closed his eyes. Nellie sat on the broken chair with Moonie at her feet and nearly fell asleep herself.

"We have another problem," Janie announced as she entered the doorway.

"Horses or no horses?" Charlie asked.

"There's horses all right, but something else, too." Janie's face had lost its pink cheeks. "Another…" she said and looked back out the door. "In the second shed. Half covered with straw. I think he's alive, but the sheriff should check him out."

It took Nellie a moment to realize what Janie said. "Another man? With bullets?" She felt it must be true—they had found a nest of vipers. "Do you know him?" That was a nonsensical question.

"Turns out, I do." Janie took a big breath. "Known as Bull Brady. An old-timer known to show up in Stanley or Custer from time to time. Selling meat usually." Janie sat down next to Charlie. "The only time I've seen so much mayhem was during the Spanish flu. At least then the men died of disease. Not bullets, or in Bull's case, something slammed against his head." She closed her eyes. After a moment, she opened them. "I'm used to wounds, but two dead men at once are too much. At least the sheriff is alive. Guess we better wake him and see what he wants to do. Ace won't wait much longer."

"How soon before another boat comes?" Nell tried to organize her thoughts. They couldn't all ride in the scow, that was clear. Janie knew it, too.

"Could be tomorrow. Could be come spring. Who knows?" Janie shrugged. "Let me see how your Charlie is doing."

"I am doing fine." Charles had opened his eyes and watched the two women. "A little green at this point." He smiled at them. Neither returned his quip.

"Charlie, there's another man in the shed outside, maybe dead. Janie just found him. A Bull Brady." Nell sat next to Charlie. "How is your shoulder?" She reached to touch the bandage. He would need another shirt. "Did you hear us talking?" She knew she sounded like a mother hen.

Janie motioned Nell to move. She lifted the bandage she had taped to his shoulder in front. "No more bleeding." She fastened the bandage again. "You look like those pictures in the Great War. Now the back."

The sheriff turned sideways, and Janie helped loosen that bandage. "No swelling, so far. How does your shoulder feel?"

"Aches. Still feels like a piece of bone or bullet is in there."

"Pretty sure there's no bullet. You'll have to have a doc look at it, maybe in Salmon."

"Nell," Charlie said and turned to her. "Let us get a photo of Bull out in the shed. Then get him down to the boat."

Loud steps on the stairs preceded Ace's voice. "Y'all comin' or do I have to leave you here?" He stood in the open doorway.

Nell, Charlie, and Janie looked at each other and then the scow driver.

Nell spoke first. "We have another body for the boat. Bull Brady. In a shed." She motioned toward the outside. "He might be alive."

"I know Bull. Dropped him off right here. Picked him up, too. What happened to him? Poison hisself with some of that bootleg liquor he liked?" He began to chuckle and stopped when no one else laughed.

Charlie gestured to Janie.

"No, Ace, he managed to bang himself on his head. The back of his head." Janie blinked her eyes, maybe holding back tears. "Those cusses musta done it." She lowered her head and then glanced up at Ace. "He was hog-tied and covered with straw. Had a gag tied around his mouth. He might've choked to death."

"Awww, gawd." Ace slapped his hat against his leg. "I can't take another body and the three of you. Sheriff, do you want to come to find the ones that got away?"

"Janie needs to go with you," Nell said. "She can explain what happened."

Charlie opened his mouth, maybe to protest. Nell continued: "The sheriff and I can ride those horses out of here. Sam the barkeep said there was a trail all the way to Salmon from here." He hadn't actually said from the ranch as he hadn't known where they were going. She hoped he wasn't wrong. "Janie can get home from Challis. We can see about finding the murderers." She turned to Charlie. "Can't we?"

The sheriff nodded his head. "There you have it, Ace."

"There's only one saddle in the shed," Janie said. "Two people on one horse might be hard on the sheriff's wounds." Her cheeks had turned pink again. She motioned to Nellie. "He should go on the boat and you and I can ride out."

"Let us see about the man in the shed," Charlie said. "If he is still alive, you will need to accompany him." He stood and motioned for Ace to go with him to the shed. "Nell, you and Janie should saddle up the horse and find a rope to trail the other one with us. We cannot leave it here to starve."

"What about Moonie? He can't go on the boat without me." Nell turned to Ace. "Do you think he can do the trail with us?"

Ace studied the dog. "I can take him. He's a nice dog, one I'd like to have."

Nellie bridled. Her dog was staying with her. She might never see Ace again.

Chapter 4

CHARLIE AND ACE SORTED OUT the bodies, one of them barely breathing, and Charlie sent them along with Janie on their way to Challis. Nellie and he had visited the horses. Nellie hated to leave the cabin in such a mess, but on the other hand, she wasn't willing to clean it up. They found what food they could, grabbed their own packs and her camera pack to tie onto the second horse, and prepared to load onto the horse that she and Janie had saddled. The nurse left Nellie a small jar of honey and some oregano to treat Charlie's wounds whenever they stopped long enough to do so, and if there was any bleeding. She took the flask with her.

"You'd better help me up, Charlie. I'll ride behind you." She smiled and patted the back side of her new husband. "That has always been one of my favorite places." When she was settled behind him, she wrapped her arms around his waist. "Does this hurt your shoulder?"

Charlie patted her hand. "You're fine. I like this, too. Ready to go?"

Nellie sighed. "I wish we were going home."

"There is a trail of sorts heading north under that cliff. It may be just a game trail, but we'll head that way anyway."

"Sam the barkeep said there was a trail all the way to Salmon. Who knows if he is right?" Nell called Moonie. He had sniffed his way around the two sheds, then perched near the riverbank. Maybe he had wanted to ride the scow again. The trail began to climb immediately. Nellie wondered if the weight of two of them would hamper the horse's progress. It seemed clear this was not going to be an easy ride. On the other hand, it couldn't be too far to Challis, the town that supplied the miners along the river. If the trail petered out, they could always find the road and travel along it. She had seen no sign of smoke anywhere. Either the fire had burned itself out, or it raged much higher than near the river. Maybe Rosy would meet them at Challis.

After more than an hour, Nellie felt the sheriff sagging in the saddle. "Let's stop, Charlie. My behind is getting chafed on the horse blanket. Maybe we should shift the saddle and all to the other horse." By then, they were traveling close to the primitive area—a huge roadless part of Idaho set aside by the federal government to protect its wildness. They had seen no sign of another person so far.

Charlie did stop and lifted himself off the saddle. He gave Nellie a hand down and then walked back and forth to stretch out tired muscles. Moonshine's tongue hung out, so Nellie gave him water from the canteen.

"I saw the sweep boat pass us on the river, Nell. Maybe we should have squeezed onto it instead of riding out." He looked at the sky. "It will get dark before we reach Challis. We will have to stop and make do for the night." He found a fallen log and sat on it, his shoulders bent forward.

"Let me look at your shoulder and leg. I want to see if riding the horse shifted the bandages."

With his left hand, Charlie unbuttoned the shirt and pulled the sleeve on his right shoulder down. A wince of pain crossed his face. "It still feels as if something is in there."

"Janie told me she pressed some oregano into the wound and that this honey would act to stop any infection." That was what Nellie had surmised from Janie's cryptic instructions. Honey was so sticky, it seemed the wrong thing to put on anything except a biscuit. Nell loosened the bandage and looked at the hole. It had bled slightly and appeared swollen and red. That couldn't be good. She found a stick and dug it into the honey jar. Then she swabbed the wound with honey and re-fastened the bandage. "Let me look at the back, too." She repeated her ministrations. "How about your leg?"

Charlie pulled his pant leg up. The white bandage looked discolored, but when Nellie pulled it open, the wound looked clean. There was no red line going up the leg, something Janie had told her to watch for. She decided to leave it alone and pulled down the pant leg. "Let's rest a while. We could even stay here for the night," she suggested. Charlie looked done in. So did Moonshine. She probably should have let him ride with Janie.

The river flowed near where they had stopped. Nellie took her canteen to the water's edge, stepped out into a shallow spot, and filled it. She could at least make tea or coffee for Charlie if she could get a small fire started. Janie had instructed him to drink water—lots of it. There weren't a lot of trees along the river, and the hillside sloped steeply—riding the horse down to the river had been tricky. Even so, several flat spots opened up beside the water to make suitable spots to camp. She lifted the saddle and blanket off the horse, released the bit, and tied a rope to the halter and around a large branch of a bush without leaves. The horse could graze on grass and dropped leaves. The other horse had already begun eating. Charlie didn't complain, so she unloosed his pack, pulling out a tarp and sleeping bag. At least, now they could share the bag. She chuckled to herself. Our first camping trip, she thought.

Rustling in the woods farther down the river drew her attention. What now? Charlie had moved from sitting on the log to sitting below it and resting his head on his knees. He might have been asleep, as he didn't respond to the rustling. Moonie sat up and stared toward the noises. He, too, didn't seem inclined to move.

A bear wandered down to the water. His fur was mostly black and his size was about the same as the bear she had seen when she was with Janie. Nellie glanced back up the hillside to see if there were any cubs. She had noticed red fish but paid them no mind. The bear certainly did. He grabbed until he brought up a large fish, needing two paws to hold onto it. The animal either hadn't seen or smelled them, or it was more interested in fishing. She could see why. Now that she watched the river closely, she saw it teeming with fish. Fins broke the surface and what she had assumed was white water turned out to be fish churning. This must be what Ace had termed a "salmon run." All the fish were stuck below Sunbeam Dam. No wonder the fishermen wanted to blow it up.

Chapter 5

THE NEXT MORNING, CHARLIE AWOKE early, feeling better. Nell had put together a meal of sorts the night before and insisted he lie on the tarp and under the sleeping bag after they ate. At his direction the night before, she hung whatever food they had left in a tree by using a rope slung over a branch and pulling it high. Moonshine laid next to Charlie and soon both were asleep. Nellie reorganized the various packs to go on the horse they had ridden, and then she walked around the campsite. The bear had disappeared, but the red fish had not. She remembered how she and Pearl, the saloon girl, had caught fish to eat the year before. Those had not been red nor as large. Nell missed a female companion.

Nellie fixed a haphazard breakfast of late summer berries and biscuits and gravy. She saddled the second horse for the sheriff and her to ride. Before they climbed on, she checked Charlie's wounds and spread the last of the honey on both. Charlie's right arm swung easily and his limp was almost gone.

"I think we should climb up to the road, Charlie," Nell said. "It will be easier going and we haven't had a hint of smoke from any fire."

"All right. You are the leader of this cavalcade." Charlie leaned over to pet Moonie. "It will be easier for you, too," he said to the dog. "But no charging of animals." Moonshine had been sniffing around but made no move to wander off.

There were game trails to follow up the slopes and eventually to the dirt and gravel road. No smoke. Their horses moved faster. Nellie cautioned Charlie to rein in twice because she thought she caught movement below the road. The second time, she slid off and called Moonshine to investigate with her. He sniffed the air and looked at her. "You don't smell anything?" Nell walked back to Charlie on the horse. "I'm sure I saw something move along below us—almost as if someone or something is following us. Something fairly large, like a deer or an elk, or maybe a bear."

"I have not seen anything." Charlie held out his left arm to help Nell back on the horse behind him. "We should move along a little faster to get to Challis."

"What are we going to do there, besides find a doctor to look at your bullet holes?"

"See about following the criminal who shot me and killed the other man at Bull's ranch. And find out what Bull knows about the whole situation, if he is still alive."

After several hours and no more sightings by Nell, Challis came into view—a line of shacks and a few businesses. Its main access wasn't on the main road but along a side road up a long slope. A few wagons lined one side of what could be called a street, along with other horses. No automobiles in sight. A one-story wood building labeled "City Hall" appeared to be the only official location. Other businesses were signed as saloons, an assay office, and hard goods, and a few structures without signs at all.

"This seems more like a wild west place," Nell whispered to Charlie. She slid off the horse, glad to stop riding. Moonie had kept up with them all the way. He climbed to a wood walkway and laid down. "Oh, Moonie! You must be so tired." She sat on the edge of the boardwalk and petted him. "You better join me, my husband. Maybe we can find a café where we could eat." She glanced at the building close by. "After we find out what we can here."

Charlie dismounted and tied both horses to a rail. "I think I would rather ride in an automobile." He rubbed his behind. "Not sure there is anything that modern in this town. I would call it a one-horse town, but there appear to be five or more." He gestured to the street. "I will go in here to see what help we can get and if Ace and Janie came along."

Nell decided to walk up the road and peer into what might be a café and ask about a doctor. Moonshine followed her. The only valuable item on their horses was her camera pack and she decided to carry it. A large sign over one door said "Saloon." A cardboard sign on the door said "Eats." The door was locked. Across the road, another house-sized structure appeared to be open. Its door stood wide and a horse was tied to a railing in front.

A glance down the street told her Charlie was still inside the City Hall. She crossed and passed the horse, noticing it was sweating. Whoever owned it must have just ridden in. She entered the small café. A woman, younger than herself, sat at a table. No one else was around.

"Is this a café?" Nell asked.

"Or something," the woman answered. "I'm hoping to get some food. Do you know this place?"

"No. I expected it to be a real town. I understood it to be where miners got supplies and so on. Do you? Is there a doctor around? We expected to meet some people on a riverboat."

The woman tossed her head of hair. She looked as worn out as Nellie felt. "Ain't seen anyone on a boat. Man who was here said he'd get me some food." Two saddlebags hung over another chair at the table.

The woman wore rough pants, a red blouse, and a scuffed jacket. Her chestnut-colored long hair might have once been wrapped on her head but had fallen to her neck. Her skin was dusty as were her clothes. Nell realized her own clothes were just as dusty. She was glad for her bobbed hair and split skirt. At least she looked like a woman and not something the wind had blown in.

A backdoor slammed and a man appeared carrying a large pot with a lid. "Ah, two customers. A bonanza day!"

Nell hoped he wasn't the cook. He wore no hat and his dark hair hung in greasy strings. His apron that might once have been white was the color of the street outside. His hands appeared clean, but the rest of him made her shudder. "What's in the pot?"

"Chili. Red hot chili. And iffen you don't like the spice, I can serve you some bread."

He placed the pot on a stove back behind a counter.

The woman spoke up. "I'll take some chili. I like it hot. Some bread and butter, too."

"Gotta heat it up. Left over from a barbecue at the town park a couple nights ago." He whistled as he set about getting out bowls, spoons, and bread. He pulled open what might have been an icebox and brought out a loaf of bread. The bread, at least, looked tempting.

"Another customer!" The cook glanced at the door.

Nellie turned and there stood Charlie. She waved him in and gestured to a table for the two of them. "There is chili and bread. Spicy."

Charlie glanced at the woman and joined Nell. He faced her and said in a low voice. "Ace and Janie are here. Bull is still alive. There's a make-shift doctor's office up at the top of this, uh, street. Keep an eye out for them. We can eat if you're hungry. Then we better find them."

"No, let's go now. The chili isn't even hot yet." And maybe, she thought to herself, they could find another place to eat. "There was a barbecue at the town park a few days ago." She nodded to the cook. "That's where the chili came from." The spices probably kept it from spoiling.

Charlie and Nell stood up. "Nice to talk to you, Miss…?" Nellie said to the woman, hoping to get a name. She nodded but said nothing.

Outside, Charlie gestured to the horses. "Walk or ride?"

"Let's walk. What else did you learn?"

"A man in a dory stopped by, but then kept going. There was a lawman of sorts at the City Hall. He said he warned the rower that the river gets rough from here on out to Riggins, especially in the primitive canyon on the way. The man said he'd stop at Salmon or North Fork."

"How far is that?"

"About eighty river miles to Salmon. The road keeps going and gets better, so we could ride the horses." Dust spiraled behind them as they trod up the street. "Salmon is a real town."

"Is Ace still here? I think I'd rather chance the boat. My backside aches! I'm out of practice riding a horse." She had to skip to keep up with Charlie. "Maybe we could find an automobile. That lawman might have one tucked up somewhere."

"Where do you suppose that woman came from?" Charlie asked. "I wonder if she is the third person who rode off from Bull's ranch. I never did get a good look at her, and I was not sure if it was a her or a him."

"We looked like two dusty peas in a pod," Nell said. "I think she'd ridden hard, just as we did. She seems young, trying to act older." Or like a man, Nellie thought.

They reached a half-rock, half-wood building, on the weary side of upkeep. Above the porch, a sign said "Doc Office." Through a window, Nell could see a dentist-type chair. She hoped this was a real doctor and not a tooth-puller. Charlie knocked, then opened the door, which led into a spartan room with two straight-backed chairs and no one in it. He crossed the room and knocked on the door on the other side. Again, without waiting, he opened that door. Nell saw an examining table and heard several voices, Janie among them.

"Wait outside, please," one of the voices said. A man.

"We are here to see Bull Brady. How is he doing? I am the sheriff from Blaine County."

Nell hovered behind Charlie, trying to glimpse Janie. Her voice floated out.

"Oh, Sheriff. So glad you're here. Is Miss Burns with you? Bull's not too good."

Nellie squeezed herself around Charlie and stepped into the room. She walked to Janie and gave her a hug. "I hope you are all right," she whispered to the nurse. Ace sat on a chair beside the door. A man with a buttoned jacket and canvas pants stood by the examining table where Bull lay. His eyes were closed. He looked dead, except for a flush on his neck and face.

"I can't treat this man with all of you in here. Get out! Sheriff, you can stay." He turned to Janie. "You can stay, too."

"I guess that means you and I have to leave, Ace," Nell said.

She turned to go out the door into the stark room. "I have some questions for you, anyway."

Ace and Nell sat on the two chairs, one of which tilted half sideways. Nell took that one. She was afraid it would collapse under Ace. "Where are you headed next?"

"I intended to get to Salmon by tomorrow, but I didn't want to leave Bull here by himself." Ace stretched his legs out in front of him. "Janie said she'd stay, but she probably needs to get to Salmon, too, to get back to Stanley." He lowered his head. "I got that dead body, too. It ain't goin' to smell so good in a bit."

"We might want to go with you. After Salmon, where do you boat?" Nell decided to stand. Sitting made her uncomfortable. "The sheriff wants to follow the dory with the killer in it. Did you see him?"

"Yeah. He moved along pretty well. Don't think I'd want to be in that tiny boat in the white water coming up. I don't think I'll have any trouble. I done it dozens of times. I know what to look out for. Doubt if he does." He lifted his arms and yawned. "I've heard of that James fellow. He's slick as they come. He sells moonshine up and down the river to everyone he finds. I'm not surprised he's a thief besides." Ace looked as weary as he sounded. "I could use some sleep. We just kept a'comin' until late. Figured I owed it to Bull to get him to the doc here." He pulled his legs in and tapped his heels.

A huge yowl interrupted their conversation. "*Get me outta here!*" Within a couple of seconds, the door opened and the large man who had been lying on the examining table burst through it. "I ain't gonna stay here! Someone stole all my money. I'm a-goin' after 'em!"

Ace stood up. "Easy up, Bull. You ain't in any shape to go

anywhere." The boatman stood even taller than Bull. Ace held his arms up, and Bull slid to a stop.

"What're you doin' here, Ace?"

"I brought you down in my scow, you ornery sheephead! Calm down! We gotta sort this out, and I gotta get back on my boat."

Charlie came out the door followed by the doctor and Janie. Janie looked fit to spit on the now-vertical patient. "Bull, shut up. Get back in there. Doc needs to check you out. You'll be weaker than a calf in about five minutes." Her voice remained under control while Ace and Bull yelled at each other. Hers was the one the patient listened to.

"All right, Janie." Bull almost fell forward. "I'm ready to fall down right now."

Janie grabbed his arm and led him back into the examining room. Bull sat on the table. The others followed them in. Nellie stayed in a corner, out of the way. She wasn't much help, but she didn't want to miss anything.

"Bull, as long as you are up and awake, you better tell me what happened. I am the sheriff from Blaine County and was ordered up here to find a bootlegging bunch of cattle thieves at your place. What do you know about them?"

Bull's face, which had been red, turned purple. Nellie was afraid he would pass out again. "I ain't got nothin' to do with them. I just told 'em they could stay at my ranch for a day or two if they'd bring me some food and liquor. Bastards, all of 'em."

"Who were they?"

"I only knowed one—James Murray. Too high-fallutin' to go by Jimmie. We've been pals off and on over the years. He likes to hunt and brought me a deer or elk from time to time. I didn't know he was a cattle thief! He sure as hell is a thief, though. I gotta find him and get my money back! That partner of his stole a whole bag of gold I been savin' up to cash in. Then I'd fix up my place and retire." His face had a woebegone look and the color gradually diminished until he was almost pale. A tear slid along his cheekbone. "Damn blast it!"

Nell couldn't help feeling sorry for him. His shoulders sagged and he began to tilt sideways. Janie stepped in and sat down beside him. She took up his wrist and felt for his pulse. Then she wiped his face with a damp white towel. It came away with a dirty splotch on it.

The doctor made no move to do anything. Charlie listened and nodded his head. "One of the others was killed. The third one rode a horse out from one of your sheds and we think headed this way. It might have been a woman. Do you know?"

Bull shook his head. He lifted his head. "Can't feel sorry one of 'em is dead. They tried to kill me." He closed his eyes. If Janie hadn't been sitting next to him, he might have laid down again. She moved and helped him down. He appeared to go to sleep.

"This man will be all right," the doctor said. "Unless he tries to chase out of here again. I can keep him for a couple of days until he gets his strength back. Janie here did all the right things." He stepped back from the table. "Find a blanket, will you, Janie? We'll just leave him right here a while. The rest of you can get out."

Charlie hung back. "Does this town have a coroner or a morgue?" Nellie waited with him for the answer.

"Morgue is the butcher shop—just like in Hailey. You're probably familiar with that." The doctor joined the sheriff and Nell at the door to his examining room. "The coroner rides circuit. I can send a telegram to Salmon and get him here, so the body doesn't spoil in the meantime."

Nell tried not to shudder. She had seen plenty of dead bodies, but they had by and large been prepared for a funeral. The ones in the butcher shop morgue in Hailey had looked not much different than the slabs of meat hanging from hooks, except they were covered. She followed Charlie out the door.

Out on the porch, Charlie stood with Nellie and Ace. "We found out something, but not much. Ace, do you know who James Murray is? Do you think he can get through with that dory he took?"

Ace's hair stood up on his head. Nellie thought he looked as well-worn as the man who brought in the chili to the café. The boatman probably needed a good sleep before he headed out again, maybe with Charlie, Janie, and her with him. There was the dead man, too. She shuddered and glanced around. First, they must find the "morgue."

"I know a James, probably the same one. He's a no-good good-for-nothin'. Slick salesman, I've heard. He peddles moonshine up and down central Idaho and sometimes into Montana. Sounds like a thief as well. I think Bull might know more than he's lettin' on. They were thick as thieves—" he said and stopped and gave a short grunt "—fits them to a tee, don't it?" He pulled his hand through his hair and then patted it down. His shoulders sagged, not unlike Bull. "They had a fallin' out not too long ago. Maybe over moonshine, maybe over that gold. James might've planned on grabbing it and running besides stealing some cattle up near Salmon. There's been a hullaballoo about cattle thieves all summer. Probably why they called you in, Sheriff. Not much law around here, specially in the little towns and backcountry."

Janie spoke up. "Let's get that dead man taken care of. I heard the doc. The butcher shop should be around here someplace."

Ace's eyes grew big as a deer's.

Janie noticed. "Ace, the butcher shop has a cold room, I'm sure. We'll leave the man in it until the coroner comes. We don't want him lying out on the boat much longer. Do you? Then the three of us can ride with you. I've really got to get back to my place. I can find a ride of some sort in Salmon." She turned to Charlie. "While we're here, let's have the doc look at your wounds, Sheriff. You don't seem to be limping anymore."

Charlie nodded his head. "Good idea, Janie. Nell took care of me, and I am doing better, but we are out of honey." He shifted around to Nellie and put his arm around her back. "Pretty soon, you can be a nurse, too."

Janie laughed. "You got plenty of honey, Sheriff." She winked at Nellie and went back into the office to round the doctor up for Charlie.

"Ace, you should find a place to take a nap before we all load to go down-river, if you will take us." Charlie followed Janie into the building.

"Let's find the butcher store." Nellie thought she should try to arrange something while the other two were in with the doctor. She didn't want to be a nurse.

Ace sighed. "Yeah, people die all the time, even in a bitty town like this one. I'm not sure where it is. You could go back to the town hall and find out. I'll walk with you and go to my scow. I need a little shuteye, like the sheriff says. You all can come with me. We'll work it out one way or another. While you're looking, I'll see if we can find the fellow's name in his clothes."

Chapter 6

FRANKIE TRIED TO IGNORE THE snoopy woman who sat down in the café near her. The town of Challis sure wasn't much. The river snaked by it a fair distance away. She had already ridden on Norman's horse twice to see if James was there. No luck.

When that man who came to Bull's ranch walked into the café, she wanted to shout "Murderer!" But she didn't want to give herself away. She tried to ignore the two but, at the same time, listen to what he said. All she could gather was a reference to Bull. That did not bode well. When they stood up to leave, Frankie pretended she didn't hear the woman's question. After the door slammed, Frankie hurried to a dirty window to see where they went and watched as they walked up the hill.

Frankie sagged from exhaustion and hunger. The cook returned to serve the chili, which was too spicy. Bread helped. She was sad about Norman but there was nothing she could do about him, except to make sure that man paid for what he did. In the meantime, she needed to hook up with James and get down river. She patted her saddlebags. Maybe the cook would let her take some bread with her.

As Frankie tied her saddlebags back onto Norman's horse, four people strode down the hill—two women and two men, all looking the worse for wear, like her. The café woman, a short plumper one, a bearded man, and the murderer. "You shot Norman!" she shouted, unable to keep her mouth shut. "You should be arrested."

All four stopped. The tall man stared at Frankie. She turned to mount up.

"I thought you looked familiar." He stopped her from mounting. "You were at Bull's ranch and rode away." His hand gripped her arm.

Frankie tried to free herself from his iron grip. "Let me go!"

"Where is your other friend? The one who escaped in a dory." The tall man pulled out a badge. "I am Sheriff Asteguigoiri, in charge in these parts right now. He shot a man at Bull's ranch and maybe you both tried to kill Bull."

Frankie jerked her arm again. "*You* killed Norm. James said so. I heard the gunshots." She wanted to spit in his face, but the badge scared her. What would a gun moll do? Lie. Pretend. She lowered her head and stopped trying to free herself. She squeezed out some tears and snuffled.

The café woman stepped over to her. "We're going to find the morgue and put your Norman in it. Come with us." She put her arm around Frankie's shoulder. The sheriff released his grip.

"What is your name?" he asked.

"I'm Frankie. Frances Bingham." He'd find out anyway, Frankie thought.

"You are under arrest, Miss Bingham," the sheriff said.

"What for? I didn't do anything!"

"As an accomplice to murder and attempted murder. You can accompany us to the morgue. I'll need to take a statement from you. Then we will take you with us to Salmon to be charged there. In the meantime, we will leave the horses with authorities here." He untied the animal from the railing.

"Wait! Those are my saddlebags with my things in them and my bread." Now her tears were real. "You can't take them."

"Charlie, let her get her bags. She had them with her in the café. That can't hurt anyone."

"Check them for a revolver. She may be armed."

Frankie untied the bags. "I don't have no gun. I'm innocent. James made me come with him and nearly drowned me. Norman can tell—" She stopped and grabbed the bags and held them to her chest. "These are mine."

"Hurry up, Sheriff." The bearded man called out. "The man at the office told me where to go. There's already someone in there. They won't be too happy, but if the coroner can get here, they'll get a crew to dig a grave. We got to offload the body from the wagon to deliver him and get back on the river. Janie here arranged for a wagon to pick up, uh, Norman. And then get us to my scow."

"Ace, deliver this horse to the office up there. I will take Nellie and Miss Bingham in the wagon to the butcher shop with Janie. We will meet you at the landing as soon as we can." A man came out of the office to help. Norman's body lay slaunchwise in the wagon, still wrapped in his blanket.

"Let me look. I want to say goodbye." Frankie, the sheriff, and the other women stood by the wagon. Frankie knelt and uncovered Norman's head. Her face sagged. He wasn't cleaned up and was being left alone and would be buried in a pauper's grave. He didn't deserve that. He had been sweet to her and saved her after she nearly drowned. Now he was an empty husk. She guessed he wouldn't care anymore. She kissed his forehead and her tears dropped on his face. Now, she was in trouble, and he had been part of it. She covered his head. No more tears for him. They would be for herself.

Chapter 7

WITH CHARLIE BESIDE HER ON the bench in the scow, Nellie relaxed enough to enjoy watching the passing scenery. When their boat hit white water, she grabbed Charlie rather than the rope holding their bench in place on the boat. The land on either side steepened into cliffs. At the same time, the river course narrowed as it rushed along its route to the sea. Bright red salmon colored the water beneath them in the less wild spots. In the frothy waves, she watched salmon jump up almost like ocean mammals as in pictures she'd seen in magazines. Janie commented from time to time about birds and small animals along the shore. She and Nellie sat on either side of the sheriff. Ace had joked about a "thorn between two roses."

The woman from the café, Frankie something, sat on the floor of the scow. She had secured her saddlebags to the bench with leather ties. She hung onto the bench itself when the scow moved through bumpy water. Ace had assured all of them that the water from Challis to Salmon was mostly calm, and then Nellie had relaxed her hold to take pleasure in the ride and look about herself. She leaned forward to inspect the opposite side of the river from where Janie pointed out a bighorn sheep. Her peripheral sight had caught an irregular shape. "Look!

Charlie! Ace! Is that a dory along there?"

By the time the two men turned their heads, the scow was deep into a giant wave. Ace pushed on the rear sweep where he stood managing the forward motion. Nellie saw that the tumble of waves continued as far as she could see ahead. She lost sight of the dory immediately and tried to hang onto Charlie's arm. Moonshine had leaped up when she shouted about the dory along the shore. The scow bounced off a house-sized rock and shot forward into what looked like a hole in the water. Its head dove and a heavy swath of green and white water poured across the four passengers. Waves on either side rocked the scow up and down and back and forth like a wooden top in a maelstrom.

Nellie lost her grip on Charlie. She grabbed for the rope she had used earlier. She missed. Another wave hit her from the side and her body lifted up and forward. Her cork life preserver threatened to pull off over her head. Her hand found her pack and grabbed at it, but it leaped along with her. Before she could take a breath, she felt herself flying over the side of the scow and saw Moonshine beside her.

With her free hand, she grabbed a strap on his cork jacket. All she could hear and see was all-white water, dark churning waves. She pulled in a huge breath and her head went under into a deep silence. She tried to keep hold of her pack and Moonie. She held her breath as long as she could. Green surrounded her as did bubbles and froth. *Charlie*, she screamed in her head. Images of him holding her against his strong chest flowed through her mind—when she was pulled up from the hole in Craters of the Moon, on their honeymoon at Lava Hot Springs. She wanted to sink into his arms, feel his strength, and rest. Her head bobbed back up in the air, all the images drowned behind her, and she coughed and choked out water. "Feet first," Lulu's voice echoed in her head. She struggled to turn around in the churning river. The sound filled her head as water sluiced into her mouth. Something slippery passed her face and then her legs. "Ewww!"

Fish. They wouldn't hurt her. Nellie stretched her legs in front of her and felt the cork hold her head up. She spit out water. Moonie rode beside her on his cork jacket. She held on to him as tight as she could, but the waves continued to rock her in directions she didn't want to go. She tried to find the boat and maybe a helping hand to lift them out. River water continued to flush against her face, so she had to close her mouth, try to breathe through her nose, and take a breath whenever there was a respite. Moonie kept his black head up higher but facing backward, so he didn't have the coughing and choking battle with the whitewater. As long as she held onto him, their cork jackets stabilized them. At last, Nellie felt the river begin to even out and the waves to lower against her face. She searched for the scow beside her. It wasn't there. Of course. It was heavier and may have traveled faster than she did, or a different route through the storm of waves and holes and rocks. No rocks had caused her to spin or sink. No logs had been in sight as they boated down the river.

Even as Nell thought her bumpy float trip would pause, she saw a large black rock in her way. Her feet hit it first and catapulted her over the edge. She lost her grip on Moonie's strap. She and her pack pulled across a flat, rough surface and she felt her cheek scrape on it. The rock crested into a sharp upward bump and she stopped, tangled with her pack. Moonshine rolled beside her, landing with his legs curled beneath him. Nell grabbed his strap again and hugged him. She felt along his legs, and they seemed fine. One ear leaked a line of blood, but he licked her face.

"Oh, Moonshine." Nellie cried, his tongue linking at her tears. The rock shone with water, but mostly, it rolled off the curved top back into the river. Only now could Nell feel how cold she was. The shock of the fall had diminished the stun of the cold, cold water. Again, she looked around to find the scow. It was nowhere in sight. She searched the shore on both sides. No scow. Back up the river, there was nothing but white water and another large boulder, maybe the one the scow had hit. What if it had shattered from the force of hitting it? Stop the panic. No, it didn't, or Charlie, Janie, Frankie, and Ace would be somewhere in the river with her. It must have held together and rammed on down the Salmon River. She inspected the water and saw several red fins and tails rushing upriver to their destiny. Dying.

Moonshine shivered close to Nell. She wrapped her arms around him under the cork. If they stayed cuddled, maybe there would be enough warmth to share. She had to think. No scow. No other boats would be coming down the river, she was sure. It was October. The scow could not come back up. The river of no return. She caught a sob. Stop the panic. What would Charlie do? She wished she had his pack. His pack. As if her words conjured up her wish, she strained her head around above the cork. There it was. She had grabbed his, not hers, when she floundered off the boat. Her pack, with its precious camera and film of the photos she took of the dead man, remained tied to the bench, unless it, too, had been knocked loose. Maybe it had drowned in all the water, but maybe not.

As if things weren't bad enough, rain began to fall, feeling as cold as the river. She watched the drops dimple the water and saw that the waves began to subside somewhat. Not much, but maybe enough to help her get off the rock. She studied the near shore. It wasn't that far away. She leaned over to see if she could see the bottom. Multi-colored rocks wavered in the water. It was definitely there but could be deeper than it looked. The current felt too strong to let her stand up in the river. Swimming seemed out of the question. Her sopping clothes and shoes would pull her down, too, or she would end up washed downriver again.

"What do we do, Moonie?" A drop of blood hit Nellie's hand, the same color as the salmon. She felt her cheek. It was scraped raw and bleeding. She had been too cold to feel any pain.

"*Arp. Arp.*" Moonie's strange bark showed he understood they were in trouble.

Shivering so hard she could barely open Charlie's pack, Nell undid the straps one by one. Inside, a jumble. She reached in to feel around and find what she could identify. First of all, a rope. It was thin and felt strong, maybe composed of some material in addition to flax. She pulled at it and pulled again. It was so long, she had to curl it as it came free of the pack. She looped it around her leg so the rushing water wouldn't catch hold and run it off the rock. "What can we do with this?" she asked Moonshine. Even her slow motions had calmed some of her shivering. She counted the loops. It must be close to twenty feet in length but much heavier, say, than the rope she had thrown when she was caught in the cave in Craters of the Moon.

Nellie eyed the bumpy edge of the rock. The rope could be looped around it. Could she throw it as far as the shore and catch it on a boulder there, one large enough to hold the line taut? Maybe Moonie's legs were strong enough to swim to the shore with the line in his mouth. But then what? Maybe he could hold it taut until she herself could get to shore. Both were worth a try. She had to get off this rock before she died of cold.

With close attention, Nell wrapped one end of the cord around the bump, careful to keep it clear of the sharper edge. She pulled with all her weight and it held, at least for the time being. Then she pushed herself to kneeling and looped the other end with a slip knot to hold the loop. She tried swinging it, paying out the line until it swooped toward the shore, and let go. The rope splashed into the river, short of the rocks and brush. Standing might get it closer, so she pulled in the rope to her, circling her left arm, while still kneeling. Her fear of tumbling back into the river slowed any attempt to stand. Moonshine stood next to her. He had no trouble keeping that position, even with water sluicing across the surface. "All right, then. If I fall, Moonshine, I can hang onto the rope and get back up with you." Maybe. She rose on one boot and then the next. Her stance wobbled. She willed herself to get her balance and feel firm on her feet. Thank heavens the flat rock itself was steady.

"One, two, three!" Nellie circled the loop and paid out the line again, wishing the strength in her arms would return. Again, the rope fell short of the shore. She sank to her knees, gasping from the effort.

"*Arp.*" Moonshine took one loop in his mouth and jerked.

Nell studied the water, searching for what she needed, or rather what would spur Moonie to reach the shore. Minutes, maybe hours, went by until she spied a short branch wriggling along nearby in the darkening water. She held onto the loop around the rock and reached for it. One leg slipped. "I have it!"

The sun behind the clouds had long left the narrow slit in the canyon above Nell and Moonshine on the rock. It was only when Nell retrieved the branch that she realized the afternoon light was waning. The white water still contrasted with the deep swirling green surges of the river, but soon dusk would fall. Where, oh, where was the scow by now? Salmon? Farther, or closer? "Oh, Charlie, I need you!" Nell couldn't help calling for him.

Still, she had his pack. "Okay, Moonshine, you have to take Charlie's place." Nell took the loop and formed a makeshift harness around her dog's shoulders and chest and under the cork jacket. "See this branch? I'm going to throw it as far as I can to the shore. I want you to go after it. Don't come back, though. Go to the shore and stand fast. Then I will come after you." I hope, she said to herself. Before throwing a long piece of the branch, one light enough to toss as far as possible, Nellie checked the rope to be sure it wouldn't tangle.

Moonshine's eyes lit up and he grinned at Nellie, his tongue hanging out in anticipation.

Once again, Nell managed to stand on the rock. She held the stick next to Moonshine's nose. "See this. I'm throwing it to the shore. Go get it!" And stay there, she mouthed. Her toss was strong and straight. The stick landed on the rocks shining in the shore water. Moonshine leaped off the rock and swam. Water flooded across him, but he managed to swim in a true line toward the rocks. The current pushed at him, Nell could see. Even so, his eyes didn't seem to lose sight of the stick. At last, Moonshine clambered onto one of the first rocks, mostly out of the water. Nell could no longer see the stick, and Moonshine appeared to search for it.

"Stay there, Moonie! Stay!" Nell screamed as loud as she could. Maybe he could hear her over the flood of water. She grabbed Charlie's pack, pushed the cork jacket up behind her head, slipped her arms through the straps, and tied the waist strap around herself. "I'm coming!"

Nellie sat on the edge of the rock and swung her legs into the water. Before she could hesitate, she shoved off, her hand on the rope slung around Moonshine, who now stood on the shore, watching her. The cork kept her afloat, although the pack tried to pull her under and the current pushed at her. The cold water stunned but she had to keep moving. Hand over hand, Nell used the rope to creep toward her dog. He held it steady, so the river current didn't send her sideways. Her strength kept her upright, but she could feel it faltering. Her feet didn't touch the bottom at first. Before long, she did feel her boots slip over submerged rocks. A few red fish continued to flash by her, intent on their own direction. "I'm almost there, Moonshine," Nell muttered to herself. "Stand fast."

Nell grabbed one rock and another and finally pulled herself ashore. She hung her head, trying to catch her breath. She had hardly breathed as she'd crossed the river. Moonie stepped down to her and licked her face, welcoming her. "I have to get out of the water, Moonshine. Help me." He grabbed her cork in his teeth and tugged at Nell, enough to give her leverage to get her body and legs free of the river.

The grass and sage on the shore retained enough heat for Nell to lie in them until the shade of the canyon dissipated all the warmth of the day. Still shivering but no longer clacking her teeth, she sat up. Moonie had lain down beside her, still attached to the rope. "I better undo the rope, Moonshine. And see if I can get it loose from the rock. We may need it later." She could hardly muster the energy to sit up. First, she had to remove some of her wet clothes and get them drying before dark descended. She untied her boots and shook out the water, then pulled off her pants. The wool hung heavy with water, so she wrung them as best she could and spread them across a shrub. Her bare legs dimpled with goosebumps. "Do you suppose Charlie has extra clothes in his pack?" The pack dripped with water, too, but the insides felt mostly dry. She searched around inside it and pulled out a holster with a gun in it. "I wonder if this got wet."

The gun was of no use at that moment, so Nell laid it aside and searched more. There were clothes. She pulled out a shirt. "Yes, yes." She unbuttoned her flannel shirt and pulled it off along with her camisole. Charlie's shirt was too big by half, but dry. She could smell Charlie's scent of oregano on it. Another search brought forth a pair of pants. Nellie hugged them. She stood up to shed her underpants and don the pants, again too long by half. Moonie watched. Nell placed all her wet things on another shrub to dry. She rolled up the sleeves and the pants and wished for a rope around the waist to keep them on. "Aha, the rope!"

Nell released Moonshine from the harness around him and took off his cork lifesaver. She had already thrown hers to the ground, thankful Lulu had insisted she take two. "All right, Moonie. I am going to thrash on the rope and see if it will come off the rock." She stepped down close to the water and shook the rope just like a jump rope. It stayed looped on the bump, as near as she could tell. "I'll try jerking it. That sharp edge might cut it." As she had done when she was on the rock, she used her whole weight to pull on the rope, first in short jerks and then a long steady pull. Nothing.

"Hmm. Let's tie it to the top of one of these little trees so it will dry out. Then I'll try again." Moonshine's head followed Nell's actions, but he didn't move from his resting place.

"What's wrong, Moonie? Are you worn out?" She knelt beside him. "Are you hurt?" His mouth appeared to grin, but his tongue dripped saliva on her, er, Charlie's pants. She checked his ears but could not find any sore spots. Where had that drip of blood originated? She took hold of his mouth. "Let me look inside." She could see little. Instead, she felt along his body. Her dog yelped when she squeezed toward the top of his body. "Maybe a broken rib?" No wonder, with how they were tossed around and then bounced up on a rock. She was lucky all her bones seemed to be in place and unbroken.

Charlie's pack still held the tarp and sleeping bag the two of them had slept under the night before. She searched around, hoping to find something to eat. Her husband's pack always held whatever they seemed to need. A cup hung on the outside, so Nellie used it to get water from the river and drink. She placed it where Moonshine could drink as well. In spite of being soaked to the bone, Nell was thirsty.

"Now, what do we do? Head back to Challis or try to reach Salmon?" She didn't know how far the scow had traveled. Which was closer? Stars began to shine in the narrow sky above her. She ached all over. She supposed Moonshine did, too. Sleeping became the only logical answer.

Chapter 8

NIGHT SOUNDS WOKE NELLIE. STARLIGHT relieved the dense darkness around her. Nell patted her bag and found Moonshine cuddled next to her. What had she heard? She held still and listened, hearing the river churning its way along. No breeze stirred the trees along the slope nor the brush next to the river. She thought she heard a nighthawk's dive with its sharp whistle before swooping back up. She sat, the better to determine the direction of any other sounds.

Footsteps, followed by a rock tumbling. Deer or elk, she thought. What else could it be? Only then did she remember the dory she had seen along the side of the river, just before she fell out of the boat. "Who is there?" Nell grabbed the revolver she had brought to the sleeping bag. The sound stopped. An owl said, "*Whoo, whooo*?" Perhaps her imagination was working overtime. Moonie's breath beside her turned into a snore. She sat and listened for what seemed like a long time, but no other sound bothered her. Finally, she lay down and slept again.

Moonie getting up to relieve himself woke Nellie, who discovered the same need. Morning light was just appearing above her in the canyon; the stars had disappeared. Her boots felt dry enough to don again, as did the socks. She had slept in Charlie's shirt and pants to keep warm. She climbed up the slope to a few trees and squatted. Charlie's pack had revealed toilet paper, for which she was thankful. She buried the paper under a small pile of rocks and returned to her nest. Moonie joined her.

"What are we going to eat?" Nell looked at the river. Fish, obviously. She wrinkled her nose. Raw didn't sound appealing at all, as hungry as she was. Surely, Charlie's pack held matches and she could build a small fire to cook. Her friend Pearl had stabbed a fish the previous summer. Nell doubted she had the same talent, but she could try. The salmon going past dwarfed the trout Pearl had caught. While Nell busied herself finding a straight branch in one of the shrubs, breaking it, and whittling a sharp edge with a knife—courtesy again of Charlie's pack—Moonshine wandered the shore, sniffing at everything. He seemed much spryer. She hoped his ribs didn't bother him, if indeed they had been hurt.

Her clothes had dried on the shrubs, so she changed into them. It was easier to move about than in Charlie's clothes. She folded them and placed them in the sleeping bag. Remembering the night noises, Nell kept the revolver within reaching distance, in case of need. Bears or a mountain lion might choose her for a tasty meal.

Nell waded into the river. Along the shore, the current didn't push at her. She watched the water and waited. A red salmon nosed by and she stabbed her sharpened stick. A miss. Moonie barked behind her. When Nell turned, she saw what he saw—several deer grazed higher up the slope in a patch of faded grass. One of the smaller deer sported two nubs on the top of his head, a male deer. She could try to shoot him. It was probably hunting season. She had no idea how to skin a deer. She turned back to the water and waited again. Another stab. This time she didn't miss.

A large wriggling red fish came up with the stick. "I'm sorry, fish. Moonshine and I need to eat."

Nellie grabbed the fish, as slippery as it was, and banged its head on a rock. It stopped wriggling. She laid it out on grass and found a flat place with no grass or small dead plants and built a fire circle in dust surrounded by stones. Last thing she needed was a forest fire. She rounded up small pieces of dried wood and plants and managed to get a fire going, thanking Alphonso, the sheepherder who taught her so much the year before. Then she took the knife and worked over the fish next to the water, pulling out entrails and slicing off large chunks of raw meat. She had no metal grill, so she hung a slab off a wet branch she found in the water. Soon, the smell of cooking salmon filled the air. While gathering wood, Nell found pieces of bark to use as a plate. Wilted dandelion weeds might taste all right, so she washed several and heaped them on the bark. "All right, Moonshine. Here is half of this chunk for you and half for me." Moonie gulped his down in seconds. Nell used her fingers to eat the savory cooked salmon. The meat felt mushy on her tongue but still tasted good. She had saved a pocket of salmon roe, thinking it, too, might suffice for a meal, as squeamish as she felt about using it. Unborn fish. At least the roe was not yet fertilized.

The leaves from aspen or cottonwood had mostly turned yellow and were too small to use to wrap the cooked fish. The autumn smell of dried leaves wafted around her. Nellie searched the shore and then climbed up the slope to see what else might be of use to save the food for later. The deer had leaped away when the fire had begun to smoke with cooking.

Sunlight warmed the canyon bottom. Moonshine dozed near the fire as it died down. Nell pulled the contents of Charlie's pack out on the tarp to see exactly what else he had. She found a folded packet and opened it. Flour! Another small packet contained bacon. He must have found those items at Bull's ranch and packed them away, always preparing for the unknown. All she had to cook them in was the metal cup. A spare bandana would work to wrap the fish.

Nell unscrewed the cap of a small metal flask and tasted. She gasped at the raw liquid. It was liquor of some sort. A sheriff carrying liquor during prohibition seemed an anomaly. Maybe it was medicinal alcohol. She screwed the cap back on and laid the container out with the other items. No bucket this time. A first aid kit of sorts contained bandages and salve, maybe for insect stings. It was like going through a treasure chest, and her heart ached for Charlie. He would know what she should do. Instead of fussing around her makeshift camp, she should begin a trek to the nearest town, pack, and dog and all.

First, she should cook the bacon. She cut up the bacon into smaller pieces and placed them in the cup. When they were cooked and cooled, she could wrap them up with the salmon, then use the cup for the roe. She built up the fire and placed the cup near the edge, turning it from time to time. The bacon smelled even better than the salmon.

Between checking on the bacon, Nell untied the rope around the little tree. She shook it, jerked it, and then pulled with her whole body. She felt it give and pulled harder. The rope flew off the rock and Nell fell backward. It was free! "Whoopee! I did it, Moonshine!" She gathered herself and stood up, pulling in the now-wet rope and looping it to be packed again.

Something burned. "Ooops. The bacon." Nell rushed to the fire and pulled the cup back. Some of the bacon was scorched, but most of it appeared just fine. She tasted a piece and wanted more. No, it should go with the salmon when it cools. She gave two of the singed pieces to Moonie, who didn't seem to mind at all.

Nell began to repack the bag. It clunked against a rock. She stopped and peered into it but couldn't see to the bottom. She reached her hand all the way in and felt a piece of metal. It had a handle—a weathered fry pan, she discovered when she brought it out. "I could have used that!" Nell finished loading the pack with the frypan on the side.

"I've decided which way to go, Moonshine. Charlie will surely head back up the river to find me. So, we will hike down the river toward Salmon. Maybe we will meet in the middle. We'll stay close to shore in case he is rowing a boat. Most likely, he will be riding a horse, maybe on the other side, so keep a good watch. I'll try to do the same." She wouldn't worry about crossing the river now. There must be bridges somewhere.

A dory with a man rowing appeared along the shore as if by magic. Nellie had just loaded Charlie's pack with the life preservers strung on the back and was ready to begin her trek downriver. She watched the man pull the boat ashore just where she had landed. This man was a murderer, according to Charlie. James, she recalled from Bull's tirade.

"Hey, Little Lady," he called. He wore Levi's and a dirty shirt, maybe once a flannel plaid. "Where you headed? Can I give you a lift? How did you get here?" He looked back at the white water churn. "Did those scalawags toss you out?" He stumbled on a rock but stepped closer to her.

The revolver was at the top of the pack in case she needed it but to get at it, she had to drop the pack. Not a wise solution, all told. She loosened the strap around her waist and eased her burden down beside her. "Did you row all the way from Challis?"

The dory's high sides hid most of its contents, but it did appear to have bags and a load of something in the front. She stepped toward the man, trying to get a better look. He moved a few steps closer to her. She didn't want him that close.

"I saw the scow go by yesterday from where I camped last night. I scouted around and saw you last night, too. Figured you'd be scared if I woke you up." He gestured to her and to the boat. "What say? Wanta come along? I'm goin' to Salmon, and I could drop you there. I hate to see a pretty lady like you get lost or drowned."

That explained the footsteps. Nellie shuddered to think he had been watching her sleep. She bent down to loosen the top of the pack. Moonshine stood beside Nell, but so far, he hadn't barked or growled. He was confused, too, maybe. "I have a dog. I can't leave him. Is there room for both of us and my pack?"

"No room for the dog." He took a step back.

"Then I can't come with you." Nell placed her hand on Moonshine's head.

"Suit yourself. I saw you was with that sheriff man. He tried to kill me." His lips sneered at her. "Did he arrest you?"

"In a way," Nell said. "A nurse was with us, too. She bound up the sheriff's wounds. Did you give those to him?"

"Nah. Another man did that. He wasn't so good a shot." The man glanced back at his dory. "I think we can fit the dog in, somewhere."

This time Moonie uttered a low growl, as if warning the man to stay put. Nell had the same reaction. The other man was dead and buried, but she decided not to mention that. Surely, this man caused the death. "I don't think my dog likes you. You better leave us to make our own way down the river. If you have any food, we'd appreciate your sharing it with us." Who knew? He might be happier if the two of them didn't accompany him. "I could pay you, not much, but something."

The man threw back his head and laughed. "Sorry. You'll just have to make do with fish." He turned and walked back to his boat and pushed at the front end, then climbed in behind the high prow. "See you in hell," He called back. "I'll take care of that sheriff, so you don't have to worry about him." The current pulled at the dory, and he began rowing downriver again.

Nell watched him go, wondering if she should have accepted the ride. She shook her head. Not with a man who wanted to murder her husband. And not with a man Moonshine didn't like. The dory rounded a bend, and it was lost to sight. "All right, Moonie. Let's load up and start walking." Maybe the man would run into the scow on his way down, and Ace and Charlie would take care of him. She wondered if he had seen Frankie on the scow and what he thought of that. Frankie wanted him for his money. She didn't sound overly fond of him when they moved Norman's body to the make-shift morgue in Challis. Maybe both of them would end up in jail. Good riddance.

The cork jackets could fit on top of Moonie, she decided. That would help with the bulk of the pack. Even so, it was heavy. Nell took her fishing stick and used it as a walking aid. She headed downriver, Moonie beside her. Walking consisted of moving in and around rocks, a few clearer spots, and then brush and more rocks. Above her, a red cliff caught the sun and reflected it down to her. The trees still with leaves clattered, and birds sang songs to speed her along. The cool morning had turned to a warm mid-day.

They could barely have trekked a mile when Nell stopped to unload the pack. "Moonshine, this is heavier than I expected. The walking is worse than I thought it would be. I guess we should eat some of our cold fish and rest a little. Maybe I'm just weak from hunger." She found a downed log, probably from an avalanche, and sat.

After Nell rested and ate some of the fish and a few pieces of bacon, she again slung the pack onto her back. She had relieved Moonshine of the cork preservers when they stopped and loaded him up again. He didn't seem to mind. The path she followed hardly qualified as a real trail. It led her around the bigger rocks but right through talus slopes where her feet threatened to slide out from under her on all the loose rocks. The Salmon River beside her weaved back and forth and so did her path. The water no longer seemed choppy and there were almost no waves that she could see. If only she had not fallen from the boat. She would be with Charlie, wherever he was.

There must be a faster way downstream. If she could cut across a curve, that would shorten her trek. The river wound so much, she couldn't see far enough ahead to determine she wouldn't lose the river itself if she tried climbing over a headland. At last, she came to a wide sweeping curve and a flat field. She decided to follow her instinct and shorten her hike by crossing the field to the end of the sweep. If she found several more like this one, that would make her hike so much easier. Nell shifted her pack and strode through the amber grasses waving along a meadow, one almost as flat as a tilled field. Grasshoppers leaped in front of her. The dried grasses smelled of fall. She let out a small whoop when she found herself back at the river, just as she planned. Moonshine trotted by her side, his tongue hanging out. He probably needed water, so she stopped at the river and sat on a rock. Moonie waded into the river, lapping. She could use some as well and untied the cup from her pack. She dipped and drank and re-tied it. "Let's keep going, Moonshine. We saved maybe a quarter-mile with our shortcut. We need to find more curves we can cut."

Chapter 9

FRANKIE AND THE SHERIFF HAD both grabbed for Nell as the water pulled her overboard. Janie hung on for her life and managed to stay aboard. Frankie slipped around on the floor of the scow as another wave flooded the whole interior. Just as she was sure she, too, would end up in the river, a strong hand grabbed her and held on.

"Geesh!" Frankie spit out water and gagged. "That café lady is gone!" She clung to the hand that held her. "You shoulda saved her instead!"

"If I could have, I would have." The sheriff's voice arose from a deep place.

Frankie had never heard him sound so desolate, not that she'd heard him talk that often. She had noticed the slight accent. He was as close-mouthed as a—what? She didn't even know. When she could sit up, and the river water flooded off the end of the scow, she pulled herself around. "What're we gonna do?" She searched for the boatman and couldn't find him. "Where'd the boatman go?"

The sheriff stood up. He, too, glanced around. Just then, Ace appeared out of the last wave, still hanging onto the sweep at the back of the boat. He sputtered, choked, and yelled. "Hang on!

Another one coming!"

Frankie flung herself at the sheriff's legs. He looked to be the strongest thing around to grab hold of. At the same time, she reached for Janie. "Hang on, nursie!" They grasped hands and held to each other until what Frankie hoped was the last wave had flooded over them. The sheriff's legs didn't move even half an inch. And then the water calmed, as if there had never been a storm.

The sheriff hustled back to Ace. "Stop this boat. We have to find Nell."

The boatman hooted. "Stop the boat? Are you crazy? This is a scow. Not no automobile! There ain't no motor on it to stop." He moved the sweep back and forth. "This current is gonna do what it will with us."

"Stop this scow, or I will shoot you!" The man drew a gun from the back of his belt. He was sopped from head to boot.

Frankie and Janie looked at each other. Frankie tried to stand to stop the sheriff. The boatman yelled first.

"And then what're you gonna do? You gonna run this sweep, you crazy man?"

The sheriff glanced around. Frankie thought he did look like a crazy man.

"I must find Nell. Take me toward the shore and I will go after her." He waved his gun.

"Calm down, mister. She looked like one tough woman. She'll get to shore herself." Frankie wanted to grab the gun but didn't dare. He might shoot her. They were all soaked, as if they had dived into the river and jumped on board again. "Where's the dog?"

With the scow moving smoothly again, Janie stood up and

approached the sheriff. "Charlie, where is Moonshine?" She moved her head back and forth. "If Moonie is with her, she'll be all right." She hung onto his other arm. "Put the gun away and let's talk about what to do. Ace can let you out, but that might not be the best thing to do. You'll just be stranded like Nellie probably is, although her dog can help take care of her. Where's her pack?"

Frankie watched the sheriff replace his gun in his belt. It probably didn't work anymore, she thought, with the soaking they all got. He sat back on the bench and held his head. "What do we do, Janie?" Frankie had never heard a man ask for help. That woman must mean a lot to him. Frankie scrambled around on the deck.

"Here's her pack." She began to loosen the top.

"Do not touch that!" The sheriff growled at Frankie. He jerked the pack away. "It has her camera in it." He stood up. "Where is my pack?"

"Sorry. Yours ain't here," Frankie said after climbing around on her knees. "You see it, nurse?"

"It went over, Charlie. I think Nellie got a grip on it as she flew out. Moonshine must have gone with her." Janie re-settled on the bench. "Thank heavens, Nellie wore her life preserver and so did Moonshine. That would have kept them from going under for more than a minute, if that." Janie sounded so positive, Frankie believed her.

"Which shore do you want to go to?" Ace asked from the back sweep.

Frankie thought the sheriff looked confused. She exchanged a glance with the nurse, Janie her name was. "That's the problem, ain't it?" Frankie tried to remember seeing the café lady land in the water, but she had been down on the deck of the scow and didn't see anything but water. "I couldn't tell. Could you?" She directed her question at Ace.

"I was too busy trying to keep this scow from turning upside down."

"I thought I saw her heading for one of those big black rocks in the middle, just like the one we bounced off of, but farther down." Janie shifted on the bench. "Sheriff, maybe the best thing to do is get to Salmon and you can get a horse and go back upriver after Nell. I'm pretty dang sure she'll head downriver to try and meet us." She turned to the boatman. "Ace, how far do we got to go to Salmon? Are there any more rough spots between here and there?"

Ace hung onto the sweep before he answered. Frankie thought he was still upset about being threatened with a gun by the sheriff. At least the sheriff hadn't tried to arrest him. "Several more hours. No more white water until after Salmon. And then it gets really wicked."

"See? In a couple hours, you can be on a horse and move back upriver. That will be much faster than trying to backtrack on the trail, Sheriff." Frankie patted his shoulder. He winced and shifted away from her hand.

"All right. Nell has my pack, I hope. It has rope and a tarp and bag in it, as well as other supplies that might help her—matches, a little food. I had all of them wrapped. Janie, that is good advice."

Frankie almost cheered. If the sheriff got a horse and packed back up the river, maybe he'd forget he arrested her. He would be in a hurry. She could hug that nurse. In the meantime, she'd try to stay quiet and out of the sheriff's way.

"Frankie, I need to check the sheriff's wounds. Can you help? I don't know if we have any dry bandages left, but that box under the bench would have them. Sheriff, put your leg out and roll up that pantleg."

The sheriff groaned, but his face didn't look so dark. With a solution from the nurse, maybe he would cheer up. Frankie wanted nothing to do with wounds, but she could hardly turn the nurse down. Were these wounds from Norm and James, Frankie wondered? All those gunshots must have hit something. Only then did she remember what the café lady—Nell—had shouted just before the scow hit the rock. "A dory!" That had to be James, so he was behind them. She hadn't lost him. There was still a chance of getting some money from him. And maybe he would pick up that Nell along the way. That would sure give him a bargaining chip for getting herself free from the sheriff. A Frankie for a Nellie. Ha!

Sure, she'd help. Then she would know how bad the wounds were. Maybe she could get the gun, too. The scow was miles down the river from where Nell had been washed out. Frankie sat beside Janie and did what she was told. When she heard Ace groan "Uh-oh," she remembered he had warned them there might be trouble when it grew dark. It was almost there, she thought. He couldn't chance hitting another rock.

Charlie turned around. "What is it?"

Just then, the scow ground to a halt. "A buried sand bar. Dad blame it!" Ace leaned over the side. "Everybody out! Now!"

Janie hurried to the side of the scow and jumped into the water. Frankie untied the leather straps and stood on the edge of the boat. She hesitated at the end. Charlie jumped down and held out his arms. How could she trust him? Janie shouted: "Jump, Frankie, He'll catch you."

"No, he'll trick me!"

"No, he won't. Jump!" The sheriff's arms caught her, and he swung her up on gravel along with her saddlebags. "Wait here," he said.

The sheriff waded back to where Ace pushed at the blunt front end of the scow. "We gotta get her off of this." Charlie turned to get his back pushing at the scow. The two of them managed to inch the boat back toward the water.

"Hold 'er there, Sheriff. I'll get a rope tied to a rock back there, so she won't get loose." He was as good as his word. The scow floated free of the sandbar but stayed in position. "You women can climb back in, but we ain't goin' nowhere tonight. There's a blanket or two in that box in there. It'll get cold out. Better shivvy up some. If you got wet things on, take 'em off, and wrap a blanket around you."

Charlie climbed back aboard, found the blankets, and tossed them out. There were only three. He jumped back down, tossed one to Janie and one to Frankie. Janie laughed. Frankie stared. Ace grumped. Frankie noticed the sheriff limped as he headed off by himself. She was surprised he didn't head off to find Nell. She glanced from him to the scow and realized Ace would need his help to get the scow back into the river current. Maybe he had already told the sheriff he couldn't leave them high and dry.

Chapter 10

THE SCOW MUST HAVE REACHED Salmon the day before. That meant that Charlie would be on his way to find her. The afternoon sun had been too warm for hiking, so Nell rested in the shade of a bent tree. Maybe he would appear any moment.

Moonshine lay beside her, but he didn't nap, as she had. There should be a road from Challis to Salmon. Nellie had kept her eyes on the other side of the river but never saw anything that looked like a road or any means of transportation following it. The river had widened and probably deepened as she and Moonie moved along beside it. For the most part, its surface seemed smooth and mostly unrippled. Once, she had stopped to wade when she could see rocks a long way out. Her fishing stick steadied her, but the water soon surged over her knees. That didn't work.

Nell debated whether to spear another fish. She was tired of the taste of salmon but couldn't think of what else there might be to eat. She couldn't bring herself to kill a deer, yet. The smaller animals like mice and voles she couldn't catch with a stick, and she didn't want to waste ammunition on them. Besides, even if she could hit one, it would probably explode.

A low growl from Moonshine interrupted Nell's reverie about food. "What?" She looked around. At first, she could see nothing to cause Moonie to respond. He stood up and would have headed uphill, but she grabbed the cork jacket. "What do you see?" A glance up the slope finally alerted her to the danger. A mountain lion had been creeping up on them but was still uphill and far enough away for Nell to react. She stood, too, grabbing a rock. Her aim was true, and the stone smacked the lion on the top of its head. She yelled as loud as she could, keeping a hand on Moonie. He would lose a fight with the cougar if she let him go after it. As soon as the rock hit the lion, Nellie grabbed the pack and pulled out the revolver. "Stay, Moonshine!" He began barking and his noise along with Nell's shouts caused the lion to pause and turn. Its body and legs, thick and muscular, lengthened as it ran uphill. Its golden coat blended so well with the grasses and rocks, she could hardly follow its progress except for its long tail. She sagged with relief when it disappeared over a ridge. She was going to have to be more alert to danger as she hiked along the river path.

"Hey!" A man's voice. Where was it?

Nellie turned back to the river and saw two men with horses on the other side. One was mounted and the other stood on the beach with his horse's reins in his hands.

"Are you all right? What are you doing over there?"

"I'm trying to get to Salmon!" Nell shouted. She circled her mouth with her hands. "How far is Salmon? Is there a bridge nearby?" She hoped her voice carried over the sound of the river.

The two men conferred. Nellie wasn't certain they heard her words. The standing man looked back at Nell. "Salmon," he said and pointed with his arm downstream, "Nine or ten miles." He stepped almost into the river. "Bridge at Salmon." The man on the horse slid off and joined the other man. "Want us to come get you?"

Nell didn't see how that was possible. She did not want to deal with two strangers. With heavy beards, they looked like miners or loggers in worn-out shirts and pants. She could see packs on the backs of both horses and rifles in scabbards. Long hair straggled from well-used hats. "No. I can get there myself." Before they turned away, she shouted again: "Did you see another horseman? A Basque?" She didn't want to mention the word "sheriff."

"No." The second man joined in. "Just us two." The two talked to each other. One man gestured downriver. The other climbed back into his saddle.

"Take care, miss," the first man said. "Wild animals out here."

Nell watched them move back into trees on the other side. The slope didn't ascend as steeply on their side of the river. She guessed there was a road there, or at least a wider path. Her shouts and Moonshine's barking must have alerted them to her presence. Maybe Charlie would have heard her as well. She and her dog should keep hiking. Ten miles sounded like such a far distance. No wonder Charlie hadn't shown up yet. A horse doesn't travel all that fast. Still, she could make several miles before twilight set in. Surely, Charlie would meet them along the way.

What if he was on the other side of the river? How would he see her and Moonshine? She couldn't keep shouting as she did to scare the mountain lion away. If the two men were traveling toward Salmon, they might run into him and tell him, she hoped, that there was a woman on the other side. She would have to stay with the river and not cross any likely flat sweeps near bends. Then they would certainly miss each other. If the men were traveling in the other direction, toward Challis, they would not run into Charlie at all.

"C'mon, Moonshine. I'll get another fish downstream where there is a good place to light a fire. I can use the oil from it in the flour to make a biscuit." She left the frypan on the outside of the pack. "At least we have plenty of water." Nell hefted the pack again, and the two of them set off downriver. Although hungry, Nell felt energized knowing how far she had to go. Three or four miles would go by quickly.

In another hour, her energy had dissipated. Worse, the slope above the river had turned to steep rock. How was she going to get around the cliff and keep going to Salmon? The river's placid surface had turned to churn again, although nothing like the stretch where she had fallen out of the scow. She wondered if the two men had meant ten straight miles. If so, the bends in the river would lengthen that distance by quite a bit. No, she figured she now had eight miles or a little less to go. The bigger problem was the rock wall. Nell stepped into the river with her fishing stick. Both she and Moonshine needed to eat something. She saw few red fish, but spied a smaller, smoother fish—maybe a trout or even a steelhead. Good. A different taste, but not as much flesh.

Her arm stabbed and she had it. Back on shore, she killed and gutted it and found a level spot to build a small fire pit. There wasn't much wood but plenty of grass to get a fire started. "Guard the fish, Moonie, but don't eat it." Nell hiked up the slope, searching for stray branches. She found a few and a larger branch she could break into pieces, enough to cook the fish and make two biscuits for them. No greens this time.

It didn't take long for the fire to leap up. Nell held the fish on the stick over the flames to let it cook. She wished her dog could hold the stick and she could mix up enough flour and grease from the fish to make biscuits. Instead, she held the frypan to catch the grease. When she figured the trout was cooked enough, she propped the stick on the pack and added water to the flour, then fried the mess in the frypan over the flame, which had now backed down enough so she could let the pan sit on its own between two rocks. The smoke trailed down the river. The odor of cooking fish probably did, too. Maybe Charlie would smell it and know where she was. She added a few pieces of bacon to the biscuits to give them some flavor. Their smell was more pungent than the fish. Her mouth watered. Moonshine paced around her, waiting for his share.

Nell used the frypan as a plate, after cutting some fish for Moonshine and passing a biscuit to him. She sat back and savored trout and biscuit herself. If she couldn't get around the cliff wall, then Charlie probably couldn't either. It would depend on whether he was on a horse or hiking like she was. Probably on a horse. She could leave the fire burning and hike up the headwall and over and down, but she couldn't see how far the wall extended. She decided to walk out into the water and see what she could see. She really didn't want to leave a fire burning. If she left fish scraps to signal to someone that she had been there, an animal would eat them. Nell remembered the arrow she had drawn on a tree during the walk up Fourth of July Canyon to alert Charlie and Gwynn Campbell where she had gone. She could use rocks to make an arrow pointing up the slope. Would he see it?

Once again, the current was too fast for Nellie to ford her way out far enough to look downriver to see where the wall ended. There appeared to be a crack further down, but then it loomed just as high again. Even if there were a shelter in the crack, there might not be one reachable later.

Using rocks from the shore, Nellie fashioned a large arrow pointing up the hillside. It was taller than she was and took a while to build. She used mostly white stones when she could find them. She placed the arrow higher than the fire ring she had built, hoping it would be visible whether Charlie came by horse across the river or hiking down her side of the river. She used her cup to drown the fire remnants. Leaving a smoldering fire was just too dangerous to contemplate.

"Here we go, Moonshine." Nell hefted her pack and headed uphill. Rather than strike straight up, she zigged and then zagged to make the climb easier. Even so, her breathing became labored. She found an animal trail, dusty, but it helped her move up and up at an angle. Moonshine led the way, sniffing here and there, stopping to look back at her from time to time. At last, she reached what she thought was the top. She dropped her pack and stepped over to the edge of the cliff to look down and around. The sight was bathed in beauty and sunlight. Sparkles danced on the river. The grasses gleamed in gold. Pine trees looked lush. They were surrounded by aspen on some slopes, their leaves the colors of pumpkin and lemons. Nell caught her breath, imagining she was the only person left on earth, and it was all hers. Gradually, details stood out. The river bent this way and that and she could see how it wound like a snake north toward the town of Salmon. There was no horse or man coming upriver toward her that she could see. Instead, far downriver, she spotted the dory, pulled into one of the bends. It appeared to be empty. Upriver, the river flowed toward her, churning white where she might have been flung overboard the day before. The black river rocks appeared to be pebbles from this height. No sign of any town showed along the water. Without the evidence of the dory, she might have been the only person left in the world. A desolate loneliness filled her, until Moonshine crowded against her legs. She lowered her hand to pet his head and rub his ears. She knelt to hold his warm fur close to her chest.

When she stood, Nell studied the tawny hills downriver. If she could find her way off the cliff, she could move more easily. Her shoulders sagged as she took a long breath. Then, she saw something. A flash? A movement? She found the dory again. Still empty. Did she just see deer or a bear? Maybe it was the mountain lion. Brown. A horse! It had to be Charlie. But where was he? She thought she could make out a saddle—an empty saddle. "We've got to get down there, Moonie." Nell strode back to her pack. She pulled out the revolver and stuck it in the back of her waistband. The pack she loaded onto her shoulders and began the long steep descent. She must find Charlie.

Chapter 11

BACK FROM THE CLIFF'S EDGE, Nellie found a trail that led down. She still carried her fishing stick, but the end had blunted and the shaft was skinny and no longer strong. The way was steep and filled with small rocks. Keeping upright became a real chore. She wanted to hurry but could not. Falling would slow her down even more than watching every step to make sure she didn't slide and splat on her back and pack.

Moonshine had an easier time of it with four legs instead of two. He seemed to have a second wind after their respite on top of the headland. He stopped every little while to sniff the air and glance around. Nell wondered if he could smell animals, especially the mountain lion. An afternoon breeze picked up as they neared the river, pushing them along and cooling them off.

Both the dory and the horse had appeared distant from Nell when she had first caught sight of them. Getting to flatter terrain helped her speed but diminished her ability to see ahead. Steep slopes above bends in the river added to her lack of sight ahead. She thought she heard a shout, although the running water beside her filled most of her senses. Riffles and a few waves from the slot by the cliff reminded her of why she was on the ground and not in Salmon. She found a small inlet with a bank leading down. She could rest the pack there and it would be out of sight of the trail she traveled. It was slowing her down too much.

"Moonshine, stay with me. No running ahead." The brush had thickened around her as she stepped forward. The sun had already gone past the opposite slope, and white and gray clouds bloomed above her. She had been lucky so far with the weather. The luck appeared as if it would end. Charlie's shirt she wrapped around her waist in case she needed it for warmth. It also hid the revolver.

Nell tried to walk quietly, letting the lapping sounds of the winding river hide her footsteps. She hoped the tall brush, willows mostly, didn't sway as she moved through them. Mosquitoes and gnats swarmed around her. After what seemed like hours, she realized she might have passed the dory and the horse. She had found neither. She must have imagined the shout. Ahead, she could see that the brush ended and the steep grassy slope of the hillside continued. Before emerging from her shield of green but eager to leave the insects, she stopped to study the water, the slope, the banks of the river. She stepped clear and walked to the river's edge. Downriver, she saw the dory being rowed. There were two people in it. But who? James, surely, but also her husband? She shook her head. She must be really tired. Charlie would not abandon her. Had he been on the horse and left it to arrest James? She knew he would do his duty, but she felt so alone.

Despairing, Nell sat by the river and scratched several mosquito bites on her arms. Moonshine knelt beside her and licked her skin. They were still two against the wilderness. She had managed so far and could again. She wished she had a telescope, but Charlie's magical pack, which had always contained everything, did not contain a spyglass. She wanted to see who rowed. The boat was out of sight by then, anyway. Tears edged down her cheeks. Nell wanted to cry out loud but that wouldn't help at all. Did a few weeks of marriage turn her into a dependent woman? No, she assured herself. Even in the cave at Craters of the Moon, she had not lost hope of getting out and finding Charlie or Rosy again. She knew they would come eventually if she didn't appear soon. She was a Chicago girl, not an adventuress. Her spirits wavered back and forth.

Across the river, Nell noticed bighorn sheep coming to the water to drink. She wished she had her camera with her, and imagined how she would frame a photograph of the river and the sheep. She wondered if the camera had drowned. Maybe she could find a used Premo camera again, one that was small enough to carry in her pack as she used to do. She stood up. If Charlie couldn't come get her, she could manage on her own. That was what she intended to do all along, wasn't it? Quit acting like a baby. Going back for his pack was necessary and she hated to backtrack, but her leftover fish and bacon were in it, as were the matches and warmer clothes and the tarp for shelter. Overhead, the sky had turned pewter gray with layers of gunmetal gray and white edges. Clearly, rain threatened. She would have to hurry.

She found Charlie's pack, grabbed it, and hiked back up the slope. She had decided rather than hike again through the brush and insects, to climb up the slope and edge along the willows. The wind had picked up even as she moved higher. "Moonie, we are in for a storm. Let's hope it doesn't get too cold." She had unwrapped Charlie's shirt from her waist and donned it. "We better find a place to hunker down." The side hill didn't flatten, so she kept moving. At the end of the willow jungle, she kept going, wanting to remove herself from the mosquitoes as far as she could, or at least until the rain started.

At last, Nell spotted a few young trees in a little grove. There she could find shelter, sparse as it appeared, and flat enough ground to camp. One tree had a lower branch she could use to fling the canvas tarp over and make a tent of sorts. Before she did that, though, she needed to make a fire ring—dig into the dirt and surround it with rocks. "Moonshine, can you find some wood?" He looked at her with a question on his face. She held up a small loose branch. "Find some of these." He panted and then bounded away.

Getting down to the shore to hunt rocks challenged Nell. All the hiking and the disappointment had exhausted her. Still, she could carry three or four rocks back up at a time and soon built a compact fire pit. Moonshine brought a dried branch, and she broke it into pieces. The pack was sheltered under the tarp. As she found the matches, she heard *pock, pock, pock*. It sounded like big drops of rain on a roof. She peeked around. White blobs fell at a faster and faster rate. Hail! *Pockity-pock-pock*.

"Oh dear! Can anything else go wrong?" Nellie grabbed the rope that had rescued her from the rock and tied it to the corners of the canvas tarp. She expanded the sheltered area by pulling the tarp out farther under the trees and over the fire pit. She would have to be careful not to let the fire get too large or it would burn the material. She should have built the little fire pit farther out. It wasn't lit, so she could move it, but not too far because the ground began to slope again. She tied the rope to branches on the small trees and scooted back to pull the sleeping bag around her and Moonshine. She would wait to light the fire.

Nell thought she would never nap with the hail storming down upon her little tarp tent. But she did. The petrichor of rain surrounded her in a misty dream. Then the smell of the fire woke her up. Flames leaped up toward the tarp. Nell jumped up and stomped the fire with her boot, scattering flaming wood away from under the shelter. She hoped the ground outside was wet enough to keep the embers from spreading. Ducking under the rope, she continued to stomp the ground downhill from her shelter. Rain poured down on her hair, her face, her clothes. When she was certain everything was out, she retreated to the tarp, shivering.

Moonshine had leapt up with Nell and pranced around. "You can't help, Moonie! Your paws will get singed." He returned to her under the tarp.

"I didn't light that fire. Where are the matches?" She groped around and found them, next to the fire pit, where a small fire persevered, small enough not to be a danger. "Did you do it accidentally?" she asked her dog. That was improbable. Maybe she had done it herself and forgotten. Improbable, too. Charlie's pack had tumbled over and many of its items spilled out onto the ground. She glanced at the matches again. Several were missing, apparently used to light the needles and wood she had stacked up in the stone ring.

As she puzzled over the fire, the rain stopped. Nell heard footsteps sliding down the slope behind her make-shift tent. A figure appeared. "You!"

A bedraggled person knelt and crawled under the tent. "The nurse was right. You and the dog survived just fine." The woman from the café. "Except you forgot to light the fire."

"Where did you come from? Where is Charlie?" Nell wanted to push the woman out past the tent and down the slope to the river. She wanted Charlie!

The woman stared at the fire ring. "You stopped the fire! Are you crazy?"

"Who are you? And where is Charlie?"

"Frankie." She lunged for the matches. "I'll get it going again."

Nell was quicker. She grabbed the matches and held them. "Your fire almost burned down my shelter." She hoisted herself to her knees. "Where… is… Charlie?"

"You mean that sheriff? He arrested James and they loaded into the dory. They're way downriver now." Frankie sat back on her haunches. "Seemed that was much more important than you are." She smirked. "He sent *me* to find you."

Nell ceased shivering. She wouldn't let this woman know how alone she had felt. She wanted to hit Frankie for finding her and shout at Charlie for taking James in the dory. Still, as far as they knew, he was a murderer and undoubtedly a danger to everyone. And a moonshiner, too. A bad man.

"I have a horse. Only he got away." Frankie glanced around. "Nice little place you got here. Any food?"

Nell calmed herself. She petted Moonshine. "How about those precious saddlebags of yours? Surely, you have food in them."

"They're on the horse. No food either." A sly smile crossed Frankie's face. "Although I could buy some."

"Good. You can pay me. I have fish."

"This bag is yours?" Frankie pushed the sleeping bag with her foot. "Looks cozy. You were sleeping like a baby when I found you."

"Charlie's and mine. It is cozy."

"Kind of like riding behind him on a horse?" She leaned toward Nell. "He's a nice man to hold onto, isn't he? Muscular and hard. And warm."

Nell eyed the frypan in the things spilled from the pack. She could hit Frankie with that and leave her here while heading downriver to find Charlie. She'd take the frypan with her and hit him, too.

"Where's the fish? I'm hungry." Frankie sat back. She stared at the pack, hungrily.

"Go catch one yourself. I only have enough left for Moonshine and me." Nell turned so her back faced the woman. The thought of her riding with Charlie on a horse together stunned her, even more than his leaving with the murderer.

"You'd feed a gol-durned dog before a hungry person?" Her voice raised an octave. "You're a bitch." She shifted to move closer to Nell. "You're mad he let me ride with him, aren't you?" Her hand pressed on Nell's shoulder.

"Don't touch me!" Nell shouted. Moonshine, who had been lying next to his mistress, growled.

Frankie scooted back to the edge of the shelter. Her nasty voice changed. "Sorry, sorry. Don't let that dog get me, please."

Moonshine's growl ceased and he lay his head down on Nellie's knee. "That is just a warning, Frankie. Don't mess with me." She turned back to the woman. "Tell me what happened."

Chapter 12

WHEN THE SCOW LANDED IN Salmon, it was near dark. Frankie rushed to get off and run. The sheriff grabbed her arm before she could even get a foot on the dock landing. "You stay with me, Miss Bingham. You are still under arrest."

Janie, the nurse, glared at Charlie. She waited for Ace to settle his sweeps, and then she climbed up and off the boat. "Frankie, let me help you."

"Keep an eye on her, Janie. I've got to find a horse." He took off, heading into the town. It wasn't long before he returned, leading a horse, a brown one. A sturdy one.

Frankie had jumped back into the scow to get her saddlebags. She handed them to Janie. "Hold these for me, will you Janie? They're all I have in the world."

"Ace, I am heading back upriver to find Nell. Can you help Janie find a ride back to Stanley? I will take my prisoner with me." He gestured to Frankie. "Which side of the river should I try?"

"I'd try the side opposite the road, Sheriff." He scratched his head. "If she were on that side, she might be here by now. It's too dark. You'll get lost. Better wait for first light. You can sleep on the scow if you want." He tied the scow with thick ropes around metal cleats. "I need to find a contract to go downriver. Maybe

I'll ask around. Could take a day or two to get that lined up." He stood on the dock, his legs braced apart. "If'n you take this gal in now, you'll be stuck at least a day. Her and Janie can get a bed in one of them auto courts. I'll arrange it and see the gal joins you in the morning." He gathered things up and left Charlie standing in the scow.

Charlie called after Ace. "I cannot wait a day or two. When I find Nell, we will come back. If you have not left, we may go with you. Depends on whether that dory is ahead or behind us." He turned to Frankie. "I'll just keep the saddlebags with me. Then I'll be sure you'll be back in the morning."

Next morning, Ace brought Frankie to Charlie. Her head swiveled between the sheriff and the boatman. She struck a pose. "I'll need a horse, too."

"There's only one. You can ride behind me." He held out the woman's saddlebags. "I now know you don't have a revolver, but you can carry the bags. They'll go along with your arrest. We can tie them behind you." He motioned toward the horse on shore. "Let's go."

Frankie grumped after him. She couldn't leave the saddlebags with him, even if he knew what was in them. And she might be able to spot James before the sheriff did and get herself rescued. She figured James wasn't strong; he didn't lead an active life. He would have to rest his arms from rowing now and then. That was why they had seen the dory. She was positive he was behind them. Maybe he had already found Nell Burns. What would he do about her? A flick of jealousy colored her face: Frankie could feel it. That woman was good-looking, and James liked them feisty.

"Wait. I need to get Nell's camera looked after." The sheriff returned to Ace. They talked and the sheriff returned before

Frankie could get on the saddle and ride away. She noticed he limped as he walked. His shoulder and his leg were still sore, in spite of Janie's nursing skills.

"Let's go, Miss Bingham." The sheriff swung onto the horse and reached his left arm out to help her load behind him.

"I'm no Miss Bingham. I'm Frankie." She landed on the saddlebags, which weren't comfortable to ride on. "I don't think this will work."

"It will have to. Hang on to the saddle."

Frankie tried and changed to hang on to his sides. He could just lump it. As she moved with the horse, she felt something hard against her chest under the sheriff's jacket. It must be the revolver he had pulled on Ace earlier, demanding to stop the scow. Gradually, she moved her hands around the sheriff and held on tighter. He either didn't notice or didn't mind, she thought.

The sheriff kept a steady pace on the horse through flatlands following the river back up. On the scow, the last part of the trip to Salmon had been smooth with only a few rough spots, once they left the steep side hills. Before long, the horse and the two of them had edged back onto the slopes beginning to climb and filled with pine trees. They passed several abandoned sheds and maybe what was once a cabin, now broken down and roofless. There were no people at all. Frankie kept an eye on the river to see if the dory came into sight. She didn't know how she would signal James if she saw him. As the horse moved down a steeper section of path, she slid into the sheriff and almost off the saddlebags. The gun. She could use it to fire a shot. James would look up and see them, she hoped.

The trail turned rocky. A sound she had never heard before—a heavy rattle—made the horse shy and then rear up. Frankie grabbed for the gun but missed it under the jacket. She fell off the back onto rough ground. She screamed and saw a huge snake with diamond markings on its coils. A rattlesnake! Its head struck out toward the horse. It stepped sideways and barely missed her legs. The sheriff sawed on the reins to control the horse and managed to get his revolver. He fired a shot at the snake. Its rattles and its head dropped.

The sheriff slid off the horse but kept the reins in his hand. He hurried to Frankie, still on the ground and struggling to get herself upright. "Are you all right?"

"Of course not! Is it dead? It bit me!" Frankie wailed. She folded herself over her left leg and sobbed. "My leg is broken!"

"You fell on your behind. The snake could not reach you. Here, I will help you up." The horse pulled back from the sheriff, who still held the revolver in one hand, and he lost his hold on the reins. For a moment, he hesitated between the horse and the woman. That moment lost him the horse. Finally, he stuck the gun in his belt, circled Frankie with his left arm, and jerked her to standing. "Put weight on your leg," he ordered.

Frankie rolled her eyes. She knew her leg was fine. Her butt hurt.

"Let her go!" A loud, bass voice rang from above them.

"James!" Frankie scurried up the hillside. "Where did you come from?"

When she reached James, he grabbed her with both arms. He whispered in her ear. "I caught the horse and tied it there to a tree." He gestured slightly to the forest line behind them. "Shhh. It has the saddlebags."

"Are you James Murray?" the sheriff asked.

"Darn right, I am. What's it to you?" James swung Frankie to his side.

"I am arresting you for the murder of Norman House. Where is the dory?"

Frankie interrupted with a shout. "He didn't kill Norm! You did, you murderer!"

The revolver appeared in the sheriff's hand.

"I lost it, just like you lost that horse." James laughed. "Now what?"

"Now, we walk back to Salmon." The sheriff aimed his revolver at James. "Frankie, you keep going and find Nell. Bring her back."

"Ha! Lost your horse and your girl, too? Some sheriff!" James said. "She told me you arrested her. Kinda like the girls, eh? Don't blame you."

"Where did you see her?" The sheriff still leveled the revolver at James. "Tell me, or you will show up in Salmon with a bullet-ridden arm." He shifted his aim, squeezed the trigger, and a spurt of dirt and rocks beside James exploded.

James jumped back. "I'll tell you. I saw her back a ways. Offered her a ride. She wouldn't take it on account of that black mutt of hers. She was wore out. Dumb dame."

"Where's the dory?" The sheriff gestured with his revolver again. "One last chance."

Frankie scooted away from James. She didn't want any bullet accidentally hitting her.

"Down there, in a cove. We can't see it from up here." He took a step or two closer to the man with the gun.

"Frankie, get going." The sheriff pointed his revolver downhill. "You go along this path. James, you show me the dory. You can row us to Salmon."

James and Frankie looked at each other. James shrugged his

shoulders. "Better do what he says, Frankie. I'll meet you in Salmon." He didn't mention the whereabouts of the horse. She wondered why. Maybe the saddlebags were safer in the forest. She wondered if James knew what was in them.

Chapter 13

NELL LISTENED TO FRANKIE TELL her story and wondered how much was truth, how much was fiction, and what she left out. It must be true that Charlie had arrested James and they were rowing toward Salmon. Whether the horse was lost might be fiction. No matter. Frankie and Nellie needed to head down to Salmon along the river. If they could find the horse, so much the better. She was tired of carrying the pack. As soon as the rain stopped, they could begin their hike.

As soon as the rain stopped. The sky had opened up and dumped what must have been held for days. Nellie shared the sleeping bag with her unwelcome guest. She kept a small fire burning while Frankie dropped off to sleep. The warmth held in by the tent made Nellie's eyes droop and then close. She started awake. One of them had to keep an eye on the fire. Moonshine slept against Nellie's legs. Something, some noise, must have awakened her. No, it was the lack of noise. The rain had stopped. The clouds were clearing, and a dusky sky opened above them.

Moonshine leapt up. He ran out of their enclosure and up the hill. "Moonie! Come back!" Nell worried he might be after the mountain lion. Before too many minutes had passed, her dog came back with an animal wriggling in his mouth.

"Hand me your knife. I'll kill and skin it. We need food." Frankie sat on her haunches behind Nell. "I won't use the knife on you." She held out her hand. "I need you as much as you need me, it appears. Too ladylike to skin a squirrel? I'm not."

"I don't know how. I cleaned the fish." But a squirrel, Nell added to herself. And kill an animal? She hadn't the heart. She wasn't hungry enough, yet. She found the knife and handed it to the other woman. "Do it outside the tarp."

"Don't tell me what to do. I'm no dumbbell."

"Unless you want a mountain lion or coyote smelling blood, you better go down by the river and clean it there. We may have to stay the night." Even as Nellie spoke, she could feel the evening slip up from the river. She'd give almost anything to move down the river another mile or two. She found the frypan and set it up for cooking over the stones around the fire. She mixed flour with some of her water, added the rest of the bacon, some fat from the meager remains of the steelhead, and fried biscuits—three of them.

By then, Frankie was back with small portions of meat from the squirrel, along with the tail that she had tucked into the waist of her pants. "For good luck," she said and pointed to the tail. "Here, you can fry these sections. Squirrel tastes pretty good. I've had it before. I used to go hunting with my pa when he was still around. Venison is better."

Nell had found some tree bark while scouting for a piece of wood to keep the fire going. She used the frypan as a plate. They all ate in silence, including Moonshine. He finished first. Frankie had frowned when Nell tossed him a biscuit but said nothing.

"We should walk a while this evening. I'll rinse the bandana in the water and wrap up the rest of the squirrel. Moonie carries the life preservers. You can carry the rope and the tarp. I'll roll it up. I'll carry the rest of the pack. Use my canteen to put out the fire. We can go until it gets too dark to see." Nell stood up. "I want my knife back."

Frankie wrinkled her nose but said nothing and handed the knife to Nellie. She helped roll the sleeping bag, doused the fire with water, and scattered the rocks at Nell's direction. She peered more closely at Nell's face. "Say, you've got quite a scrape there. It looks as if it's still bleeding."

Nell gently touched her cheek. "I know. I'm not sure what to do about it. If we could find some yarrow, I could use that to stop the bleeding." A tear rolled down her cheek. "I don't want a huge scar."

"I don't think it will scar. It just looks mean now. I think I saw some dried yarrow by the river when I cleaned the squirrel. I'll go get what I saw." Frankie hurried down the slope and came back with dried flowers in her hand. "These are dry. I'm not sure they'll do any good." She handed the stems and flowers to Nell.

Nell squeezed the stems in her hand and rubbed the scant amount of plant juice on her cheek. If anything would help, maybe the yarrow would. "Thank you, Frankie—for the squirrel and the yarrow."

Frankie nodded her head an inch.

They loaded up and moved down the slope to walk nearer the river. Moonshine stayed in front of them. Carrying the pack without the rope and tarp helped Nell move along faster. She had been careful to put the revolver on top of the pack's load and kept it hidden.

When Frankie stumbled behind Nell for the third or fourth time, Nell stopped. "I can't see either. Moonshine has better eyes, so I've been following him. Let's find a spot to set up our tarp tent again. The only food we have are the squirrel scraps. You were right. They taste all right."

"Be careful, there is a dead snake around here. I think I know where we are." Frankie stepped cautiously along the trail they had been following. "Here it is. There's a flat spot right up there. C'mon."

Nell wondered if it was possible to eat dead rattlesnake. She might be hungry enough to do so. Maybe it was poisonous. She followed Frankie's voice and found a tree with a sweeping branch. Perfect for the tarp. "Can you eat rattlesnake?"

"Dunno. I never did. Heard it tastes like chicken."

Nellie laughed out loud. Frankie echoed her. They laughed together, sitting down to unload their burdens. Moonshine barked. After a while, the dark descended and they could hardly see each other. "I'll find the matches. Here's the knife. See what you can do with the snake. Can you see it?"

"No. But I remember where it is."

"Wait. I'll bring the candle and give you some light. I need to get some rocks for a fire pit."

Later, the two women sat by the fire and under the tarp. Nellie yawned. "You're right. It does taste like chicken." Frankie began giggling and soon they were both laughing again. "You sleep, and I'll keep watch."

"How do I know you won't ditch me?" Frankie scooted back under the tarp.

"You don't. But it seems we need each other. I have to trust you when you take the second watch. By the way, there was a mountain lion around earlier. One of us must stay awake and keep the fire going—a *small* fire." Moonshine stayed alert next to Nellie. She was glad for his company, and, in a way, for Frankie's company.

Salmon Moon

Frankie reminded her of Pearl from the summer before—both mountain women, brave and resourceful. Nell thought of her days in Chicago. They seemed far away and much too sedate and sedentary. Something she'd rarely seen in the city were the wide swaths of stars above.

As she watched the stars, a bright moon—a salmon moon—entered the scene, and the stars faded. She felt as if she could truly see a man in it. In her imagination, it was her husband searching for her. A silver streak floated on the river waves, brightening the whole canyon with sparkles. A path lit by a river moon. Soon it moved beyond the opposite hills and disappeared. Time to wake Frankie.

Still, Nellie hesitated. Frankie's story of Charlie and James told little of how James had been where he was, what happened to the horse, and why Frankie had been sent to find Nell. She didn't trust Frankie at all. Even Charlie's tale of what happened at Bull Brady's homestead seemed truncated. He never really said how he had been wounded. They must have been wild shots to pierce a leg and a shoulder. In a dory with James, Charlie would be doubly vulnerable, she worried. She could understand Sheriff Charlie leaving a deputy to fend for herself, but why leave her? She was his wife. Maybe she should have taken the deputy position, not the married one. No, she thought. She could take care of herself, and Charlie knew that.

Nell recovered the revolver from Charlie's pack and put it in her waistband. She hid the knife under the corner of the tarp, and then she shook Frankie awake. The woman woke so quickly, Nell wondered if she had been awake for a while. "I'm sleepy, Frankie. Your turn. Moonshine may keep you company but keep your eye out for the mountain lion. I don't think a coyote would come near the fire. Who knows about a lion?"

"Huh. I'm wise to you. You just want to scare me." Frankie crawled over to the fire and leaned against Charlie's pack.

"Don't get into that pack. We need everything in it." Nell laid down. As much as she thought Frankie needed watching, she did sleep.

* * * * *

"Nell. *Hsst.* There's someone up in the woods." Frankie's hand pushed on Nell's shoulder. Her voice was a whisper.

Pulled from a dream of water and fish, Nell shook her head to clear it. A flush of almost dawn outlined their surroundings. "What did you hear?" She whispered, too. "A lion wouldn't make noise."

"Footsteps. Then a thrashing in the trees."

Nell pulled her revolver out and unearthed the knife. "We should be armed. Just in case." She handed the knife to Frankie. "Let's stand up. We won't be so vulnerable."

Outside the tarp, Nell searched in the dim light to see what she could above them. A large presence moved against the trees. Not a mountain lion. Maybe an elk or moose.

"It's the horse!" Frankie yelled. The animal backed up into the trees. "I'll go get it." She flung down the knife.

"Wait! You'll scare it. Let it come to us. It must be curious about the fire." Nell hurried to put her revolver in her back waistband before Frankie could notice. Maybe the horse smelled the two women.

As the early morning light increased, they waited. And then another animal screamed like a woman in pain and leaped at the horse. The horse neighed and screamed, too, an unearthly sound, and shied back. Its front legs jabbed at its attacker and knocked it back but not far enough. A large cat hunkered down and then leaped again, closing in on the neck of the horse.

Moonshine rushed up the slope and entered the fray, growling and snarling. He jumped at the lion and knocked it sideways. Frankie screamed. Nell brought out the revolver and tried to aim at the mountain lion. The horse, in a frenzy of shying and pounding with its hooves, made a moving target, and she couldn't get a clear sight of the mountain lion. She didn't want to shoot and risk hitting Moonie, as black as the river behind them. The women could only watch and hope the horse and dog would prevail. The horse's hooves jerked and struck again and again. At last, the lion lay still on the ground. Her dog circled the animal. The horse's chest heaved as it stood and trembled, its head hanging down.

"Go get it, Frankie, but gently! I'll keep an eye on the lion." Nell followed Frankie up the slope, both of them stepping slowly and carefully, Nell with her revolver out and aimed. "Moonshine, come here, boy." He heard her because he glanced up but took his time leaving the carcass. "You helped save the horse. Good boy." She knelt as he neared and moved her hands over his body, trying to see if he had been hurt by lion or horse. He was wet with sweat. "Are you hurt?" She felt nothing awry. Daylight might tell a different story.

When the women and dog were back at the tent, with the horse's reins tied to one of the branches, Nell replenished the fire. "Where did the horse come from, Frankie? Did you tie it up in those trees?"

"I didn't. James did." She stayed close to the reins. "I forgot about it when we were setting up camp and eating the snake."

Nell could feel her companion shudder. Her own goosebumps spoke for themselves.

The light quickened. Nell checked Moonshine again where he lay near the sleeping bag. "It's time to get moving. With this horse, we can get to Salmon, maybe in time to meet Charlie and his prisoner, er… James." She stood and began rolling the tarp. "I doubt if they slept out overnight, though."

"They would have to stop and let James rest," Frankie said. "He couldn't go all the way without resting, so maybe they did camp." She, too, stood and began gathering their camp detritus. She patted the horse and removed its saddle and the saddlebags. She peeked at Nell who didn't seem to notice any of her movements.

"You better water the horse. It must be so thirsty!" Nell had watched Frankie surreptitiously, afraid the woman would get on the saddle and ride away. "Take the frypan and do it or take it to the river." She almost kicked herself for suggesting that. It would be so easy for Frankie to abandon Nell. "And bring water back up to douse the fire. I'll fill my canteen before we leave."

Hanging the pack around the saddlebags appeared impossible. Maybe the saddlebags would hang over the pack. The two of them would have to squeeze onto the saddle. Nell wondered how capable and flexible the animal could be. It must be used to carrying mining gear and maybe even gold. Frankie had removed the saddle to give the horse a rest. Nell shook out the saddle blanket and smoothed the horse's back with her hands before it went with Frankie to the river. Bareback might not be the woman's preference, and Nellie knew her companion wouldn't leave the saddlebags.

Frankie brought the horse back up to the camp, along with water in the frypan to douse the fire. It was full daylight before the saddle blanket, saddle, pack with the tarp, sleeping bag, camp gear, and saddlebags had all been loaded onto the horse. "Does it have a name?" Nellie asked.

"I don't know. That sheriff of yours never told me if it did." Frankie had not been happy for the bags to go on top of the pack, although Nell convinced her to try it. The two women weren't too heavy, so the horse should be able to carry everything. At least the dog wouldn't ride on top.

"I'll take the lead. Maybe we can change along the way. It depends if you get uncomfortable. Let's go." Nell managed to get her foot in the stirrup and Frankie boosted her up, then Nell helped Frankie climb on behind. "Come along, Moonshine. We're almost there!"

Chapter 14

FRANKIE ASKED TO CHANGE PLACES as the pair reached the farmland and flat fields around Salmon. She knew they were close and wanted to be in charge. They had not seen James and the sheriff along the river as they rode north. She hadn't decided what to do if James were in jail. She certainly couldn't row the dory alone on the river as it flowed through the primitive area. If the sheriff waited on the dock in Salmon, she was lost.

To her surprise and delight, James waited on the dock. No sheriff was in sight.

"Where's Charlie?" Nell craned her head back and forth. She slid down first. Moonshine had walked and trotted along beside the horse the whole way.

"He decided to get off back there a ways." James grinned and helped Frankie to the ground. "Glad you ladies found the horse."

"Frankie said you were under arrest and that the sheriff was going to take you to the county jail." Nellie glanced around, trying to see if Charlie lurked anywhere. There was no sign of him. "What do you mean, 'he got off'?"

"I had to rest my aching shoulders, so we pulled into a bitty cove back there." He waved his hand in the air. "He had to see a man about a horse. So did I. I got back first, shoved off, and rowed right up to town. He'll probably come along soon, madder'n a hornet, I suspect." James untied the saddlebags. "You want these?"

Frankie felt herself blush. "You bet I do." She grabbed them from James.

"Pretty heavy for a sweet thing like you." James wrapped his arm around her waist and pulled Frankie to him.

"Don't!" Frankie pulled away. "I'm not too sweet on you, James. You left me more than once. What are we gonna do now? If you're here when the sheriff returns, he'll put you in the slammer. Then what will *I* do?"

Nellie faced them. "He'll put you both in the county jail, although I doubt you'll be in the same cage." She turned to the horse and untied the pack, swinging it down in front of her. Moonshine sat on his haunches close by. He looked like a black guard. James took a step toward them, and the dog snarled a warning. Nell placed her hand on his head.

"Guess we better hightail it outta here, Frankie. With two of us to row, we should be able to get to Riggins and maybe on to the Snake. It's all downhill from here." James's laugh sounded raspy. "We can leave the sheriff empty-handed. Hah!"

"If I go with you, you gotta treat me right. No more drowning." Frankie frowned, not certain she could trust James.

"I was just fooling with you. Can't you take a joke?" James's face adopted a hang-dog look, mouth down, head lowered. He lifted both and grinned again.

"That was no joke. If it hadn't been for Norman, I woulda drowned." Frankie leaned toward James and swatted his arm.

Nell reached for Frankie, with her hand outstretched. "Don't go. It's too dangerous. I'll talk to the sheriff, tell him how you helped me. Besides, aren't you hungry? I bet there's a café nearby.

Come with me." Nell patted Frankie's arm. "If James isn't lying about Charlie, he should be here any minute."

"That's damned right, Frankie. C'mon. Get in the boat. I brought some food for me, but you can have it. If you decide to stay, though, I want those saddlebags."

"No! They're mine." She swung away from both James and Nell. "Let's go, James. We can fuss over the bags later." Frankie had spotted the dory at the dock as soon as she and Nell approached the landing on the horse. Who knew if Nell could talk the sheriff into letting Frankie go? "Help me get in the dory, James. And this time, treat me right." Frankie swung her hair around, waved to Nellie, and stepped over to the dory. "I can't say it's been a good time, Nell. But it wasn't the worst I've ever spent." She pointed to the horse. "You better get him looked at. He's got a couple of deep scratches from that mountain lion."

James assisted Frankie in, untied the rope, and climbed in himself. He pushed off. "Tell the sheriff I said to leave off. I didn't kill Norman. Next time, I'll beat the stuffings out of him!" He pushed against the dock stanchion and the boat moved with the current downstream.

Frankie sat in the back, hanging onto her saddlebags. She turned and waved to Nellie. She wished she had taken more time to think about heading off with James. Even Norman might have been safer than his partner.

Chapter 15

NELLIE SAT ON A TUB turned upside down and Moonshine joined her. The horse stayed near Moonie. It was as if they had become friends after the fight with the mountain lion. She should head back to Challis, but maybe Charlie was on the side of the river she and Frankie had just traveled. She couldn't understand why it had taken Charlie and James so long to get to Salmon. They had left the day before. And where was Charlie now?

Activity stirred around her. Two men loaded a small scow tied up near her. She approached them. "Have you seen a tall Basque? Or Janie the nurse?"

"You mean that sheriff from down towards Ketchum? Yeah. He was at the city jail just an hour or so ago. A doc worked on his shoulder. He got it banged up bad."

The second man chimed in. "Janie headed back to Stanley with someone going that way." They both went back to work.

Nellie breathed a sigh of relief. Charlie was all right. What had happened that he didn't take James to jail? She was sorry Janie was gone.

Ace came striding down the dock. "Hey there, Miss Burns. You ready to go again? The sheriff is on his way. We're going after you-know-who. Charlie's got your pack and all. Janie found a ride."

"Ace, you're still here! I thought you would be long gone."

"Nope, I needed a contract to go downriver. I got one from the local police. I'm a gonna chase the—" he said and looked around. He lowered his voice. "That murderer James Murray. The sheriff's been charged to get him." He almost laughed, but seemed to realize this was deadly business. "Got some more business, too. We'll be taking mining gear and such to a rancher along the river. He's up the Middle Fork, but we'll meet him where the fork meets the main. We been wondering where you been."

Nellie stood up and saw Charlie walking toward her. No limp, at least. She hesitated before approaching him. After all the hullaballoo since she fell off the boat, she wasn't certain how she felt about him or how he felt about her.

"Nell!" Charlie hurried his step and surrounded her with his arms and chest and neck and head. "Thank god, you are all right. I hated to leave you up the river. Forgive me, please." He stepped back, still holding onto her shoulders. "I know you are a survivor, but I did not want to make it harder on you. Only, I did have to." He held her again and she felt safe, as she always did in his arms.

She clasped her arms around his waist and pressed her cheek against his chest. Nell couldn't stop herself from crying. She knew her body shook while tears streamed down her face. "I didn't know how—" "I didn't—" "You were gone—" She gulped after each effort to explain her crying. "You left me—" Charlie just held her. After a short while, Nell stopped crying. "I'm your wife, not some deputy!" Her tears turned to anger. "Why did you let that woman ride on the horse with you?"

Charlie let her go. "You are angry about that?" He began to laugh but stopped short when he saw Nell's face. "Be angry that you fell in the water. That you had to survive in the wilderness, or that I left you and sent Frankie to find you. Or that I took James in the dory—or rather he had to row the boat with me in it." He wrapped his arms around her again. "I am truly sorry, my dear Nellie. I knew how strong you are. I really had no choice. I could not let a murderer go. And now we must catch him again."

Ace harrumphed. "Let's go, you two. I ain't got all night to watch you make up. Got your life preservers, Miss Nellie? The river gets a sight more dangerous from here on. That murderer and his gal certainly may end up in it. The sooner we go, the closer we'll be to pull 'em out when they do." He motioned for them to follow him. "We're puttin' you in the middle, Miss, on the bottom. There's ropes to hang on to and stayin' low should keep you safe unless the whole kit and kaboodle goes ass over—oops, sorry. I'll do my best to keep us goin' right side up. I done this dozens of times."

Charlie had taken the horse back to the ground at the end of the dock where a deputy waited to take possession. Nellie called for Moonie, following the horse. He returned to her but glanced back at the horse, who neighed. "I can't go yet. I've had almost nothing to eat for several days. I have to eat!"

Ace and Charlie glanced at each other. Ace sighed. "I'll go up to that local café and get you some vittles. You two get settled. I don't want to lose you and have to go searchin'."

The sheriff assisted Nell onto the scow and placed her where Ace pointed. "I am tying your pack to you, Nell, although those cork things do not help. I will load my pack on my back. If we go over, we should keep our belongings with us. Your camera is dry. I checked." When she was settled, he added, "I am going to stand up to help Ace when he needs it." He leaned close. "Your revolver is dry, too."

Nell whispered back. "Your revolver is in your pack. I almost had to use it, once." Ace returned in short order, and she watched as he pushed the scow off the dock into what was calm water. "Now tell me what happened with you and James."

The river was loud enough that Nellie couldn't hear all of what Charlie said. She understood that James had used his oar to knock the sheriff down, striking at his right shoulder. She wondered how the outlaw knew about that. Probably Frankie had said something. Sitting close to him on the horse might have alerted her to his wound. James had tied his victim's arms and legs with a vine. It had taken Charlie the better part of the night to get himself loose. He walked the road to get to Salmon, seeing no one on his way. He had seen the empty dory at the dock, but he had to get help for his shoulder first. By then, he saw James and a passenger heading downriver.

Nellie followed with a brief summary of what she had been through after she fell off the scow. Then she reached up to touch his shoulder with a tender touch. "Did the wound open again?"

"Not only opened, but the oar split the skin. A doctor sewed it up. It is painful."

"I don't see how you are going to help Ace with the sweep. That would probably just pull the stitches out. Too bad Janie isn't still with us."

Charlie nodded. He turned his attention to the river and to their boatman.

Nellie opened the sack Ace had brought to the boat. Inside were rolls, pieces of ham and cheese, several apples, three pieces of apple pie (for all of them, she guessed), and a cloth napkin. She tried to be ladylike in eating and failed. Neither Ace nor Charlie watched her, so she fell to, giving Moonie pieces of everything except the pie.

Chapter 16

NELLIE WAS TORN BETWEEN FEAR of landing in the water again and serenity at being *on* the water again. The depths of deep green on which they moved and the palette of colors around them helped distract from the fear. Sitting next to Moonie and his warm fur comforted her as well. She wrapped her hand around the rope holding in mounds of mining gear and the bench on which Charlie sat. From time to time, he followed Ace's instructions to push or pull the sweep at the front end of the scow. She watched as he babied his right shoulder. She had insisted on viewing what new damage he had sustained. There were stitches, but both the bullet wound and the tear appeared to be healing well.

A road followed the river as they headed north. The river flowed smoothly with almost no white water, and when it did rage, Ace managed to keep the scow as level as possible and few waves buffeted them. Around noon, they reached the North Fork, where the river made a turn and headed west. The next destination was Shoup where a smattering of buildings and a dock greeted them. Ace maneuvered neatly to land the scow.

"I'll go ashore and get more supplies," Ace announced. "You two wait here. I'll see about a report on the dory. It can't be too far ahead of us. The river hasn't moved that fast."

Moonshine stood as if to follow him. "Stay with us, Moonie. There's nothing up there for you. He'll get you some jerky." Nell poured water from her canteen into a small pan she had found in Salmon. Moonie lapped it up and settled down again. "Charlie, what are we going to do with James and Frankie if we catch up with them? Ace said the next town was Riggins and not big at all." He had also warned about all the white water between where they sat and the town. Nell tried not to focus on his doom-and-gloom predictions. She released her hand to give it a rest.

Charlie rested his arm on her shoulder below him. "I do not know. We will have to wait and see what happens on this part of the journey. Ace said the dory they were in will have a rough go from here on out. In Salmon, I telephoned Rosy in the office in Hailey. He will try to meet us in Riggins, so we could return home from there with him. If we do not round up the criminals, I will leave it to the federal marshal in north Idaho to finish the job." He frowned. Nell knew he hated to fail at finishing anything. He was a dogged lawman.

Ace returned. "I got a report. The dory passed here last night. They docked until first light and headed out again. They paid for supplies with gold dust."

"I bet that's Bull's stash they're carrying. Those saddlebags weighed too much to just carry supplies or clothes," Nellie said. She pondered a moment. "If they end up in the river, the bags will sink to the bottom. Poor Bull."

"He ain't so innocent, Miss Burns." Ace leaped back on the scow after untying it from the dock. As he pushed on the sweep to get them back in the current, he turned to her. "Say, why do you have a different name than the sheriff here if you two are married?" He paid attention to what he was doing and then turned back to her.

"Because I had my own name and wanted to keep it. Charlie didn't seem to care." Not that it mattered if he did, Nell thought to herself. She had considered suggesting he take her name but decided that was one step too far, even if his was impossible to pronounce. He had explained once that in his native language, Euskara, pieces of his name referred to places in the Basque country of Spain.

"Tighten up them life jackets, Miss Burns. We're comin' to some hot spots." He called to Charlie. "I'll take the front. You come back here. Miss Burns, there's a bailin' bucket. You'll need to work that, but hang on tight, too."

The river had settled into a glass-like surface, a mirror of the side walls. Then, the air resounded with booms like thunder. Nell thought at first a lightning storm was headed their way, but the skies were blue. When she realized it was the river booming, she nearly froze.

"Ready? Here we go!"

Not ready was Nell's only thought. The front of the scow froze in space and then fell and the rear stood up straight. Ace's bulk leaned on the sweep with all his might. Water completely covered him as it surged onto the boat and swept across Nellie and then Charlie. She saw them pass a huge rock where the water boiled and sprayed from the side onto the scow. Holding onto a rope and a timber on the floor of the boat, she felt herself lifted by an impossible force and then let go before her hands turned limp. The scow turned sideways but stayed with the current. A steep rockfall beside them flew by. When Nell could see, more white water thrashed on all sides. She had looped one of the ropes around Moonshine and he stayed low on the scow floor. He bit at the water surging over him but seemed safe. Ace shouted a time or two to Charlie but she couldn't hear the words. And then the roar of water, the boom of the scow in it, all ceased. Serene green water took the place of the maelstrom.

"Folks, you made it through Pine Creek Falls." Ace's arms stroked the sweep and he stood tall.

When Nell looked back, she saw they had come down several feet of falls. Her heart still beat like a timpani, but gradually, her breathing slowed. She took the bucket and filled it with water to sling over the side. Charlie released the back sweep and stooped to help her, taking the bucket. She let him and crawled to Moonshine to release the rope around his middle. He licked her face.

"I never done this without a back sweep and bailer. You two did just fine."

"Was that the worst?" Nellie asked.

"Nope. We got more to go, but first, we'll stop at where the Middle Fork meets this here Main Salmon. Maybe we'll pick up our criminals in between. I didn't see no dory leavings back there. They musta made it through."

Nellie touched Charlie's shoulder. "How did your shoulder do?"

He smiled and patted her hand. "The stitches held."

Ace shouted out "Hang on!" a few times but the remainder of the afternoon, they followed the moving current. Another series of white water stretches felt nothing like Pine Creek Falls. The cliff walls grew steeper and taller, and the river course narrowed. Nell watched for wildlife, hoping to see more bighorn sheep. They passed structures fitted onto narrow byways and near creeks tumbling into the Salmon. Ace didn't comment and Nellie didn't ask about them. Mining claims had peopled the route of the

Salmon for fifty years or more. The areas appeared deserted.

When Ace directed Charlie to the back sweep, and Ace headed to the front again, Nellie was forewarned. She wrapped Moonshine again, found the bucket, and the spot where she could hang on the tightest. Instead, Ace directed them to the riverside. He jumped with a rope to a rock and pulled in the scow. "Gotta look this one over." Charlie went with him.

Both men came back, their faces lined with worry. On board, Charlie whispered to Nell. "There is a big hole we need to avoid. Otherwise, we will be fine."

Nell watched Ace. He didn't look fine. He stood with Charlie at the back sweep and gave instructions, words Nell couldn't hear. "I thought we were going to land at the Middle Fork and Main Salmon before the water became really dangerous," she said.

"These falls are worse than usual because of the low water," Ace answered. "You'll be fine."

That word "fine" was beginning to sound in Nell's ears like a particularly bad swear word. She decided to stay close to Moonshine and hope for the best. She was afraid to wrap a rope around both of them in case the scow turned over and they wouldn't be able to get loose. Landing in the water was much preferable to being stuck under the wooden boat filled with mining gear. It would probably sink.

Once again, the scow's front end hung in the air for what seemed like minutes and then dropped, the tail end standing straight up. Nell saw the hole in the water. It looked like it led to a deep green hell. Ace shouted to Charlie. He shouted back. Then water swamped all of them, and Nell was certain they had overturned. She gasped all the air she could hold, grabbed Moonshine, and hung onto him. What felt like a ton of water shoved her under the bench and pulled her out. Just as she lost all sense of up or down and her lungs emptied, her head came out of the water. Ace and Charlie clung to the sweeps and the boat scooted along the edge of the hole. More water swept across the scow, but not as heavy nor as deep this time. If the river was low, it didn't feel that way to Nell. She looked back and saw the seven- or eight-foot height of the falls. Water dripped from her whole body, as it did Moonie's. She tried to squeeze out her clothes but gave up and bailed water instead.

Ace whooped. "Middle Fork next stop!"

Chapter 17

FRANKIE TOOK HER TURN AT the oars of the dory when James grew too tired. He bossed and cajoled and gave her instructions. She ignored him and rowed as hard as she could down the middle of the Salmon. When she heard the booms ahead of her on the river, she pulled the boat to a calm eddy beside the shore. "What is happening down there?"

James grabbed a tethered rope and jumped to the riverside. "Maybe we should take a gander."

"You look. I need to rest." Her arms and back ached. No wonder James got tired. She had thought she was stronger than he was, but maybe not. "I'm hungry. I need one of those pastries you brought aboard from Shoup. Where are they?"

"Not good for you," James said. "They'll slow you down." He grinned and walked along the riverside to look. He came back, his face appearing to have lost all color. "Not sure you can do this one. I better take the oars again."

Frankie moved from the middle seat to the back one. She didn't want to be in front and get the brunt of white water. She wished she had a life preserver. She should have taken Nellie's from the scow before they headed out on the dory. Or at least taken Moonshine's. Dogs swim from instinct, don't they? "Go ahead.

Hand me a pastry, please. I'm starved."

James grabbed a bag from under the rower's seat and passed Frankie a maple bar. He took one for himself as well. He must be hungry, too. Too bad there hadn't been any ham or bacon at Shoup. It was almost a ghost town, now that most of the mining had stopped.

Frankie helped James push the boat back into the current. She decided to sit on the floor of the boat and hang onto the rear seat. It had a space between the seat and the tail end of the boat. She hugged the whole seat and grasped her hands together underneath. She closed her eyes, so she couldn't see what they headed into.

James shouted. Water poured over the deep front of the dory and across the whole boat. Frankie held on as tightly as she could, her mouth filling with water. Sitting on the floor had been a bad idea. She choked and coughed and her head finally came free of the huge wave. At first, she thought James had been swept off the boat, but he had merely ducked to let the water flow over him. He sat up, and he worked the oars like a machine to free the dory from the foaming water. Before long, they slowed onto calmer water.

"You okay back there?"

Coughing and spitting water, Frankie answered. "Oka-a-ay." She watched the falls behind them and could hardly believe they hadn't dumped over. "You did it, James." She spit out more water. It tasted green.

After a while, Frankie heard the booming again. "There's more falls up there! I want out. I'll walk around."

"Nah, these won't be as bad as the last ones." James kept rowing.

"James, let me out!" Frankie shouted. She had eaten another

maple bar and it felt like a lump in her stomach. Another bad idea. She made a motion to put her legs over the side. "Take me to shore! If you don't, I won't row again." The rocks on the riverbed shown bright and clear. It couldn't be too deep.

The threat worked. James headed to shore. Frankie knew she had to jump as she doubted he would do anything to help her gain land. Her foot slipped on a rock as she leaped to shore and she fell forward, skinning a knee and her hand. *Jerk*, she thought. Then she realized she didn't have her saddlebags. "Wait!"

With one of the oars, James pushed the dory back into the current. "I'll see you downstream a mile or two. There's no landing after these next falls until the Middle Fork meets this big river. And then it's huge! Want to walk all the way to Riggins?" He laughed and his belly shook. "If you make it, we can split the gold then." His mouth grinned as wide as a Cheshire Cat.

Frankie didn't think he would wait for her. Still, the booms reverberated all through the canyon. She stood and began to struggle down the river to the sound, slipping on moss and tangling with brush. She reached the next waterfalls just as James and the dory arrived there, too. The dory hung in midair for a few moments and then dived down. Frankie shivered at the boiling white water and then saw what looked like a dark green hole in the water, a whirlpool with no apparent bottom.

She saw James's eyes widen and his face blanch. He lurched at the oars like a madman, pushing and pulling to miss the whirlpool. He almost made it.

Chapter 18

"ACE! CHECK OUT THAT WOOD floating over there!" Charlie shouted at the boatman.

Nellie looked up from bailing and glanced toward where Charlie pointed. There was movement along the shore as well—a person scrambling over rocks and brush, apparently trying to keep up with the log in the water.

Ace worked the sweep to get closer to whatever floated. "Might could be the dory," he called back to Charlie. "Upside down. No surprise." He moved the scow to be in front of the floating boat. "No good place to land here."

"Charlie, I think I see someone scrambling on shore. Maybe one of them is under the boat." Or floating in the water, she didn't add.

Charlie leaned over as far as he could from the back end of the scow. "Does not look too deep. I could jump in and see if I could turn the dory upright." He lifted his head to check with Ace. "What do you think?"

"You should stay at the back sweep, Charlie. I don't think it looks too deep, either. I could get in and peer underneath." Nell could bite her tongue. She did not want to jump in the water. What if she lost touch with the scow?

"You could not lift the boat. You are too small." He pulled off his shoes and jacket. "I will go. Okay with you, Ace?"

"Yeah, check it out, Sheriff. Seems like whoever might be under there is yours." Ace continued to work the sweep to keep his boat in line with the dory.

Nell studied the shore. The person she thought she had seen was no longer visible. The screen of rocks and brush provided good shelter. She hoped it had been Frankie, not James.

Charlie jumped in. The water came up above his waist. He waded to the overturned dory and grabbed the edge. His muscles strained. Nell worried about his shoulder. This could split the stitches. She didn't think she could re-sew them. He stumbled with the current but held on. The boat slowly lifted.

A man, looking like a drowned rat, appeared. He lifted his arms and helped Charlie tip the boat over. His wet hair hung over his face and neck. "My god! You came along at the right time. I couldn't get any leverage to push the boat over." He must have recognized who helped him. He spit into the water.

"Where is your companion?" The sheriff held the boat in place as he waded toward the scow, the back of the dory in hand. "Is she all right?"

"How do I know? The bitch stayed on shore." He shook his head like a dog shaking off water. "She coulda helped with that damned whirlpool."

"Call her," Charlie directed. If she were on shore, she could not have seen that James still lived. The boat was in the way.

"*You* call her. I ain't interested."

Nell heard the back and forth. "Frankie! Where are you?" She called. "James was under the dory and is all right. Charlie has him." She watched the shore and waited. Soon the bushes flailed, and Frankie stepped onto a rock in the water.

"What about my saddlebags?" Frankie answered. "I couldn't reach the boat."

Ace's voice interrupted. "Come on out and get on the scow. Charlie, bring that criminal over here. We can attach the dory behind us and take everything along to the Middle Fork. Then we can figure it all out."

"I can't," Frankie wailed. "The water's too deep."

Charlie shoved James to the scow, still holding onto the dory. "Wait while I tie up the dory and I will come get you."

"You're gonna have to tie it up alongside, sheriff. Otherwise, we can't use the back sweep, and we'll need it ahead." Ace nodded to Nellie. "Can you help him? I gotta keep my hand on this here front sweep."

Nellie loosened her grip on the cargo rope and shuffled to the side. "Hand me the rope, Charlie, and get yourself at one end or the other of the dory. The back end, I'd say. I can wrap it around some struts here, but you'll have to tie the knot. I don't know anything other than a slip-knot." She turned her head toward James. "You climb up the back, behind me. Moonshine will keep an eye on you. No tricks, or I'll let him go on you."

Without too much time passing, Nell and Charlie secured the dory. She could see what looked like the saddlebags tied around the seat in the back. Frankie would be relieved. Charlie waded to shore and picked Frankie up with his left arm. At first, she squirmed. Then she calmed down and let the sheriff bring her to the scow, her legs trailing behind. She climbed over the side and flopped down next to Nell. "Hello again," she said.

Moonshine ignored Frankie and instead watched James. He stayed in the rear of the scow. Charlie took up his position at the back sweep. Nell wanted to check his shoulder but didn't want to alert James that the sheriff was still damaged, and even more so because James had shoved him with an oar. Frankie sat down on the floor of the scow and sulked. There appeared to be no weapons at hand, but Nell didn't trust either one of them a whit.

"Frankie, come and help me bail. Ace, is there another bucket?"

The boatman nodded and picked up a bucket from the front of the scow. He tossed it to Nellie, who caught it before it tumbled back toward James and Moonshine.

Frankie crawled to Nellie. She grabbed the bucket. "All this water come from those last falls?" She managed to sit, still holding onto one of the ropes. "I wouldn't ride the dory because the sound terrified me." She hung her head. "You're a lot braver than I am."

"I think you may be smarter than I am. I didn't go look at the falls with Charlie and Ace. They looked worried when they returned. Did you see the dory go over?"

Frankie nodded her head. "Looked like ass over teakettle to me. I was sure James had drowned when he didn't appear in the smoother water." A brief smile flitted across her face. Nell decided there was no love lost between the two.

"We're comin' up to the Middle Fork where it joins this here Salmon River," Ace warned. "We're gonna pull into a side eddy. There should be company waitin' for us. Charlie, get ready to leap to shore with a rope. James, don't move."

Nell watched the shore. Sure enough, she saw two men, bulky in size wearing Levi's, heavy work shirts, and slouch hats, unshaven and dirty to boot. When the sheriff leaped, they hustled to catch him and the rope and pull the scow to shore. Another man joined them, cleaner in appearance and not as muscled. Not a miner?

"Hiya, Milt. I got a load of gear for you. How's tricks? Any shows?"

Milt waved at Ace. "We need the gear you brought us." He turned and talked to his men, giving them directions. Back up the shoreline, a wagon with two mules pulling a long sledge with wheels waited.

Frankie and Nellie moved to the far side of the scow and let Ace uncover the gear. The two men began to heft it out of the boat to carry it up to the sledge. Almost everything appeared to be metal, rusted metal at that. Nell surmised it came from other mining claims, not so different from equipment she had seen at Vienna, Custer, and Bonanza, ghost towns in the Stanley Basin. It was a wonder that mining still carried on along the river. Flywheels, skinny metal lengths, gears, wood and metal, too. Before long, the boat was cleared of most of the gear and rode higher in the water. She wasn't sure that would be a good thing when floating downriver and through the whitewater. Or maybe it wouldn't be so vulnerable to the rocky depths.

Nell kept an eye on James. He didn't offer to help, but then Moonshine probably wouldn't let him do so, anyway. Resting while the others worked would let James gather his strength. Not a good thing at all.

Within an hour, Charlie climbed back on board and back to the sweep. Milt and his miners pushed them off, and soon Ace had the scow riding with the current again. The two women had been busy during the offload, bailing any water left from the ride over the falls. Both seated themselves near but not on the bench. That had been too vulnerable to sweeping waves.

"What's coming up, Ace?" Nell called. She wanted to know how to prepare. She did not want to end up in the water again. Her glance back to Charlie told her he might feel the same way. He had touched her arm while he helped the men unload and asked her how she was. She wanted to hold onto him and stay in one place for a few hours. That was not to be.

As they floated down the river, James began to talk. "I didn't kill Norman, Sheriff. You gotta believe me. Just ask Frankie there." His voice whined at a higher register than Nell had heard before. "I carried him into the back bedroom at Bull's place. He was dead by then. There wasn't nothin' I could do."

Nell answered for Charlie. "You shot the sheriff."

"How'd I know he was a sheriff? He didn't wear no badge or clothes like a lawman. I was just protecting Frankie there. All I could see was Norman going down. I thought this strange man shot him. I sure didn't. He was a pard' of mine."

"Then who did it?" Nell thought it was strange that Charlie didn't say anything. She guessed he was busy with the sweep.

"Darned if I know." He glanced at the sheriff. "Maybe the sheriff did. Maybe Bull did it. Maybe that cowboy who rode in did it. Happened while Norm stood on the porch like a target waiting to be shot. Dumb."

"Norman was not dumb!" Frankie's head had moved back and forth between James and Nellie. "You told me it was the sheriff who shot Norman!" Her face wrinkled up and she squeezed some tears out. "Norman was a good man, and he trusted you. Told me you and him were gonna do some jobs together." She gestured back upriver. "That Salmon was where we were going to go in that dory. It couldn't even hold all three of us!"

"And whose fault is that? You wouldn't catch and hold my scow." He growled at Frankie, then crawled toward her. Moonshine barked and stood up. James backed down. "We coulda fit in there just fine. Besides, you took the horse and left, paying me no never mind. You stole the—" James clamped his mouth shut.

Nellie glanced over at Frankie, who hugged the saddlebags, even though she had tied them to the rope holding the bench in place. In the distance, she heard churning water. Almost at the same time, Ace shouted.

"Hang on. Here we go again!"

This time, the scow floated right through the whitewater as if guided from beneath by an unseen hand. Water splashed along the edges of the boat, but the boat, other than moving up and down, glided through the waves and to smooth water at the end. The dory slipped easily along with the bigger boat. The only difference it seemed to make was to pull the scow a little to the right. Ace guided his sweep to keep both wooden boats in line. Nellie watched Charlie at the back sweep. He and Ace seemed to work together on this stretch, keeping them all level and in place. That was easy, she thought, but it brought to mind her sensations when she had been washed overboard, her images of Charlie, her lover and husband. She smiled at him. If they had been alone on the boat, she would have managed to crawl to him and stand up to wrap her arms around him, sweep be damned. Instead, she turned to Frankie. "Are you all right?"

Frankie nodded. "I'll be glad to get off this boat. It's no safer than that dory was. Maybe going to jail will be a welcome relief." Her hair dripped from the water that splashed over the side. Her Levi's looked soaked as well.

"Move closer to me, Frankie, and stretch your legs out. Maybe your pants will dry a little faster." Nellie motioned to the woman. The water could just as well come in on the other side next time, but maybe they could help each other.

The river ran between steep mountains on both sides, one with rock cliffs climbing higher and higher. A few trees managed to grow in isolated spots. Nell had to lean backward to see the tops of the cliffs. The other side rose not as high and bunches of evergreen trees hung on to the slopes. After the Middle Fork, the Salmon spread out wider, except for the water they had just run through. When she looked back, the gap in the mountains, the blue sky, and scattered white and gray clouds reflected off the water. She wished her camera were easier to use on the scow. That scene would have made a perfect postcard.

Ace called out to Charlie. "We're gonna stop at the ranch comin' up. I got mail to deliver and maybe we can get us some fresh vegetables, maybe even a meal, if the owner's feelin' generous. Just follow my lead." He stepped around his sweep and guided the boat to the river left, where the steep slopes had diminished down to a long, level flat of land. Several log structures sat back from the shore, and a man and a woman headed down to the water from one of the cabins. The man hailed Ace.

"Howdy, Elmer. I got mail for you, and a few supplies the Shoup store said you needed. Help me land this darned boat." Ace threw a rope to Elmer. "We got some passengers we're takin' to Riggins. Got any grub we could buy from you?" No mention of criminals.

Frankie perked up. She pulled her wet hair back and managed to tie a string around it. Nellie, once again, shook her shorter hair, glad it was shorn to below her ears. It dried fast and held its shape. Charlie prodded James with his knee. "Get up, James. You can stretch your legs if you wish. Do not try any tricks. I will take off the handcuffs. I have my eye on you and so does the dog. If you get out of hand, I will re-handcuff you."

"Moonie, come with me." Nell waited for Charlie to step to her side after James passed and jumped onto the shore. He ignored Frankie and she let herself down, with a hand from Ace. "Wait,"

Nellie whispered to Charlie. "How is your shoulder? Do you want me to look at it?" She wrapped her arm around Charlie's back, feeling his strength and the damp from standing at the sweep. "If nothing else, I can dry the bandages or put on new ones. Janie left a bunch for us."

Elmer, bearded and with long white hair, and the woman, with deeply lined face and hair turning gray, stood on the shore next to the scow, a married couple, Nell guessed. "Good to see you, Ace." The woman held out her hand to shake, but Ace grabbed and hugged her. "You're looking good, Mary Rose. How are things?" He shook the man's hand. "Elmer." Ace handed over a small leather bag and motioned to the scow. "Got a box of supplies for you."

"I will get it, Ace." Charlie stepped forward.

"We brought mining gear to Milt, back at the confluence. We're so light now, it's like guiding a pine cone down the Salmon, except for that darned wooden boat tied up to us." He pointed to one of the boxes in the front baggage area. Charlie picked it up and carried it to the side. "Water has been good since Salmon," Ace said. "Not too shallow. Not too deep. Early October may be the best time on the river, unless there's a fire. So far, so good."

James and Frankie stood to one side. Nell wasn't sure they were talking to each other until she saw Frankie nod her head. Uh-oh. Plans were being made. She nudged Charlie's back and gestured to the pair. "Better take the handcuffs and slow James down," she whispered. "I think they have something in mind."

"Y'all come up to the house," Mary Rose said. "I can fry up some elk meat and greens and taters from the garden. You look tired and in need of a rest." She turned and walked with a hint of a sashay up the flat section of land. She turned back. "You, too, Ace. I got your favorite cake. Didn't know you were comin', but it was a nice day, so I thought you might could appear."

On shore with her dog, Nellie knelt to Moonshine. "Watch him," she said in a low voice and pointed to James. Louder, she turned to Elmer, "This is a lovely oasis. Do you mind if I take a photograph of your cabin and outbuildings? It would be nice to get one of the river, too, from your viewpoint."

Elmer shrugged his shoulders. "Sure."

Nell introduced herself and Charlie. She left off the designation "Sheriff." She pointed to James and Frankie and identified them as well. "We are all going to Riggins, courtesy of Ace there." Charlie heard her and climbed back up to retrieve her camera bag. Water poured off the canvas.

The whole party crossed the field together with Ace leading and Charlie at the back. Nellie stopped to set up her tripod and situate her camera. It was completely dry, as was the film pack. The canvas bag had done its job. "Wait," she called. "Turn around and I'll get a photo of all of you—for posterity." Only Ace and Elmer and maybe Moonshine looked happy about being photographed. James, Frankie, and Charlie scowled at Nell. "Okay. Keep walking. I'll get the cabin after you are all in it. Frankie, you help Mary Rose, please."

Frankie stuck her tongue out at Nell. She turned and entered the cabin, grabbing Charlie's arm as he neared her.

The boat crew appreciated the food. They had been eating pastries, snacks, and jerky. Fried elk meat and the fixings satisfied their hunger pains. "I gotta—" James motioned to the outdoors. "Where is the—" he blushed.

"Out that door and up behind the cabin," Elmer said.

"I will go with you," Charlie said. He stood up and waited for James to do so. They both walked out the door.

After a stretch where no one said anything at the table, Nell rose and picked up plates. "Thank you, Mary Rose. That was delicious and indeed welcome to our weary crew." She heard a privy door slam, boots running, the loud sound of a punch landing on someone, and a muffled swear word. She doubted Charlie would swear, so she assumed he had hit James. Ace leaped up and hurried out the door. Frankie winced.

A loud voice shouted. "I didn't do it, I tell you!" That was James. "Take these off."

Ace came back to the door. "We gotta go, folks. Head on down to the scow. I'll help Charlie with—you know."

"Where is Moonshine?" Nell hurried to the door, too. Her dog stood on one of the steps, watching the activity behind the cabin, unseen to her.

"What's goin' on?" Elmer crowded Nell from the doorway and stepped out.

"Just another ruckus," Mary Rose said. She stayed behind to clear the table.

Ace herded Charlie and James down the front grassy area to the scow. Nellie waited for Frankie, and they walked together. Nell turned and waved to Elmer and Mary Rose. "Thanks," she called.

The river ahead looked smooth. Nell doubted it would stay that way. The conversation at the table had referred to various names of whitewater, camps, waterfalls, beaches, and danger.

Chapter 19

"ACE, HOW MUCH FARTHER TO Riggins?" Nell wanted to know what lay ahead but wasn't sure how to ask without sounding like a sissy. Would they have to stay somewhere on a beach? She had seen several with broad sand sweeps and others with smaller beaches but groves of evergreen.

"Depends on the water. Looks like we'll have a storm, maybe this evening. I don't like the look of those black clouds. We're pretty light right now. If it rains hard, it'll raise the river and give us more rapids to go over. They might be easier, and they might be harder."

Nell watched Charlie. He was definitely favoring his right shoulder. There had been no time to consult Mary Rose about it. Nellie looked ahead. The river stayed calm for quite a while. She joined Ace at the scow.

After the two of them talked, Ace called out. "James, you ain't been doing nothin' on this trip. Time you took the back sweep. We got a lot of water comin' up, and I know you've had some experience on a scow. Charlie, take off his handcuffs and set him up at the sweep."

A flash of relief crossed Charlie's face. He let loose of the sweep and stepped over to James. "I will take the handcuffs off again,

James. Both Moonshine and I will have you in our sights. Do not try anything to upset this boat or to get away. There is no nearby town like on the stretch from Challis to Salmon." He released the handcuffs and shoved one cuff into his pocket with the other hanging free. "Moonshine, keep an eye on James. If he lets go of the sweep, jump on him." The dog eyed Charlie and seemed to nod his head. He sat near the sweep, his head alert, his eyes on James.

The next few hours passed peaceably. The sun disappeared behind clouds, and soon, the river appeared to be a hallway between steep slopes and under a pewter sky. Nell gave Moonshine water to drink. She shared her own canteen with Charlie. She checked to be sure Frankie had water and suggested she take some to James, which she did. She didn't talk to him and crawled back to the bench and riggings to hang on.

The few stretches of white water didn't create waves and Ace slipped the scow easily down the river. "See that beach down there a ways?" He directed his question to James. "We'll stop and eat something. Then we'll keep going if the storm holds off. Otherwise, we'll camp for the night."

The two men on sweeps managed to push the scow toward a white sand beach. Charlie jumped with the rope into the water and pulled it close. He wrapped the rope around a rock that appeared just for that purpose. The dory rode high on the side of the scow.

"We're right in the middle of the Idaho primitive area," Ace said. "No roads. No nothing along here, except a few ranches or mines grandfathered in. There might be a bear or two. Keep an eye out for deer, and we might could have venison for supper." He, too, jumped off and helped Nellie and Frankie to the beach.

James hesitated. "I don't want no handcuffs on."

Charlie nodded. Moonshine jumped down after the criminal. He ran up and down the beach, probably tired of being the watch dog hour after hour. The sheriff threw a stick and Moonshine ran after it, bringing it back to Nellie. She hugged him, took the stick from his mouth, and threw it into the water. Moonie chased after it.

Nellie watched her dog and decided she would like a bath in the water. Ace, James, and Frankie had moved up the beach and sat in an area with a few trees for shade. Charlie lowered himself to lean against a log and rest his head. "I'm going in, Charlie." Nell whispered. Behind a large rock, she stripped off her bedraggled clothes, down to a camisole and bloomers, and jumped in the water. It shocked her at first with how cold it was, but she dog-paddled around the small eddy and ducked her head under. She needed a bar of soap, but just swishing around in the water made her feel cleaner. Moonshine stood close to the shore. She crept up, grabbed the stick, and threw it down the beach so he could get more exercise. At last, Nell climbed out of the water and shook herself off. She did have a clean shirt in her camera bag and dug it out. Her split skirt would have to do for the rest of her.

Ace called for Nell and Charlie to get something to eat and drink. Nell waved and called. "We'll be there shortly." She wanted to look at her husband's leg and shoulder first. Charlie opened his eyes. Clearly, he had been asleep.

"Undo your shirt, and I'll check out your shoulder. I don't think James can see it from here, nor Frankie either. I'd just as soon not show them how bad it is." Nell kneeled and pulled the shirt off to the side of the bandage and loosened it. A couple of the stitches had broken, but the bullet wound seemed to be healing. The torn skin from the paddle hitting him looked angry and a little swollen. Nell wished she had more honey to cover it. "Let me look at the back." The other side of his shoulder had not changed. It was healing. "All right, now pull up your pants."

The bullet wound in Charlie's back calf also appeared to be healing. "Does it hurt?" Nell asked.

"No, and I do not think I am limping anymore. My shoulder hurts, though."

"If we stop at another rancher's place, I'll try to get some honey and mercurochrome and see if I can help that shoulder." She put her arm around Charlie. "I'm sorry you are so banged up. I'm glad James is on the sweep for now." She stood up. "We better get something to eat, so we can take off again. I think it's quite a ways to Riggins."

Already, Nell's camisole had dried, but the bloomers under her split skirt still felt damp. She walked next to Charlie toward the others. Just as they arrived, a few raindrops splashed down. She reached down to the small spread of food and grabbed jerky and an apple. She handed them to Charlie and grabbed another handful. She noted the tin with the rest of the elk stew from Mary Rose no longer held anything but scraps. "You all were hungry." She glared at Frankie. "You could have saved something for us."

"Don't look at me. Ace and James acted like they never had eaten a thing back there." Frankie held out her hand. "Here, there's a roll left. I saved it for you. That sheriff can get his own food."

Nell split it and handed half to Charlie. "Thanks, Frankie."

Rain began to fall harder. Rolling thunder crashed and echoed between the walls of the canyon like a bowling ball hitting pins, like in the Rip Van Winkle story. Everyone jumped. Ace scrambled up. "We better find a dryer place," he shouted. He glanced at Nellie. "'Course, you're wet already." He smiled at her. "Grab your packs from the scow and head to that overhang of rocks." Ace pointed up the slope behind the beach. "We should stay dry up there."

James had nothing to retrieve. Frankie and Ace grabbed a few items, but nothing so formal as a pack. Nell and Charlie hustled toward the rocks with their packs, Nell trying to cover her camera pack with a jacket. She picked up her damp shirt from a bush as she scuttled after Charlie. Her hair was still wet from her swim and threatened to get wetter still. A jagged spear of lightning flashed right down the river, followed by a crack of thunder louder than anything she'd ever heard. "Charlie! Wait for me!" He pulled up and grabbed Nell's hand.

A stray thought occurred to Nell. This would be the perfect time for James to escape. Escape to what? She asked herself. More mountains. An electrical storm. Rain. No roads. She hurried to climb over the rocks to an overhang. "What are we going to do? This is a serious storm!"

Ace grunted. "If it weren't for the four of you, I'd keep going. A little rain ain't gonna hurt anything and might make the going better." He curled up on the ground with his knees near his head. "Sorry 'bout the food. I got a few pieces of jerky in my side pocket." He pulled it out, but Nell wrinkled her nose at how many pieces of thread and gravel were stuck to it. She took it and handed it to Charlie. "Anything else?"

"Piece of candy." He held out a piece of peppermint.

"I thought you stocked up at Shoup."

"I did, but the box is down in the scow. As soon as it stops storming, we can get it and set up camp here for the night. Maybe we can get a fish or two, or even a little venison."

Nell salivated, but she didn't want to get a deer killed. Still, venison might be better than squirrel, and that hadn't bothered her at all. It depends on how hungry one is, she thought.

The rain and electrical storm continued for what seemed like hours to Nell but probably stopped after thirty minutes. By then, dusk was in full swing. Moonshine had joined the group under the rocks and fallen asleep. Nell had dozed once or twice but jumped every time she heard thunder. Ace disappeared. James and Frankie huddled under a heavy jacket, probably belonging to James. He stood up, pulled the jacket off Frankie, and donned it. He glanced toward the sheriff and then away, stepping out from under the rock ledge. Nell watched him and wondered if he was considering running away. Elmer and Mary Rose's place was some miles upriver and across it. What was down the river was a mystery, but James might know, if he had been on the river in the past.

Ace returned, carrying two grouse by their feet. "Dinner!" He dropped them next to Frankie. "You girls know how to get the feathers off? We need to set up a fire pit on the beach. James, you and I can do that. Then I'll get the fire and some water goin'." He turned to Charlie. "You want to get a tarpaulin set up in that small grove of trees where we sat a while ago? We can all sleep under it for a few hours and then get going again." Ace crooked his finger at Nell. When she stood next to him, he said: "Fetch the food box from the scow and see what we can add to the grouse for dinner. Biscuit makings should be in there. Maybe some side pork."

Nell nodded and made her way down the slope, sliding and falling once. At the scow, she found several boxes and located the box Ace wanted. It looked damp, but when she opened it, there was an extra layer of cardboard over the food, so it had stayed fairly dry. There wasn't much. A can of beans. Bacon. Flour. A can of evaporated milk. Enough to make do, she thought. There was still a frypan in Charlie's pack, so she walked over to the grove where he worked on spreading the tarpaulin overhead by tying all four corners to branches of the trees. "I need the frypan." She hugged him around the waist as his arms worked at tying one corner. He dropped them and hugged her back.

"I am sorry you ended up in this mess, Nell. It is my fault."

"You needed a deputy, didn't you?" Nell brushed his face with her lips as he leaned over her. "Just think of me that way for a while." As if he hadn't already, but she didn't say that out loud. "Why not just let him go? Maybe he didn't kill Norman."

Charlie unwrapped his arms and stood up again. His mouth closed in a straight line. His eyes bore into her. "What kind of sheriff would do that?"

"I doubt if the marshal wanted you to catch a killer. All he wanted was to stop a cattle thief and a moonshiner. You've pretty much done that, haven't you?" She began to walk away but turned back. "Let the marshal go after James."

Ace roasted the plucked grouse parts on sticks over the fire. Nell fried the side pork, then the beans, and finally the biscuits. She had found some mullein leaves to use as plates or scoops. Dinner wasn't so bad, after all. The scow group sat around the embers for a while. The boatman brought out a bottle of something unidentifiable. He, James, and Frankie drank from it. Nellie took a sip, but it was godawful. Charlie shook his head. Moonshine lay next to his mistress and slept. Once, he stood up and watched upriver for a while. No one else could see what he was watching.

"I got some blankets in the scow," Ace said. "I'll use one and James, you and Frankie can use the others. The married couple here can spoon up in a sleeping bag. We all better get some sleep. Nell, thanks for the biscuits. We can eat the rest along with that side pork in the morning. Sorry no eggs, folks." He wandered to the scow and came back with a bundle of blankets. They weren't wet, only slightly damp on the edges.

The huge moon Nellie had seen the night before, her salmon moon, crept up from the top of the canyon. Before long, it was only a glow in the sky, playing hide and seek with clouds scudding across it. She ducked inside the tarp to the sleeping bag. Everyone soon huddled under cover. Nell noticed James took the far edge facing downriver. She wondered again if he would try to run.

Morning came much too early. Nell had heard someone get up in the night. Moonshine had left and returned. She sat up and saw Ace rekindling the fire. Charlie had disappeared. So had Frankie. James snored. So, he hadn't escaped. She had heard more rain before any light had appeared, but she could see no clouds in the narrow opening above the river. The scow had been pulled up tighter on the rock, and the river sounded louder than usual. Nell headed up the slope to find a private place, change her shirt, and take care of business. Frankie passed her coming down.

"Thought he'd leave, didn't you?" Frankie whispered to Nell. "He's no murderer, even if Norman is dead." She motioned uphill toward some evergreens. "It's private up there." She pulled tissue from her pocket. "Need some?"

Nell nodded and took it. "Charlie has a job to do, and he'll die trying if he has to."

Frankie studied Nell a moment. "You better keep a sharp eye on him. You and that dog."

Nell continued uphill. Frankie's words sounded like a threat. Did she and James cook up something during the night? Ace and Nell couldn't stop them if Frankie and James acted in concert.

As far as she knew, neither of them had a gun. Ace probably did, maybe in the same place where he kept the blankets dry. Where had Charlie gone?

When Nell returned to the camp, she saw Charlie, or someone, had folded the tarp and cleaned up the nest. Both hers and his pack had been taken down to the scow. The blankets rested on the scow bench, neatly folded, too. Everyone stood around the fire pit, keeping warm. Frankie stood next to Charlie, a little too close, in Nell's opinion.

"We're going as far as we can today," Ace said. "We won't make Riggins, but we might make an old mining camp where there's a road in. Some of these old camps have boats with motors on them. Maybe one could take you all to Riggins instead." Ace had the bailing bucket filled with water. "I'll put this here fire out and let's get goin'." He turned to James. "You're on sweep again. We might get some rough rapids."

Chapter 20

ACE TOOK FRONT SWEEP. JAMES held onto the back sweep. Moonshine sat in the back and watched James. Charlie, Nell, and Frankie stayed near the bench. Frankie tied her saddlebags to the ropes securing the bench and stayed on the floor of the scow. Charlie sat on the bench, and Nell sat near Frankie on the floor. These had become their normal places the previous day, except the sheriff had stayed closer to James in the rear. Nell thought her husband looked tired and discouraged. She wondered if that was a pose to lull James into the same condition. So far, being married wasn't all that she had imagined or expected. Perhaps, she really didn't know her husband well at all.

Mostly white water ahead was signaled by roaring and booming waves. Sometimes, Ace shouted a "heads up!" to alert his passengers to hang on. The day had turned sunny and mostly warm, except when water sloshed over the boat and dampened everyone. Nell tried to remember what she and Charlie had been doing before getting on the scow. She conjured up sunny days, lavender blossoms, and warm nights at Last Chance Ranch. She would give almost anything to get back there safely with just the two of them—and Moonshine.

The scow entered a long stream of rough water. Nell had

loosened her hold on the ropes and grabbed Charlie's legs. Both of them began to slide toward the rear. Frankie screamed. Nellie raised her head above the sweeping water. The dory wobbled and then let go, loose from the scow. It floated away, rising and sinking with the waves. James leaped off the back of the boat. Moonie followed him, barking sharply and then disappearing under the waves. Ace struggled to steer the scow through a labyrinth of waves, rocks, and holes.

"Get Moonie, Charlie! Save him!"

Charlie crawled to the side of the boat and reached over the edge. James tumbled by, his feet in front of him. He stayed clear of Charlie's grasping hands. Just then, Moonshine surfaced, his head held up by corks, and the water shoved him into the sheriff's arms. Charlie grabbed and brought the dog up in one strong motion to propel him to Nellie. Moonie stood up and shook all over. If Nellie had any dry spots left, she no longer did. Frankie shouted, but her voice was lost in the maelstrom.

Nellie could feel herself slipping in her cork life preserver on the sluice to the rear and possibly over. She, too, screamed. Charlie leaped, grabbed her foot and held on. Ace maneuvered to the side of the last rapid and sagged over his sweep.

"That was a humdinger!" After a few moments, he stood again. "Everyone all right?"

He glanced around. "James is gone," he said, followed by what sounded like, "and good riddance."

The rocky shore and steep cliffs left them no room to beach the boat. Even Charlie could see that, Nell thought. The current pulled the scow more slowly through the river, giving each of them time to recover.

"Any more like that?" Nellie asked. "Maybe I'll get off and walk the rest of the way." She was only half-joking. She sat with her arms around her dog. There was a scrap of warmth where her body touched his. Charlie took off his shirt and wrung it as dry as he could. His torso shone with water. Frankie watched him—admiringly, in Nell's opinion. So did Nell. She was tempted to yell at Frankie: "That man is mine!"

"Sorry, folks. I shoulda checked out that rapid ahead of time. I miscalculated." Ace's shoulders drooped.

Charlie stepped up to the back sweep. "I can help out now," he said. "How far is the mining camp?" He grabbed the sweep as it jiggled loose in its framework. "Will James get there first?"

Ace's forehead wrinkled. "That was Salmon Falls. I'd guess another ten to twelve miles. Another hour or two, given how the river is actin'." He glanced downriver. "I don't see him or the dory. I'm surprised it let go the way it did."

"Do you think James can swim that far?"

"Doubt it. He ain't that strong. He had a hard enough time with that sweep."

"Huh! James is a sissy." Frankie's opinion had not been offered quietly. "That's why I don't think he killed Norman." She fondled her saddlebags.

Nell piped up. "That leaves you, Frankie, or Bull, and he didn't look to be in any condition to be shooting a rifle or a shotgun." She stared at where the dory had been tied. One of the ropes swung loose. "Look at that. It was cut." Nell turned to Frankie. "Did you do that?"

"No, I swear I never touched it." She reached her hand out to Nell. "I didn't shoot Norman either. That leaves the sheriff here or Bull. Those two were armed. I wasn't."

Frankie crept up to sit on the bench, trying to smooth water out of her Levi's. "Didn't you see the shotgun there in the horse shed? I sure did." She gave up and sat on the floor again. "That's why I lit out. I didn't want him shooting at me."

All this was new to Nell, and she suspected, to Charlie, too. Charlie had said Norman hit Bull, who appeared unconscious when they found him. Even Janie had thought he might be dead. James *must* have been the killer. He was closer. He dragged the body to the house, perhaps to hide him, and then left in the dory. Maybe he planned all of it from the beginning, except, of course, the sheriff arriving and then Ace, Janie, and Nellie. Now, it seemed Bull wasn't unconscious. Maybe Frankie had hit him. Bull would have been furious with Norman for taking, or planning to take, his hoarded gold. What had become clear to Nell was that Frankie had the gold in her saddlebags. Why else would she guard them as if they were her life? In a way, maybe they were. She glanced at Charlie. She wanted to talk with him and hash out what they thought and what they planned to do about James, if the scow caught up with him.

Nell needed a real rest. Everyone else on the boat did, too, she assumed. She wondered if the mining camp had bunks for workers. That might be a stretch of her imagination. She was certainly too damp to sleep on the scow. Frankie's eyes were closed, but Nellie could see the muscles in her arms gripped her saddlebags close.

"There he is!" shouted Ace. "Got himself into that dory, he did."

"He is rowing upstream, Ace." Charlie stood at the sweep. "Can we maneuver to keep him from going by us?"

"Doubtful. Get out your gun and shoot him. That'll stop the criminal."

Charlie didn't move toward his pack. Nellie doubted the sheriff would shoot James in the dory. It would be like shooting fish in a barrel.

Frankie got to her knees. "Hand me a gun. *I'll* shoot him."

Ace, Charlie, and Nell all stared at Frankie. "What?" she said. "I'll just wing him so he can't row upstream anymore."

James was rowing facing upriver. He maneuvered closer to the scow. "Throw me a rope!" He shouted loud enough to be heard. "I want back in the scow! We can let the dory go." He looked down. "It's sinking!"

Ace laughed like a hyena. "Go 'head, Charlie. Toss the man a rope. Looks like he wants to turn himself in!" He bent over double, laughing. "Now I've seen everything!"

Frankie's lower lip stuck out. "I don't want him back. Let him sink. Serves him right."

Charlie tossed the rope and James caught it. Each pulled at it until the dory moved close to the scow's end. "I'm jumpin' in," James called. He stood on the dory end seat and jumped. Charlie caught his arm and shoulder. The dory slipped sideways. The high front tipped up as the rear of the boat sank into the river. Within a minute, the whole dory disappeared under the dark, sluggish water. The scow swept on its way downriver. A burble of water marked the burial site and then, it, too, disappeared and the sheen of the water returned.

"Hey, Ace! Got one of them blankets? I'm colder'n hell." James stalked back to the boatman. He helped Ace dig a couple out from a large tin box. He passed one to Frankie and Nell and helped himself to one. "I'll take back sweep once I get warm again."

The others glanced at each other, maybe too dumbfounded to say anything. Ace and Charlie paid attention to their sweeps. Nell and Frankie leaned against each other, and Moonshine huddled between them, his head on Nellie's knee. Frankie whispered to

Nell, "He has mean eyes, don't you think? He is a villain." She closed her eyes and dozed. James didn't say anything more. Maybe he slept.

Nell thought about Frankie's words. She watched James for a while. He did have mean eyes. They were hard to read and often stared without blinking. His pomaded dark hair had fallen to one side in the water, exposing a small bald spot toward the back when he turned his head. Charlie's hair, black like most Basques, grew full and thick. James resembled a drowned rat.

Nellie watched the river behind them. The scene of faraway mountains and steep side slopes felt like a dream. She wanted to share her thoughts with Charlie, but this wasn't the time. That was all right. Since she had known him, a few of his serious edges had softened, at least toward her. He had never blamed her for letting that man die in the north Idaho mines. She echoed Ace in her head: Good riddance. Maybe she had taken on a rough edge or two from Charlie. She decided they made a good pair.

"Don't get too cozy, you all. We got Big Mallard Rapid comin' up. It can be as bad as Salmon Falls. James, you better get on the sweep. Give the sheriff a rest." Ace leaned on his sweep to push the boat toward the left going downriver. "One of the river runners said the left side was best, so that's what we'll do. Everyone else, get ready to get wet. Dump those blankets in that big tin. I don't want them wet."

The roar of Big Mallard met them before they saw the whitewater. Both Frankie and Nellie sought cover under the bench this time. It didn't keep them dry, but at least they didn't get soaked, and best of all, they didn't get swept to the rear of the scow. Nell knew Charlie could handle himself and Moonshine. Maybe James would get swept over again. Ace maneuvered the front sweep with all his might. Soon, the scow scuttled out of the rapids onto a flatter section of river.

"Not so bad, huh? You're gettin' to be river rats." Ace stood up straight and shook his wet hair and beard. He looked like Moonshine shaking off too much water. "The mining camp is there on the right. Let's all take a rest on land."

Chapter 21

"GET READY TO DISEMBARK." ACE maneuvered his front sweep toward the shore. Two men waited to grab the rope he threw. "I got some mail for this here camp. And one box of something."

Frankie reached for her saddlebags. They were still tied to the bench and caught between her legs. She was tired of their burden. Maybe she should have left the bags hidden in one of the outbuildings at Bull's. No one would have bothered them there. She could have ridden a horse back when they finally reached civilization. She glanced up at the men pulling on the scow. Long, scraggly beards covered their lips and chins. Their clothes looked worn and filthy. One of them spit tobacco in the river. Maybe she would just stay on the boat. She doubted they could even see the saddlebags and wonder what was in them. James knew. Ace probably guessed. Charlie and Nellie had both looked inside, so they knew. She stayed where she was and wondered when the sheriff would take them away from her.

The sheriff and Ace helped unload the last box of gear to the miners. Ace knew them both from prior trips. He asked about a boat with a motor, and whether the road had been traveled recently. Frankie perked up to listen. She was as anxious as James to get away from the sheriff, but she didn't want to go with James either. There had been a pile of paper money at Bull's. She wondered if James had it somewhere on his person. It would be mighty wet.

"We got a motorboat, but the motor don't work," one of the men said. "We hoped someone comin' down the river could fix it. Do you know how?"

"I could take a look. I'm better at sweeps." Ace jumped down to follow the men. "We all could use a good meal. Our supplies got washed out over Salmon Falls."

Frankie hadn't noticed any particular "washing out" of supplies over the wicked section of whitewater, but if Ace could get some food for all of them, she'd eat it. Still, she wondered how old the supplies at the mine might be. Still again, if there was a road, probably not too old. She looked around to see if any mining activity was going on. It would be gold this far down the river and away from civilization. Most other gold sites had played out a long time ago. If these men were sluicing gold, there wasn't much evidence. Maybe the creek running into the river was the source. She'd have to wander up with Ace to find anything, she decided. That would mean either carrying the saddlebags or leaving them on the scow.

Ace called back. "C'mon everybody. We'll get some eats up here. These fine gentlemen said there was lunch fixings."

James sidled over to Frankie. "Are you all right, Frankie?" He put an arm around her shoulder.

Frankie shoved it off and stepped sideways. "A fine lot you care. You didn't tell me you were going to jump off the scow." She tried to keep her voice low, but her anger kept it too high. She saw Nell listening.

"I thought I'd help you get away here at this mining camp. That road looks used, so someone has a truck to get in and out, even if the motorboat is laid up." He moved away. "I planned on hiding in one of those buildings up thataway. I been here before, you know."

"Did you steal all that paper money in Bull's cabin?"

"Shhh. Don't let these others hear you." James's whisper was almost louder than Frankie's question. "That's for me to know." He hustled closer again. "What do you care? You got all that gold." He nodded toward the saddlebags. "Want me to carry them for you up to the food? You better eat something."

"I was going to find out where the mining went on up there." Frankie decided she'd better keep hold of the saddlebags. She'd seen James cleaning up last night's camp, folding blankets, and so on. He probably cut the ropes on the dory back then.

The group entered one of the outbuildings. It had a kitchen area with cupboards and presumably some food. Frankie glanced around and back at Nellie, who was behind her.

"You gals can fix up somethin'," one of the miners said. "There's pancake fixin's. There's an icebox with ice if you need that. Might even be a dab of butter." The two men grabbed Ace to go with them.

Frankie stared at the miners. So much for feeding them. She sighed. She hated to cook.

To her surprise, Charlie stepped up and nodded to Nellie. "I am not a gal, but Nell and I can whip up some good pancakes for us." He waved at Frankie. "Maybe you could find a few berries to go with."

In October? Frankie questioned herself. The canyon held heat a lot longer than the mountains around them. She decided to escape outside. She handed her saddlebags to Nell. "Look after these, will you? I'll find berries." She found cups in the cupboards and left. James followed her.

"Make yourself useful," Frankie said and handed him a cup. "There just might be a few huckleberries in the bushes around here." She thought this would be a good opportunity to find out what was in the other low-slung buildings and whether the road could be used to get out of the Salmon River primitive area.

The outbuildings looked as if they were used for storage of broken equipment of various sorts. She even saw an automobile without tires and up on wood blocks. That one hadn't used the road in a long time. Frankie found some berries near the road, so she poked around. Grass grew in the middle but the road had been used not too long ago. She could see a small patch of spilled oil. It was dry, but still black, not yet absorbed by the dust. She had lost sight of James. Maybe he had left by the road. No footsteps showed, though.

"Frankie. Any berries? We're ready." Nell's voice called from near the riverfront.

"Coming. I got a few." Frankie looked around for the miners. Two deer bounded off from where they had been browsing leaves on syringa bushes turning orange. She watched them. Maybe they could get venison for the rest of the trip. Nah, she thought. They must be getting close to Riggins. She'd ask Ace.

Charlie, Nell, Frankie, and James, who appeared at the sound of Nellie's voice, sat around a table in the make-do kitchen area. The miners weren't hungry, Frankie guessed. She wondered if they had a stash of gold anywhere. She had checked the saddlebags the minute she arrived back to get breakfast. It didn't look as if the buckles had been moved.

The sheriff placed a huge stack of pancakes on the table. He had scrounged syrup of some kind. He rinsed the berries and placed them in a bowl and passed a small slab of butter. No one talked except to ask for syrup. Nellie had found forks and knives and laid them out. Ace came through the door. "I hope you saved some for me."

"Could you fix the boat?" James asked. "I know how to steer one. Did that a dozen times on this here river."

Frankie snorted but said nothing. The saddlebags were now between her feet under the table.

"Nope. Need some parts. I'm gonna order them when we get to Riggins, and I can call up to Salmon." Ace added a pile of pancakes to a plate, pouring syrup over them plus a few huckleberries. "These look mighty good!" Ace made short work of the food. "They hit the spot and removed it. Thanks, you gals!"

Frankie tried not to laugh.

Nell did and said, "Charlie did most of the cooking, Ace. He is multi-talented, as you can see." She fetched one more cake onto her plate. "I don't think there will be any left for the miners." She pointed to Frankie and James. "They found some huckleberries. The last, I'm sure, before winter arrives."

"Are we near Riggins, Ace?" Frankie sure hoped so. She was tired of getting wet and tired of the river. She wanted to be on land, except not in jail. So far, the sheriff seemed dead-set on James being the killer. All of his protestations appeared to fix the idea in the sheriff's head. The morgue in Salmon could possibly point to someone other than James, depending on the kind of bullets in Norman's body. She felt sorry for her sometime-boyfriend. He hadn't known what he was getting into with James, the full-time criminal. Neither had she.

"Ways to go," Ace said. "The South Fork of the Salmon comes into this main river in around a half dozen miles. The water will be a lot higher then." He stood up. "We gotta get going. If we get a big piece today, we'll get to Riggins tomorrow. There are quite a few mining sites and some ranches from now on, even a few bridges over the river."

"Bridges? That must mean there are roads. Where do they go?" Frankie asked. She perked up. "Let's get going. The miners can clean this place up."

"I've been heating water on the wood stove. I'll do the plates and cutlery, then I'll come down to the boat. It'll take you all that long to get ready to go." Nell pulled a metal bucket off the stove and filled a pan in the sink along with some soap she found on the sideboard. "Charlie, bring the plates here, and I'll get this done."

All the activity gave Frankie time to whisper to James in an aside. "If there's roads down river, maybe we can get off and catch a ride with someone. Those roads must go somewhere." She pushed at him. "Keep an eye out, James. I'm not going to jail with you."

Even the short time on shore had given the scow floorboards time to dry out. Soon, all were back to their regular spots. The sheriff settled down with the dog and James took the sweep. With Ace in front and James in back, maybe the boat would move faster. As they moved west, the steep cliffs softened into slopes with trees.

They swept through a series of whitewater sections, none as bad as the earlier rapids. When they reached the South Fork, the descending river did indeed grow larger. Several quiet sections slowed their progress. Frankie liked those better. She didn't have to hold on so tight, and the river looked so beautiful, like a dark mirror.

James began to whistle a tune. Frankie looked up at him, and he did something with his hand on the sweep. It looked like a diving motion. What did he mean? Then he scrunched up his face and winked at her, turning it slightly so the sheriff wouldn't see. "Lookie ahead," he called. "A bridge." All heads followed his pointing finger, all except Frankie. She saw him pull a gun from under his shirt in back. She'd thought he lost it in the water. He aimed at Ace and fired.

Moonshine jumped at James and knocked him away from the sweep. Ace fell off the boat into water beginning to tremble into whitewater. Frankie and Nellie screamed, and Nellie jumped forward to try and catch Ace, to no avail. The sheriff grabbed the sweep and tried to maneuver close to Ace in the water.

James dove into the river and swam to the bridge on the far end. Frankie was not going to jump in with him, not with the saddlebags. They would pull her under. That must be what his hand sign had meant—dive into the river. She watched him, angry but relieved he was gone. Something in the water followed him—a bag maybe or a fish? He climbed up the rocky shore and pulled the thing after him. As near as she could tell it was a canvas bag, probably filled with money. That must be what he had been up to when he disappeared while picking berries.

"Frankie, help me!" Nell's cry woke her out of her stupefaction. Nellie had grabbed Ace's shirt and pulled, trying to get him back on the boat. Frankie hurried forward to help. Without Ace, they might never get to Riggins. If that bridge's road led back to Salmon, James would get away and she would be the one to end up in jail. She needed Ace. So did the others. Only James did not.

Chapter 22

NELL PULLED ON ACE'S SHIRT until she had an arm. Frankie leaned down and helped grab the other arm. He was a big, heavy man. His head lolled but his eyes opened. He managed to grab a boat edge. The two women held the boatman up, and Ace gathered leverage by using the sweep.

"Here, I have him." The sheriff's hand grabbed Ace's wrist. "Everyone together now, pull." Ace flopped over the side like a big white whale. "Where are you hit, man?"

Ace gasped air and spit water. He lay on the boat bottom. "Grab the back sweep, sheriff, or we'll turn over in the next waves."

Charlie jumped to the back sweep again. Moonshine stayed near Nellie. She and Frankie tried to sit the boatman up. Nell shoved a box toward his back. Frankie pushed his legs around. "Where did the bullet go?" Nell asked. Both women ran their hands up and down Ace's bulky body.

"I dunno." He leaned forward, feeling his own chest. "Maybe he missed and just knocked me into the water." His breathing slowed down. His eyes closed, and he slumped sideways.

"He's bleeding." Nellie pointed at the floorboards. "Look."

A river of red seeped from under Ace's hips. "We need to turn him over. Quick."

Turning Ace took as much strength as pulling him out of the water. At last, Nell found the bullet hole in the middle of his lower backside. He must have been turned when James shot. Nell tore his shirt off, folded it into a big bandage and pressed over the hole in his pants. "We need to pull his trousers off," Nell called to Frankie.

"He'll be naked," Frankie said. Her expression said what she was thinking—curled lips, wide eyes, and a wrinkled nose.

"We can't lose him. Tie the sweep and help me. You can go back as soon as I rig a bandage sling. We need him." She turned to the rear. "Charlie, can you keep us in a straight line in the white water? I need Frankie's help."

"I will try. Hurry up if you can. There is more bad water ahead. Ace warned me a while back." He leaned hard on the sweep pole to get the boat back to the middle of the river.

Frankie eased Ace's shoes off and grabbed the bottom of his pants. Nell had managed to undo the belt around his middle. She hoped he wore underdrawers, but it didn't matter. She needed to get the bleeding stopped, or they would lose him for sure.

Ace's buttocks gleamed white and fleshy. His underdrawers barely covered them. Nell didn't want to touch him, but the bullet hole still leaked a small but steady stream of red. She re-folded the shirt material and pressed on the hole. When she and Frankie tussled with Ace's lower half, she hadn't seen another hole. The bullet must still be inside the man.

"Charlie, he is wounded in his backside. I think the bullet is still in there. What do I do?"

The sheriff struggled with the pole and sweep paddle. Nell could see that behind the scow, the water reflected a back-and-forth trail, no straight line as he had intended.

"Stop the blood, if you can. Raise his feet higher than his head." The boat skidded off a hidden boulder. "Hang on. Grab Moonshine. We have a rough ride—" The pole jerked out of Charlie's hands. He nearly fell over but righted himself and grabbed the sweep again. The scow had slipped half-sideways, but Charlie managed to steady the boat back to a straighter line. "Frankie, keep your sweep straight on."

Moonshine curled up next to Ace and near Nell's arms, so she could wrap herself around both dog and man. Ace served as a living anchor. She tried to keep one hand on the shirt bandage. A huge wave splashed over Frankie, Nell, Moonie, and Ace. Once the water sluiced off, the scow bumped down a series of smaller waves until they reached quieter water. Frankie let her sweep go. She moved a box to place it under Ace's legs.

"Thanks," Nell said. "I think I have the blood stopped. Now I need to strap the bandage in place." Nell found a length of rope caught under the bench and tied it around Ace's mid-section, over his drawers and around the soaking wet cloth bandage on his hind end. He didn't wake, but Nell was sure he was still alive.

Charlie tied his sweep in place and helped the two women get Ace into a better position, head cushioned and legs up. "We will need to get the bullet out, but not until Riggins. Maybe there is a doctor there."

"No doc in Riggins," Ace said, surprising them.

Moonshine licked the boatman's face. "*Arp.*"

"Where'd that sonofagun go?" Ace growled.

"He swam to the bridge," Frankie answered. "He's long gone now." Her scowl matched Ace's voice.

Ace winced. "Ha. The road goes to Riggins." He tried to motion backwards and failed. "The other way, it goes to a deserted mine.

We'll get to town first." He laughed and then choked. "Water."

Charlie held his head up and Nell helped him sip from her canteen. "We'd better rig up a fishing line," she said. "We'll need food tonight if we camp again."

"One of you better keep on a sweep," Ace said. He closed his eyes. "If you sit me up better, I can tell you what to do."

With Ace's directions and Charlie's and Frankie's efforts to follow them, the scow continued down the river in a semi-orderly fashion. Nellie kept her eye on Ace and checked his bandage from time to time to be certain the blood had not re-started. Ace marshaled his strength and ate some of the jerky Nell found to give him. Before long, they approached what appeared to be a ranch along the river.

"Not there," Ace called out. "Keep going. We need to get farther along while it is light out. There's more places to stop."

Nellie eyed the ranch house, which appeared to be occupied. "Why not there?"

"That's the Bemis place. They don't like strangers."

"Polly Bemis? I've heard of her. I heard they were real hospitable," Frankie said. "Maybe we could get some food there."

"Aye, we probably could. We just need to get farther down the river." The wince on Ace's face said he hurt.

Nell figured he might not want people he knew to know he'd been shot in his buttocks. Moving him wouldn't be easy, either. Still. She motioned to Charlie, pointing with her head to shore. They could get dried off. He paid no attention.

Stream after stream entered the Salmon River. The river grew deeper, but Ace said it was low water. Many of the would-be streams had dried out by fall. The hillsides grew steep and then eased off. There were more signs of cabins and some mine workings, most of which were deserted.

"What about Polly Bemis? Who is she?" Nell was surprised Frankie knew anyone along the river.

"Don't you know? She was a Chinese woman sold into slavery here in Idaho. They say Charles Bemis won her in a poker game and married her. They moved along the Salmon River a while ago. James said… I heard they had their own place here and saved more than one fool who came down the river or over the hill looking for gold." Frankie hung onto the sweep pole and kept her eye on the river, just as Ace had instructed. "I'm hungry. Any more of that jerky?" She stared at Ace. "We shoulda stopped there."

"Charles Bemis died a while back, and Polly lives there by herself. She don't need no trouble from the likes of us."

"Too late now," Nellie said. She scrounged around her pack and then Charlie's and found more jerky. That looked like the extent of any food they had. She handed a piece to Frankie and another to Charlie, saving a small chunk for herself. Jerky always made her thirsty. "How is your wound doing?" She moved to sit by Ace and hold Moonie. "Are you hurting?'

"Yes. Damned embarrassing to have two women fixing me up and a hole in my backend."

"Is that why you didn't want to stop?"

"We gotta keep goin' so we can make Riggins tomorrow. If we stopped at the Bemis place, we gotta play nice, eat some food, talk a while. You can't just run off if people feed you." He patted Moonshine. "Hey, Charlie, there's some more whitewater comin' up. Front and back sweeps need to work together here." He tried to get up, without any luck. "We better rig somethin' up here in front so I can take a hand."

"Aren't I doing a good job?" Frankie pouted.

"Sure you are. You just ain't strong enough to keep that sweep in a line in the bad water." He thought a moment. "You might better bring up the paddle and let the sheriff there keep track of where the scow is goin' from the back end in this next section. Duck down. You, too, Miss Nell. Hang onto your dog. I can hold onto the bench here."

Nell wanted out of the boat. She shivered from being wet. Her clothes never seemed to dry. Even Moonshine looked bedraggled. She would have liked to have met Polly Bemis, maybe even take her photograph. She looked around for her camera pack and found it lodged under the bench and clear of any water on the floor. Thank heavens. She had forgotten for a while that she was a photographer. "Charlie, do you need any help?"

He smiled at Nell, who smiled back. "No, I am learning how to run the sweep. Ace is a good teacher. Maybe see what you can find to help him get back to the front sweep, after we get through these next falls." He nudged the pole. "And finding fishing gear is a good idea. We will all be hungry by the time we stop. Good thing we had a hearty breakfast back at that mining camp."

Nell felt the scow bump across a boulder. Charlie shouted, "Here we go! Hang on!"

Water drenched all of them again, but the scow cleared the whitewater and continued running the river. "When can we stop, Ace?"

"Another mile or two," Even Ace sounded dispirited. "All we need now is rain," he complained. As if conjuring up a storm, the sky darkened and before long, hail pelted down on them.

Nell tried to protect Moonie from the hailstones. She felt their sting herself and pulled a jacket from her pack, damp as it was.

Charlie had dropped his coat a while ago, so she grabbed it and handed it to him. "Frankie, do you have a wrap in your pack?"

Frankie shivered so much, she could hardly hold onto the pole. "I don't even remember. The pack is under the bench, next to your camera. Go ahead and look in it."

Nell eased Frankie's pack out from the bench and opened the top. She jabbed her hand inside and tried to feel if anything was still dry. Her hand ran up against what felt like a pile of paper. She glanced up at Frankie, who stared back. "Just ignore all that stuff," she said.

Nell didn't feel like confronting Frankie in the middle of the river, so she kept searching for something dry and found a heavy sweater. "Here," she said, as she pulled it out. "This'll keep you warm for a bit, but if we go through more water, it will never dry out." She scooted to the front end of the scow and handed it to Frankie, who donned it immediately.

"How about you, Ace? Anything around to keep you warm?"

The hail turned to rain and then stopped. The sun peeked around the bank of clouds and soon brought enough warmth to the voyagers so they removed jackets and sweaters. Nell struggled with the cork preserver so she could take off a sweater. "Is the river always like this?"

"It is in the fall. Summer is nicer, but you can always get a squall, even then." Ace tried to shift his bulk. "Charlie, in two more bends, head for the right side of the river. We should come to a big campsite at Sheep Creek. Doubt if anyone'll be there, but it's a good place to tie up for a while."

The current pulled the scow forward. Soon, Nell saw a large flat spot along the river. That must be Sheep Creek and Camp. Ace called to Frankie, "Can you jump and tie us up, Girly?"

"No!"

"I can try," Nell said, "but I might not be big enough."

"Nell, come back here and hold the sweep. I will tie up the boat." Charlie held the pole for Nell, then hurried forward to grab the front rope and jump into the water. He landed the scow on a quiet, flat spot. He grabbed the boat and pushed it alongside the landing. "Can you swing a leg over, Ace? I can handle you all right, I hope."

Ace maneuvered toward the side through a portal in the low wall. Nell tried to help but she was of little use. Frankie released her sweep and managed to lift one of Ace's shoulders. As strong as Charlie was, he had some difficulty getting the boatman over the side and situated on a dry spot. "Next!"

Nell could climb over herself. She pulled her pack with her. Frankie jumped down. Both women scouted the campsite. No one else occupied it. Frankie found a food pack hanging from a tree. It held moldy biscuits, but also a side of bacon. "We got something to eat!"

The sheriff started up a fire in a rock ring. Nell found a hook and line in her pack at the bottom plus the frypan and an envelope of flour. "Good. You can stir up a few biscuits with the bacon. I'll see if I can catch a fish." The sun had disappeared behind the steep slope rising across the river behind them, but it was warm enough to shed jackets. "Frankie, here is the tarp. See if you can rig up a shelter for Ace. Moonie, you should prowl around, see if there's anything to worry about back there." Nell found a lively insect to hang on a hook and headed for the water along another section of camp. "Ace, is there a shelter of some kind around here?"

Ace had slid to his side without the bullet hole. He looked better than in the boat. "Might be. Man name of Crowfoot had a cabin here long time ago. People lived on the Sheep Creek Bar out there, but it's gone now. Upriver a ways is a grave marker."

"I will scout around, Nell," Charlie said. "Can you clean a fish?" Charlie watched the fire, then added more wood.

"Of course, I can. I'm not a sissy." She flung the line into the water. "I got along fine without you or anyone for days out here."

"Two," Charlie mumbled. He hastened after Moonshine.

Frankie stumbled back to the fire. "Ace, I think we just heard the newlyweds in their first spat." They both laughed.

The temperature cooled down considerably after the group ate the food they had found or caught. Nell gave some of her bacon to Moonshine and one biscuit. The sheriff took a long piece of fish, cleared it of bones, and tossed it to the dog. Moonie ate every morsel.

Nellie sidled up to Charlie. "How are your bullet holes? I should take a look in the firelight." She sat beside him and held onto his arm, the arm without a wound. "You had no trouble landing the scow."

Charlie leaned toward Nell and placed his hand over hers. "Shoulder seems fine. My leg still pulses from time to time. We are out of honey or herbs to slather on that one. Leave it until we get to Riggins." He patted her hand. "You better sleep next to me tonight to stay warm. Ace can have the tarp. Frankie, too. I found a couple of blankets that are mostly dry. James did us a favor folding them all up and packing them in the tin boxes." He took his arm and circled Nell's back. "I wonder how he is doing in the bad weather and now the cold. That revolver will not keep him warm."

* * * * *

Next morning, Nell woke early. She had slept warm all night cuddled next to her husband and with Moonshine beside her. She fried bacon and fish for breakfast over the fire. The sheriff helped Ace back into the boat. Frankie cleaned up. All four worked as a unit. The women had fashioned a make-shift seat for Ace near the back sweep at Charlie's suggestion so he wouldn't get as wet as he would up front. They also managed to boost him up so he could maneuver the sweep if he needed to. Charlie took the front sweep, leaving Nell and Frankie to their usual seats around the bench on the floor. Moonshine rested close to Charlie and looked back across the boat.

"There's a good current for a long stretch," Ace said. "Figure about three to four hours and we'll be in Riggins." He lifted a cup of water in a toast. "Of course, we gotta go by Ruby Rapids to get there." He grinned.

Chapter 23

THE RIVER BOATERS PASSED MORE creeks splashing into the Salmon River. From time to time, Ace called out landmarks, including the Riggins Hot Springs. "Nice place to stop if we weren't in a hurry. Plenty of hot water. A little stinky, though." No one called out to stop. For once, they all stayed dry for quite a spell.

"Better pull over to the left, Sheriff. You should scout the Ruby Rapids, see if you can get a good line to go through. In high water, these are dangerous. Might not be so bad now with the river getting lower." Ace's ability to move around had improved overnight. He took hold of the pole to help Charlie aim toward the left beach. "You can jump here and pull the boat up on the sand. One of the gals can keep hold of the rope. The water is quiet right here."

Both women jumped out and helped Charlie with the boat. Nell hated getting her boots wet again. Frankie jumped further and landed above the water. Charlie was gone a short while. When he came back, he reported, "These rapids don't look too bad. There is a hole off to the right that we can miss by going closer to a hefty boulder on the left. Does that match with what you know, Ace?"

Ace rubbed his head and stroked his beard. "That sounds about right. You don't want to hit that boulder, though. It'll send you right into the hole. Think you can thread the needle?"

"I can if you can manage the back sweep." Charlie pulled his hand through his hair.

"I'll try. My butt feels a lot better today. Gotta thank Nellie for stopping the bleeding."

Nellie felt her face burn. Handling Ace's rear end had been a new experience. Frankie chuckled low. "You got good hands, Nell."

"All right, crew. Let us get back into the scow and on our way." Charlie took the rope from Nell and Frankie, and after they climbed on, he pushed the boat into the current. "We will probably get wet again."

Nellie gulped when the boat crested the rapids and she could see the hole and the boulder and a churn of whitewater, green and dark with foam on top. She grabbed the rope by the bench and hid her face in Moonshine's fur. Ace whooped from the back. Frankie let loose with a "Hot damn!" Water rushed into the scow in front. When it felt as if the boat was turning sideways, Nell straightened up. She would have to jump. Before she could decide to do so, the scow plowed out of the whitewater and back into a smooth-running river. "You did it!"

"Nice work, Sheriff. Let me know if you ever want a job as a sweep man." Ace settled back into the high seat Frankie and Nell had fixed up for him. "I gotta rest now. Only one more set of tricky water at Lake Creek."

Several bridges crossed the Salmon as they moved toward Riggins. Ace remarked on a couple going to mine workings and places where people had built houses and then lost them, either to landslides or fire. He pointed out a small sheep operation, name of

Hayward. "He just keeps herding along." Ace chuckled to himself.

Nell commented to Frankie, "So lonely out here. Getting in and out must be difficult. At least Bull's place was closer to the road. I wonder what happened to that horseman. He was the reason I'm even here."

"I saw him head out on his horse. Where did he go?"

"He showed up in Stanley and warned the barkeep there that the sheriff had been hurt. The barkeep telephoned to Hailey and managed to send a message to me. That's when I was able to get on Ace's boat and then saw you in Challis." Nell watched Charlie man the front sweep. He did look as if he knew what to do. She turned to see what Ace was doing. He appeared to be sleeping. "Hang on, Frankie. I am going to check on Ace. His wound might be bleeding again."

Nell crawled to the back of the scow. "Ace." The man didn't move or wake up. "Ace," she called louder. Ace's head moved.

"I'm going to look at your wound. See what's going on. All right?"

Ace grunted and turned just enough so Nell could find the bullet hole. Blood seeped again. The bandage had slipped down his side. Nell gripped the folded shirt, shook it out, leaned over the side of the boat to wash it, squeezed the water out, and refolded it. "I'm going to press on your backside again, Ace. It might hurt. Hold still if you can." The skin around the wound had swollen and turned red. She tried to think if she had anything in her pack to help. "Ace, is there a first aid kit anywhere on this boat? In your pack?"

Frankie spoke up. "I might have some bandages and that red stuff." She opened her pack and searched in it. One of the pieces of paper dropped out, and she scooped it up as fast as she could.

Nellie saw that it was paper money. She pretended not to see it. Frankie pulled out a small tin box and crawled to Nellie with it. "Look in here."

"Nellie, give Ace some of that leftover fish in my pack." Charlie pointed to his pack that still lay in the back, near Ace, tied to the pole's stand. "That should help him some."

Nell opened the tin box. She found gauze and a bottle of mercurochrome. "I'm going to put some of this stuff on the wound, Ace. It will sting but it might help. We'll need a lot more when we get to Riggins. Hang on."

A loud groan came from the boatman when Nell poured mercurochrome on the bullet hole. He glared at Nell. "Tryin' to kill me, are you?"

"Nope, trying to fix you up. Sorry it hurt so bad." Nell re-wrapped the bandage, this time with some gauze, and pressed it on the wound. "Here, press on the bandage with your hand. You are stronger than I am. You might have better luck stopping the bleeding." Nell closed the tin box after replacing the medication. She crawled back to Frankie and handed it over. She wanted to warn Frankie about the paper money but decided that was not her place. She glanced up at Charlie. He concentrated on keeping the boat in line with his sweep. She crawled to the back, found fish in the pack, and handed it to the boatman, who ate a strip of the red meat.

"These fish are dying. They're pretty beat up and mushy. Amazing how far they've come though. All the way from the ocean, you know—waterfalls, rocks, tree branches, and bears." He pointed to a bridge. "That's Lake Creek bridge. Could be more whitewater. Next stop, Riggins!"

Nell checked the bandage. The bleeding had stopped again.

Ace called to Charlie to stay to the right in the heavy water, and they made it through without dousing everyone. It was another hour or so, and then buildings on both sides of the river began to appear.

"There's the Riggins Mercantile, up there above the landing, Sheriff. You can pull in here. I'll help with the back sweep." Ace had recovered some and stood to grab the pole. Frankie and Nellie kept their eyes on the town and on the landing, wanting to arrive and not sure what it meant to be in a town again, albeit a small one.

"The post office is in the Mercantile," Ace announced. "This is a real town. Not like some of the other shanty towns in Idaho. There's even a hotel and a saloon, along with a shearing shed. A steel bridge crosses down the river." When Charlie had the scow secured, he helped Ace out of the boat. The climb up to the buildings looked too much for the wounded man.

"Ace, I'm going to find some help to get you up there and settled, maybe at that hotel. Is there any other place you want to be? Is there any law around here?" Charlie looked at Frankie and her face turned red.

Frankie ducked her head and concentrated on getting out of the scow. She helped Nell unload and they both brought their packs to the shore and away from the water. "What am I gonna do?" Nell didn't know what to say. She assumed Charlie would re-arrest Frankie, but how could he get her back to Hailey? And what about James?

A loud *"helloooo"* came from the top of the riverbank where Charlie was climbing up. Nell could hardly believe who she saw. "Rosy! What are you doing here?" She turned to Frankie. "That's Rosy Kipling, the deputy sheriff from Hailey. He must have come up from McCall to get to Riggins." Now there would be a way to get Frankie to jail. Nell felt a twist of emotions. Frankie had helped save her far up the river, and they had managed a bond of two women in trouble. "Rosy is a good friend of mine."

Nell clutched Frankie's arm. "Frankie, turn over that money. Tell Charlie and Rosy that James strung you along, and you didn't know what was happening." She surmised that was at least half-true. "You were a victim as much as Bull was. And you'll have to hand over the saddlebags, too. Say you were saving them for Bull so James wouldn't get them." Nellie was surprised at herself. This was not the right thing to do. What would Charlie think? He always chose the right way to proceed. He would not approve of Nell giving Frankie an excuse for her behavior.

Rosy came walking with sturdy steps down the slope. He wore his ever-present miner's boots, a flannel shirt, and Levi's. Sometimes he wore a patch over his blind eye, but today he did not. His eye appeared as a small cloud in his head. When he met up with Charlie, they shook hands. "You are a welcome sight, Rosy. We have a wounded man, and I need help getting him up the bank."

"Rosy! Charlie is wounded, too. Have you found a doctor here in Riggins? Ace said there wasn't any." Nell grabbed the former miner's arm and hugged it.

"I brought Janie with me. I knew Charlie had been wounded. He sure looks like he's doing okay." Rosy gave Nell a big hug. Moonshine added his voice, "*Arp, arp!*" "Now who is this young lady?"

"I'm Frances Bingham. I'm called Frankie. I was kidnapped by the outlaws back at Bull's ranch." She stuck her hand out, at the same time winking at Nell. "The sheriff there thinks I'm an outlaw, too, even though I saved Nell from a fate worse than death. I never did try to run away, unlike the kidnappers, James and Norman."

"Rosy, help me with Ace," Charlie said. "Ladies, get your packs and gear and go up to the street. We'll meet you there." He gestured up the trail. "And don't try to run away now, Frankie. We have some talking to do."

A worn trail cut into the bank, leading to the town. Nellie and Frankie, with Moonshine, managed it fine. Nell noticed Frankie was out of breath at the top. They found a bench and waited for Charlie and Rosy to arrive with the boatman. When they appeared, Nell stood and nudged the other woman. "You can give Ace a rest here until we know what to do. Rosy, where is Janie?"

"She's in the Mercantile, replenishing her supplies. I dragged her out of her cabin near the Middle Fork. We didn't have time to stock up." Rosy hitched his pants up.

"How did you get here?"

"We crossed over through Lowman and up to McCall. They're all dirt roads. Idaho has a lot of work to make it easier to go north and south in this state. My old tin barely made it." He looked around at the boat crew. "Not sure how we'll get everyone back in and home again."

Nell leaned against the back of the bench. They had been on water so long, she felt her legs might give out on dry land. "How about the hotel? Could we go there and nurse all the bullet wounds? Maybe stay over a night?" She watched Charlie to see if he objected. A long automobile drive sounded terrible. The sheriff, Rosy, Nell, Frankie, Janie, Moonshine, and Ace. They couldn't all fit.

Jane came out of the Mercantile carrying several packages all tied up with string. "Sheriff, how are your wounds? I've been worried about you."

Nell cringed. They both had said little about his wounds. She guessed it didn't matter anymore with James and the threat he posed gone. She remembered what Ace had said. James might get to Riggins, too. She looked up and down what looked like the main and only street of Riggins. A few automobiles sat in front of businesses, as did a carriage or two. She saw three horses tied up in front of a saloon. She guessed James would be there if anywhere, an anonymous miner or rancher among others.

"You could look at my leg, Janie, but we have someone with a worse wound. Ace the boatman here." He moved so Janie would see Ace on the bench. "We need to get him to a place to lie down and with some privacy." He whispered to Janie as she came close. "He was shot in his backside. Nell worked to stop the bleeding. The bullet is probably still in there. Do you have a sharp knife?"

Janie nodded and turned to the boatman. "I have a room at the hotel. Rosy slept in his automobile. Can you walk, Ace?"

Rosy helped Ace stand up. Nell stepped over to Charlie. She whispered, too, keeping an eye on Frankie, who carried her saddlebags. "Remember, James may be here. I suspect the saloon might be a good place to check. Should I do that?"

Charlie shook his head. "You would stand out like a—"

"I know. A sore thumb."

"No, a rose among thistles. There will only be men in there and maybe a saloon girl or two. I doubt if they pay any attention to Prohibition, this deep in the Idaho wilds."

Moonie sat next to Nell. She thought of him as her perpetual guard. "I can take Moonshine. He'll recognize James, I think."

"Rosy, can you and Janie take Ace? Nell and I have a chore to do. Frankie, you can go with them or come with us, but you are not staying here alone."

"I'll go with Ace." Frankie looked tired enough to drop. Her saddlebags almost dragged on the ground. "I could sleep standing up."

"Rosy, keep an eye on her," the sheriff said. "She is an accessory to a crime, and we are taking her back to Hailey."

Frankie drooped at his words. Then the four of them walked up the street with Rosy and Frankie helping Ace hobble.

Moonshine poked his nose on Nellie's leg as if to ask, are we going, too? Nell rubbed his ears. "What is our chore? Going to the saloon?"

"Yes. I thought I would go to the door and let Moonshine walk in. If he does not react, then the two of us will follow. We both look as if we lived on the river for a month. I doubt anyone would recognize us, except James. He probably looks the same, unless he arrived much sooner than we did." Charlie held out his elbow, and Nell circled her hand around it. She was savoring the reference to a rose.

A wooden walkway led past a hard goods store, an ice cream parlor, a café, and then stopped at the saloon. The door featured glass at the top, crossed boards at the bottom, as if it had once been glass as well. "You wait here. I will take Moonshine inside and see what I can see."

Nell nodded and sought out a place to sit down. The only resting place was the edge of the sidewalk. "All right. I'll perch here until you return. Don't let Moonie get hurt." Her dog looked back at her when the sheriff rubbed his shoulders and said something low to him.

The door closed behind Charlie as someone yelled, "Take that dog outta here!"

No sheriff and no dog. Nell waited to see what would happen.

And then a man came running out of the door and collided with Nell, knocking her into the street. She grabbed his arm and hung on. He tried to shake her loose. By then, Moonshine had followed the man and grabbed his pant leg, growling. The sheriff came out next, accompanied by a couple of patrons and a man in a supposedly white apron shouting, "And don't come back!"

Charlie grabbed the man's collar. "James. The third time you escaped, the third time you have been caught. Settle down, and I will release Moonshine." He fumbled with his coat and brought out handcuffs. "Let go, Nell. I will shackle him."

James hung his head. "Damned sheriff. Don't you ever give up? I told you, I didn't shoot Norman." He was as disheveled as Nell and Charlie. His hair stood up on top and hung in greasy strings around his neck. His clothes might have come from a rummage sale.

"If you did not, that will come out when we investigate. In the meantime, you are my prime suspect." Charlie pulled at James's shackled arm and marched him down the street toward the hotel. "I will see about a place to lock you up until we can get you back to Hailey and probably on to Salmon." He turned to Nell. "Come with us. We can get a room and clean up, then find food for everyone." He leaned down to Moonshine. "You did what we wanted you to do, Moonshine. Thank you." He rubbed Moonie's ears and patted his sides.

The clerk at the hotel confirmed there was no jail in Riggins. No hospital either. And no doctor. He suggested the sheriff rent a room for his prisoner or contact the forest service office. Yes, there was a telephone to use to call out. Nell arranged a room for herself and Charlie. She found out where Janie and the other members of their group were—in the dining room of the hotel. Ace had been treated by Janie and now rested in a hotel room.

"Bring James in with the others, Charlie. Then you can arrange something for him, either here or at the forest service office. I'll meet you in our room." Nell whispered the number—10—to Charlie. She did not want James finding them if he was able to escape a fourth time. The room was next to Janie, then Ace, and then Rosy. No arrangements had been made for Frankie yet. "Maybe you should take our room, and I can room with Frankie."

"No!"

The sheriff's vehemence surprised Nell, but she was glad he wanted her with him.

"We can find the same kind of lodgings for Frankie as we find for James. I will arrest both."

"Didn't you hear Frankie tell Rosy that she was a victim of all this?" Nell wanted to tell Charlie that story had come from her, but she kept silent.

"Yes. A good story. Not sure I believe it. Do you?" Charlie cocked his head and stared at Nell. "Frankie didn't shoot Ace like James did. But I think they are still planning to escape. James is guilty of assaulting our boatman. We all saw it, as did Miss Bingham."

Nell tried not to blush. She walked away and then back again to Charlie and James in the foyer. "I think I believe her. She is naïve enough to have become embroiled without knowing what was going on." She stood close to her husband. "And as you say, James shot Ace. Frankie had nothing to do with that."

Charlie rolled his eyes. "True. But she might be a smart cookie with her tale of woe."

James laughed out loud. "Frankie? She thinks she's smart. She wanted to be a gangster moll and get the gold." He lifted his shackled hands. "And she did. What do you think is in those saddlebags?"

Nellie faced James. "And where is that stash of paper money that you had when you climbed out of the river? Or did you think we didn't see what you were doing?"

James turned away from her. "Ain't none of your business."

"The others can wait a little longer, Charlie. I am going up to see about a bath and a change of clothes, if I can find anything dry in my pack." Nellie took the key from the clerk and walked over to a curved staircase. "I hope you find a good, secure place with no windows for that criminal."

Chapter 24

FRANKIE WATCHED THE CLOSED DOOR to see if anyone else would come in. The hotel room where she had been lodged by the sheriff was little more than an attic room, barely large enough to hold a narrow bed, one chair, a stand with a basin and pitcher of water. Nell, who had accompanied the sheriff, pointed out a metal pot under the bed. Frankie was sure the woman blushed, embarrassed by the lack of facilities. One window, three stories up, looked out on the river. Charlie tried the window and found it painted shut.

"This is your room for the night, Miss Bingham. Rosy will sit outside to make certain you stay in here."

"Where is James?"

"In a room like this one. Rosy will keep an eye on that one, too."

"Is he next to me?"

Charlie ignored the question. "Tomorrow, we will journey to McCall. You will not be on the river again."

Frankie sighed with relief. She sat on the bed. "How is Ace? I had nothing to do with James finding a gun at that last stop. Or him deciding to use it. Did you get the money sack?" She leaned forward to untie her shoes. "That was Bull's money. Norman found it." Frankie had given up her saddlebags to Rosy when he asked. She now regretted giving out the "victim" story that Nell had advised. She could see Nell was not going to help her. She, Frankie, was on her own again, and always.

Poor Norman. He had been sweet on her. Already she missed the idea of his being her beau. He was not as exciting as James, had always been polite and never overstepped his bounds. Still, when she saw him outside the shed at Bull's ranch, she knew he was coming for the gold and his horse, the one she had already saddled for herself. Polite, maybe, but out for himself, too. Weren't all men? At least James didn't hide it.

Once the sheriff and Nell closed and locked the door, Frankie collapsed on the bed and cried. All she could do was wish for the money and go to jail.

Someone knocked on the door and then unlocked it from the outside. Another knock, so Frankie slid off the bed and opened it. Nell and Janie stood there, Nell with a tray of food in her hands and Janie with her nurse's satchel.

"I thought you might be hungry." Nell laid the tray on the bedside table. "Janie wondered if you had any cuts or bruises from our river trip. Ace thought you might."

"Ace did?" Frankie eyed the supper tray. She thought the boatman didn't like her at all, but maybe he did. She realized her whole body ached from the river trip. She groaned. "No cuts or anything, but I sure do ache."

"I have some laudanum, Frankie. Do you want some? You'll sleep better, but you should eat first." She turned to Nellie. "I've already worked on your poor face, Miss Burns. You sure skinned it on that rock. I hope the arnica works its magic." She touched the side of Nellie's face where the lotion lay thick. "Are you stiff, too? You both spent a lot of time on the river, in and out of the water, and sleeping on the ground, too, I imagine."

"A good night's rest should help my aches and pains, Janie. Thank you." Nell backed up to the door.

Frankie eyed the door. She could try to make a run for it. She knew she could move faster than Janie, but probably not Nell. She'd already seen how strong Nell could be and how determined. The welt on Nell's face had subsided, and Frankie felt a little guilty that Nell's looks had been affected by the scrape. She wasn't as pretty.

There was a to-do down the hallway. James's voice rose and fell, boots clomped on the stairway, and then what sounded like a body falling, wood breaking, and a loud groan. Nell and Janie stepped outside the door. Nell closed and locked it. Frankie was only concerned that James didn't get free. She would get the brunt of whatever the law found as punishment if James weren't around. She banged on her door. "What is happening?"

More bangs and thuds sounded outside. After a while, a door slammed and then another and then silence. A key entered her door lock, and the sheriff opened the door. He glanced at her food and then at Frankie. Neither Nell nor Janie appeared behind him. "Are you all right, Miss Bingham?"

"What happened to James?"

"He is now tied in his room. Do you want the same treatment?"

"No, no I don't. I'll be no trouble. Thank you for the food." She tried a tremulous smile, hoping for a response from Charlie.

He moved outside the door, not turning his back. "That was Nell's idea."

"Could the nurse come back? I could use her medicine." Frankie wished she could see James. "Did James get hurt?" She wanted to throw something at the sheriff, but then she would be tied up in her room, too, she supposed. "Could I see him?"

"He has not once asked about you," the sheriff said. He looked ready to shut the door.

"He got me into this fix, but I don't want him to suffer the way Norm did." Frankie tried to look chastened. If James did manage to get free, she wanted to go with him. She knew she couldn't manage on her own. She and Nell had worked together fine, but alone? No.

The sheriff gave her a sharp look. Frankie ducked her head and hoped she looked apologetic and caring all at once.

"All right. Maybe he will calm down for you." The sheriff took her arm and walked her three doors down the narrow hall. Smells of cooking cabbage seeped up from below. The staircase was almost as steep as a ladder. He kept his hand on her arm, as if she might try to escape. She could see that would not be possible. That must be why the sheriff allowed her to visit, a warning of sorts of what would happen to her.

Frankie saw that the banister to the stairs had broken, and the rug had split on two of the stairs. James must have put up a terrific fight. When Charlie opened James's door and she looked in, she saw a bandage around his head and his right arm in a sling. He wasn't going to be much help to her. Frankie could see his legs were tied to the legs of the chair where he sat—a sturdy wood chair, probably from the dining room.

"What do you want?" James's surly voice held no appeal. Still, Frankie might need him sometime or somewhere.

"Are you all right, James? Did this sheriff hurt you?" She really didn't care but tried to make her voice sound as if she did.

"Yes. He pushed me down the stairs." He half lifted his slinged arm as much as he could with handcuffs on. "I think he broke it."

"Did the nurse look at it? She would know."

"I doubt it. She's no more a nurse than you are, you b—" James cut off his own words.

Frankie backed up. "You don't care at all about me. You dragged me into this whole fix, you criminal. I didn't know you would kill a man, steal money, and endanger all of us with your 'escapes.' And then shoot at Ace! How could you? He helped save your life!"

"I didn't kill anyone. And if I didn't, who did?" James glared at Frankie. "*You* did it, Frankie. Don't try your story on me." He turned his body on the chair, so his back faced Frankie.

Rosy Kipling climbed the stairs behind the sheriff. "I heard that, James. I saw what happened. You pushed off Charlie here and fell all on your own. You always were good for nothin'. You landed yourself in trouble. It ain't the first time."

Frankie studied Rosy. "Do you know James? How do you know him? He could be telling the truth."

"Ha! Liar is his middle name. If you ain't learned that by now, you're a slow learner." Rosy motioned to Charlie. "I need to talk to you. Some good news and some bad news."

The sheriff sighed. "All right. Let me get Miss Bingham back to her room. She and James here do not agree on much."

Back in her room—her cage, Frankie thought—she pressed her ear to the door, hoping to hear what the two men said. Rosy never used a soft voice. She heard a reference to an extra automobile and the road to McCall. A snowstorm. Boise was mentioned several times. Weather must be closing in. Soon, all was quiet. Frankie ate some of the now cold stew and drank water from the tray. She slipped off her clothes down to her underthings and climbed into the bed. It was much softer than the ground. She dreamed about James and pushing him into the water.

In the morning, Nell unlocked the door and entered with Moonshine beside her. Frankie was ready for her. "Nell, what is going to happen to me? I came and found you. I saved you." She was now dressed again and felt stronger. Outside her window, it was mostly dark, and trees swayed in the wind. A blustery morning. Frankie kept her voice low, so Nellie stepped closer to hear her.

"You are right, Frankie. If you hadn't come along the river for me, I don't know what I would have done. Maybe starved. Maybe lost my way." Nellie lowered her head. "What would you have me do?"

"Help me. I know we are heading south today. To McCall. Maybe to Boise. Don't let them put me in jail in Boise." She touched Nellie's arm. Moonshine made a small sound and Frankie stepped back. "I don't deserve that. At least take me to Hailey where I know people. I don't know anyone in McCall or Boise."

"I can try to get you to Hailey. More than that might not be possible. Get your things together. We'll have breakfast and get on the road. You, Janie, Moonie, and I are taking Rosy's automobile. Charlie, Rosy, and James will be in another auto, one from the forest service. Ace is going on down the river in his scow when he is better. He wants to sell the wood in Lewiston." Nell stepped back to the doorway. "That is the plan anyway. The weather is turning."

Frankie didn't have much to gather without her saddlebags. She felt empty. "Where is James?"

"He's already down in the hotel foyer, eating some breakfast. Rosy is standing guard."

"Did he say anything more about me?"

Nellie turned her head. "Nothing important."

"Did he accuse me again, that liar?" Frankie stomped her foot. She sat back on the bed and burst into tears. "I thought he loved me. I should never have believed him."

Chapter 25

NELL WANTED TO HELP FRANKIE. She owed her, but Frankie involved herself in nefarious doings—theft, a killed man, an injured man, an attack on Charlie, a lawman, and who knew what else. Once before, Nell had proven a woman guilty of murder. That woman had never helped Nellie at all, and indeed, made life difficult for many people. But Frankie and Nell, they had helped each other in bad circumstances. Without Frankie's help, she might not have made it back to Charlie. What could she do to help the other woman?

On the way down the stairs, Nell insisted Frankie go first. If she didn't trust Frankie behind her, then why was she struggling to decide about assisting her? Nell knew why. They had suffered along the shore, getting rocks for a fire, catching fish and a squirrel and cleaning them, shivering in rainstorms, keeping each other's spirits up. Frankie had looked for and found yarrow to rub on Nell's scraped cheek. They had even eaten rattlesnake together.

In the hotel foyer, breakfast awaited and so did the sheriff, Rosy, James, and Ace. Janie joined them, too. Moonshine circled the rug near the table and lay down. Nell found an empty dish and filled it with water for her dog.

"Well, I'm gonna miss all of you," Ace said "We had quite an adventure. I never had so many souls on board and so much hurley-burley." He faced Nell. "I'm sorry about your spill, Miss Burns. I thought the sheriff here was gonna rip my head off for not stopping to find you." He made a sound like a laugh. "It was Janie here who could see I couldn't stop the scow, even if I wanted to, and persuaded him to wait until we got to Salmon to get a horse to come get you. We both saw that your dog went with you. Charlie would find you faster on a horse."

Nellie turned to Charlie. "You never told me that." She knew her face flushed because heat crept up from her neck.

"Yeah, I ruined the rescue." James laughed out loud, curled his lip, and pointed at the sheriff. "He decided I was more important than a damsel in distress. Ha!" His shackled hands rattled when he lifted both.

"I didn't." Frankie jumped in with her comment. "I saved Nell, or maybe we saved each other. We could get along fine with the dog here. We didn't need you *men*." If she could have flounced out, Nell thought she would have.

"Who do you think tied up that horse for you?" James's face flushed red. He half-rose from his chair at the table, glanced at the sheriff, and sat back down.

"James, you shut your mouth," Janie said. "You've already caused more trouble than you're worth. You weren't on the scow to see how much trouble we all were in. Ace handled it like the professional he is, and the sheriff listened to reason." She served herself eggs and sausage. "Now, eat up everyone. We have a long day ahead of us."

Ace blushed. "Mighty kind of you, Janie."

"We river folk tell it straight," Janie said.

The rest filled their plates and ate.

Nellie followed the sheriff. In front of her, Rosy was riding shotgun for Charlie with James in back, hands shackled. She knew Rosy would grouse about the road. James might sleep in back. Janie sat beside Nell in Rosy's automobile, and Frankie perched in back to look out the front window. Moonshine sat in the front well near Janie's legs. The nurse didn't seem to mind and petted Moonie's ears from time to time. The two autos left the river and headed south on the dirt road. Nell had driven Rosy's auto all one summer going back and forth to the Stanley Basin, so she felt capable of driving on the road behind Charlie.

Soon, both autos left the canyon and climbed to a high valley. Cattle and sheep grazed in fields where crops had been harvested. Clouds darkened and lowered. The forest service automobile ahead of her moved steadily on. Nellie wished Rosy drove his own auto, and she rode with her husband. He thought James was too dangerous and with Nellie in that auto, he would try to overpower her and hold her as hostage to escape.

Nellie had tried to argue with him, reminding him she was young and strong and would have Moonshine. Rosy was getting older and weaker. With Moonshine protecting her, she thought she could handle James. Charlie said no. Nell wasn't certain she could handle Frankie. She was strong and even younger and sly as well. As she steered the auto, Nell wondered what had happened to the gun that James had used to shoot Ace. He couldn't swim with it. Maybe he had put it in the bag with the money. Where did the money go? James had plenty of time and distance to hide it. If he didn't kill Norman, he would be charged with assaulting Charlie and Ace. How many years would he get in jail?

Nell's meandering thoughts distracted her from watching Charlie's automobile. Pulling her attention back to the road, she realized snow had been falling for some time. More than an inch lined the roadside. She had lost sight of Charlie ahead of her. The falling snow came directly toward her, making it difficult not only to see the auto ahead but even the road. Rosy's auto had wipers on the windshield, but they only worked sporadically and needed help with a lever inside. "Janie, can you keep the wipers going? I'm having trouble staying on the road." Soon there was a buildup of snow and ice on the windshield. She would have to stop and clean it off. Nell had turned on the front lights early on, so Charlie could see her. When she pulled to the side of the road and braked, her auto slid sideways. "Stay here, both of you." Fortunately, Nell wore the gloves that had been in her pack and dried at the hotel in Riggins. They were mittens, though, and not handy to sweep snow off the front window. They clumped with snow and turned soggy. Nell peered ahead to see if she could see Charlie. Surely, he would realize she had stopped and either slow down or come back to see what the problem was. Maybe his back window screen was covered with snow, too, and he couldn't see her at all.

Nell did the best she could and climbed back in behind the driving wheel. Her windshield looked as if she had done nothing. The wipers now had clumps of snow in them. "Well, that was no help. I'll have to try again. Any suggestions on how to clear the snow and ice away?" Janie and Frankie both shook their heads.

"Wait," Janie said. "I have a straight razor in my bag. Maybe that would work. Or something else. I have to get into the boot." Janie opened her door and it almost slammed shut again on her. The wind had risen.

"I'll help," Nell said. "Frankie, you stay here. You don't want to be out in this storm." Frankie nodded. She had insisted on bringing a blanket from the hotel and now wrapped it around herself. Nellie thought she looked far too innocent. If Frankie tried to get away in the storm, it might be the end of her. Perhaps she would prefer that to going to jail.

Nell helped Janie with the boot. The nurse found a straight razor and a pair of scissors that might be useful. Nellie tried both on the front window. The razor didn't work at all, but the opened scissors did scrape the ice off the wipers. Janie used her leather gloves to clean the window. They both climbed back into the auto, and the wipers began to work. Frankie lay down in the back seat, huddled under the blanket. Nell reached back to touch the bundle and felt Frankie's leg. Maybe she slept. Moonshine slept in the front well.

The auto moved easily out of the slide, and Nell began the trek along the road again. Before long, she could see Charlie's auto in front of her. He had definitely slowed for her to catch up, or perhaps he had trouble seeing, too, and had to clean his windshield. She crept closer and closer. The auto was not moving. Nell pulled her auto alongside to see if Charlie needed help. What she saw frightened her. Rosy lay toppled against the far window, and James held a gun to Charlie's head. When James looked out and saw Nellie and Janie, he motioned with his gun for her to back off.

James must have ordered the sheriff out of the automobile, as the door opened and Charlie stepped out. James kept his revolver aimed at the sheriff, and they both walked back to Nellie's auto. James motioned for Nell to get out. "Janie, stay here," Nellie whispered. "Wake Moonshine up and let him out your side."

"I want Frankie. Get her out." James yelled at Nell.

The sheriff nodded his head.

"What is wrong with Rosy?" Nell wanted to delay as long as possible, so Moonshine could get around the auto.

"James shot him," Charlie said. "He needs Janie."

Nell turned back to Janie. "Go help Rosy. He's been shot."

"Don't move," James shouted. "Get Frankie out here."

"She's asleep." Nell knew that made no difference, but she tried to give Charlie a chance to stop James, if he could.

James moved the revolver to aim it at Nellie. His voice turned to a growl. "You heard me. I want Frankie!"

"Nell, get Frankie out here," Charlie ordered.

Nell reached for the back door handle and opened the door. Frankie had not moved. Nell pulled at the blanket and found only Frankie's pack spread out to look as if a woman lay under it. Frankie was gone. Nell's tripod had been her leg.

"She's not here," Nellie said. "We had to stop and clear the windshield and get into the boot. She must have snuck out the door then while Janie and I were working to get going again."

"How far back was that? And don't lie to me, or I'll shoot all of you."

Moonshine leaped on James with a loud snarl. The gun went off before he dropped it and fell to his knees. "Get him off me!"

"Hold him, Moonshine." The sheriff picked up the revolver.

Nellie kicked at James. "Good boy, Moonie." She turned to Janie. "How bad is he hurt? Do you need your satchel? I can get it. Frankie fooled us."

"He's hurt in his side," Janie said. "It bled a lot, but I have it stopped. Yes, please bring my kit. I need to bandage this wound. That man there is a wild shot. I hope you or Charlie now has the gun. Good boy, Moonshine!"

"Go ahead and get the kit, Nellie. I will keep James covered until I can get him shackled again. This time, I will lock him to the automobile itself. James managed to tangle himself up with the back window and I stopped. Rosy opened the back door. James took Rosy's gun and shot him and then aimed the gun at me. I am glad you came along when you did. I was worried the snow had detained you." He put his arm around Nellie. "Don't worry about Frankie. We'll find her. She will not get far in this storm."

Janie huddled with Nell and Charlie. "There is a doctor in McCall. We should have brought Ace, too." She lowered her voice. "How far have we come from Riggins, Sheriff? I think you should go on with James and Rosy. Nell and I can backtrack to find Frankie."

"I agree, Janie. Nell, what do you think? Want to turn around and search for Frankie? Or let her go." He released his arm and wiped some of the snow off her face. "I doubt if she can survive this storm, especially without her pack and that blanket." He thought a moment. "I think we have come thirty miles or so, maybe less, maybe more. This snow disoriented me, too. The forest service automobile has a gauge, but it is broken. The snow didn't begin until we entered this long valley."

Nell wanted more than anything to go with Charlie, but Rosy needed the doctor. "Janie is right. If we don't find Frankie in the next hour or two, then I say we head back toward McCall. Do you want to wait for us there, or do you want to go on to Boise and get that criminal locked up?" Before she turned back to her automobile, she whispered to Charlie. "Search him. If he had the revolver, he may have the money, too. Where are the saddlebags?"

"They are in your boot. I did not want them anywhere near James." Charlie pulled on his ear. "I will wait a while in McCall. If you do not come within the next hour or so, we will go on to Boise. You can find me through the sheriff's office in Ada County."

Nell knew Charlie was upset. His Basque accent slowed his speech down. Oh, oh, Nell thought. One more thing to go wrong. "If Frankie managed to get out while we worked on the windshield, she'll have the saddlebags, too." Nell hurried to the boot and opened it. She was right. Frankie, the sly one, not only escaped, she took the saddlebags with her.

Chapter 26

NELL HUGGED CHARLIE AND ROSY each goodbye. James, in back, snorted. Then she and Janie climbed back into Rosy's automobile. The snow still fell and seeing ahead remained difficult and dizzying. She tried turning off the headlights, but it was too dark to see anything. Nell turned them on again and watched the side of the road through Janie's window. That helped because she could glimpse the pile of snow there. They had a goal: Find Frankie before she died of the cold. She turned the automobile and headed north. This felt a little like getting on the scow again, a never-ending story.

When they reached where Janie and she had opened the boot and scraped the windshield and wipers, Nell stopped the auto. Enough snow had fallen that Nell could not see the exact place until she spotted the skid marks, faintly visible. "I'll see if I can find any tracks leading up the road. You stay here. I am leaving the headlights on so I can find my way back."

"Better take that blanket," Janie said. "If you do find her, she'll be darned cold. And don't go too far. We can just keep stopping and looking."

Nell extracted the blanket from the back seat. She tried opening and closing the door without making a sound. That didn't work.

She and Janie must have been noisy as they worked to clear the snow and ice or they would have heard Frankie leave. Maybe the door wasn't completely closed when they looked for Frankie later.

Walking on the road was a slippery exercise, so Nellie moved to the side where the snow was deeper. She wished she had a flashlight to shine a wider path than she could see. Janie called to her. "I have a flashlight in my satchel. Take it." Nell made her way back, picked up the light, and began her search again. She thought she could see faint foot marks, but with the wind, they could have been anything, especially an animal. She retreated to the automobile.

"Our best chance is to drive slowly and see if we see her. I can't tell if I can see footprints of anything, let alone a woman walking," Nell said, as she climbed back into the auto. "We'll go slow. We both need to stare out the front and sides." Driving in the snow reminded Nell of her first trip in snow from Ketchum to Hailey traveling with the Chinese couple who wanted her to photograph a dead body. A chill ran down her back. Stop, she thought. Look for Frankie.

Snowflakes aiming at the auto window resembled a kaleidoscope of white and made Nell sleepy. "Do you have the time?" she asked Janie. It felt like late afternoon.

"Around 11:00, I suppose. Or lunchtime. I'm hungry. We expected to be at McCall by now so we didn't pack a lunch. We should be back to Riggins soon. 'Course we've been going slow. I'm surprised we haven't seen Frankie. I bet she hid if she saw us."

Nell stopped twice more and climbed out to study the road. Neither time could she find foot tracks. The snow piled up, as much as four or five inches on the road. She was damp and cold behind the steering wheel. A deer appeared in front of the auto, as if it had been dropped from the air. Nell pushed on the brake. The tire failed to grab, and Rosy's auto spun in a circle, avoided the deer, and crashed into a large white bush. With a whoosh, the bush dumped its load of snow onto the hood covering most of the window. She leaned over the wheel and tried not to cry with frustration.

"Are you hurt?" Janie's voice sounded far away.

Nell lifted her head. "I'm not. Are you?" The dark was so complete, she thought she might be blind but she was certain she hadn't hit her head. "Janie, where are you? I can't see you."

"I'm right here, Nellie. The snow has covered the windows, and we are in the middle of a bush. We need to get out and clear the snow off." Janie's matter-of-fact voice steadied Nellie.

"Damn that Frankie. I could tie her up and leave her to freeze. The motor stopped. The headlights are either off or broken. I'm not sure I can get us going again." Nellie ranted.

"Calm down," Janie continued in her nurse's ordering tone. "First, we need to get free. Does Rosy have a shovel in the boot?"

"I don't know." Nellie sank lower in her seat.

"Can you get out?"

"I don't know."

Janie heaved a huge sigh. Nell heard her push on her door, and it opened a crack, enough to let daylight, as dark as it was, to lighten the front seat. "I can't get it open. You have to try your side or climb in back and try one of those doors." Janie reached over to Nell. "Can you do that?"

"I don't know." Rosy should have been driving his own automobile. She should be with her husband.

Janie's hand rubbed Nell's shoulder. "Straighten up, Nellie. You have been in worse situations than this. Rosy told me you were stranded in a cave in Craters of the Moon. You were in a cave-in at a mine. This is only a fall snowstorm."

Nellie knew this was all true. "All right. I'll try my door." She did and it opened nearly halfway. She squeezed out and backed up to assess the situation. It was just a bush. Except for the load of snow dumped on the front of the auto, there should be little trouble getting free. Nell climbed back in and started the motor. It rumbled without any trouble, and she backed from the bush and onto the road. "I'll have to clean off the snow from in front or we'll never be able to see."

"I'll help." Janie, able this time to open her door, jumped out and used her coat sleeve to whisk the piles of snow away. Nell worked on the windshield. The headlights still worked; they had been covered with snow. The cold air had refreshed both women, and they motored on. Moonshine had moved from front to back and fell asleep in the back seat. Oh, to be a dog, Nell thought.

Janie sat up straight, peering through the front window. "There's someone in the road and walking our way. Who in thunder?"

Nell eased the auto to a stop. Janie opened her door to the walker. "What in thunder are you doing out here in this blizzard?"

"Are you Nell Burns?" A wool scarf hid most of the man's face. He carried what looked like a make-shift walking stick. Snow covered most of his head, where a knit hat was pulled down over his ears. Janie gestured to Nell.

"I'm Nell Burns. Who are you? You'd better get inside before you freeze." The man opened the rear door and climbed in. "What are you doing out walking on a day like this?" Moonie sat up and sniffed at the man, who reached over to pet him. Satisfied, Moonie lay down again.

"I was heading for Riggins in my own auto, and this woman

stopped me. She was walking in the blizzard. She was almost dead from the cold, so I picked her up. When I finally got some sense out of her, she said a Nell Burns would come along to get her. It sounded as if you threw her out of this here automobile and left her on her own." His anger sounded through the scarf. "How could you do that?"

Nell rolled her eyes. "She escaped from this automobile. Sheriff Azgo from Blaine County and I have been taking two prisoners from Riggins to McCall and then Boise. One may have killed a man, and both stole money and gold from another and tried to kill him. The woman you picked up is Frankie Bingham and is possibly guilty of both crimes. Because she escaped, she knew we would come looking for her."

"At first, she sure didn't seem like a criminal to me. She shivered so hard when she was telling her story, I was afraid she would go into convulsions." The man lowered the scarf. He wore a neatly trimmed beard and no mustache. His pasty face resembled an underdone pancake. Nellie didn't know him, but Janie exclaimed.

"Why, you're Shep Hayward. I'm Janie the nurse from the Middle Fork. Seems to me I set a bone for you once."

"Where is she now?" Nellie asked. "You were crazy to walk along the road. We might have gone on to McCall." Nell re-settled behind the wheel. "We better catch up to your auto and Frankie. I hope you kept the key, or you might find it gone."

"That's the problem, see. I left the auto running to keep it warm. I opened my boot and gathered up a blanket and spare water to try to make the lady comfortable. I thought she had passed out. She scooted over to the driver's seat, and I'll be damned if she didn't get it going and left me to wonder what to do next. I knew there weren't many people out in weather like this. Coyotes and wolves maybe, but not more automobiles." He slumped back into the seat. "Sure glad you came along, see, just like the lady said you would. You or a Charlie."

"Not this time," Nell mumbled to herself. "Where were you going, Mr. Hayward? And where did you come from? You didn't pass us."

"We just passed your sheep operation on the river, Shep. Ace pointed it out." Janie kept herself turned toward the back.

Nellie fumbled with the gears. Her back ached from driving. She wished it had been Charlie who came back for Frankie. No, he had to deal with James. Frankie must have thought the sheriff would give up Janie for her.

"I'm supposed to catch a ride with a scow to get up to Lewiston. I need some sheep salve and other supplies for my animal operation, see. Got myself some cattle, too, and I do a little gold sluicing from time to time. Enough to pay some of the expenses, but not much more." He pulled off his hat. Nell saw he was completely bald. "I was going as fast as I could to get to Riggins. Came in from a side road that runs along the river a ways. I didn't need to pick up that lady, but I couldn't leave her there, now, could I?"

"How far down the road were you when you began walking?" Nell kept her face forward to keep going on the road.

Shep pursed his lips. "Not sure. I might have walked a mile or more. I think I walked about an hour and kept slipping. That's why I found this stick, see."

"So, Frankie could be in Riggins by now," Janie said. "I figure I know where she'll go."

"Where?" Nell had begun to worry about how to find Frankie in the town. As small as it was, that didn't mean there weren't hiding places.

"Ace," Janie said. "She'll want to get out of Riggins as soon as possible and that is one sure way, if he is able to handle the sweep by now. If we're lucky, it won't be snowing yet in Riggins." Janie peered out the front window. Even as she talked, the snow seemed to be letting up.

"Ace is the one I was supposed to get on with." Shep nodded his head. "Is he still there? I guessed he'd be gone by now."

"One of the prisoners we're taking south shot him." Nell turned back to the steering wheel, getting ready to drive again. "He is recuperating in Riggins. Janie fixed him up, so he'll be able to go, maybe once this storm stops."

"Your lucky day, Shep," Janie said. "You could probably help Ace with one of the sweeps. You may meet your lady-in-distress again."

As the auto continued north, the road sloped down. Before long, the snow turned to sleet, clumping along the windshield wipers. Nell stopped and slid out her door to clean the wipers. She looked for automobile tracks but saw none. Was Frankie that far ahead of them? Shep Hayward seemed a little sketchy to Nell. He met Frankie, no doubt. Still, Frankie had managed to fool Nell and Janie both. Fooling Shep took no stretch of imagination.

"Nell, you are going too slow," Janie said. "Do you want me to drive? I do know how, and you could use some rest is my guess."

Nell looked over at Janie. "Yes." She stopped the auto and prepared to climb out. Janie slid out her door and came around the front. She stopped by one of the headlights.

"I can see a tire track!"

When she joined Janie, Nellie could see it, too. "Those are the first we've seen. Frankie must not be too far ahead of us. And Riggins should be near. You can drive the rest of the way, Janie."

Back in the automobile, Shep was slumped in the back seat, dozing beside Moonshine. "Let's let him sleep," Janie said in a whisper.

Indeed, Janie drove much faster. Nell would have fallen asleep, too, but she worried the auto might slip and cause another spin or hit a tree. She finally relaxed just as they entered Riggins. Shep, too, had awoken and leaned over the front seat.

"There's my automobile," Shep shouted. "Right there on the side of the road by that saloon! Let me out."

Janie slowed. The man hurried out the back door, waved a hand, and slipped into his own auto. "I'll wait to see if the engine starts up. Frankie might have taken the key."

"No. He's going, Janie. Let's find Ace."

Chapter 27

FRANKIE FOUND ACE IN HIS hotel room. She knew she looked like something the cat dragged in, but then, so did Ace. "I've been through hell trying to get back to you. I want to go with you downriver, to wherever you are going." She slung her saddlebags onto the floor. Her wet and muddied Levi's and her skimpy jacket felt as if they would rip to pieces any minute. Even her sweater underneath sagged below her waist. "Are you paying to stay here? How is your behind? When do we leave?"

Ace showed his surprise by his struggle with words. "How…? Where…? Who…?" He had been slumped on his bed when Frankie opened the door and entered quickly.

"Try again," Frankie said and laughed. "I know you didn't expect me. I didn't expect to need you, either. And you need me. I can handle the sweep, front or back. You just tell me what to do. How is the river from here to Lewiston?" She walked to the single window and turned. "Is there a lot of whitewater here on out? Maybe you could teach me to be a river guide. Nellie Burns is a photographer. Janie is a nurse. There's no reason I couldn't be a river guide. I don't have to be a gangster's moll, after all." She took off her jacket and tried to straighten her sweater.

"Where is James? Is he with you?" Ace tried to sit up straight, but he was half-tangled in bedsheets. "I thought you all were on your way to the jail in Boise. That's what Janie told me."

"Well, he is. But here I am!" Frankie spread her arms out like wings. "Will you take me?" She didn't know what she was going to do if he wouldn't. After all, the River of No Return only went one way. She could hardly go back to Hailey or Twin Falls. Maybe she could take the car she stole and begin the drive north. She had no idea how bad the roads were, probably worse than the river. If she did that, she would be a real criminal—a thief.

When Ace didn't answer, she looked out the window. It felt as if it should be dinnertime or later. Outside, the car she had borrowed and left at the entrance to town came put-putting down the street. Oh, oh. Nell and Janie would be in hot pursuit. "If you'll take me, I'll stay on the scow until you're ready. Should I pick up any supplies? Food? More blankets? Gear of any kind? I'm your servant from here on out."

Ace still didn't have his power of speech back, except in important ways. "Yeah, I guess I could… Someone on the other sweep would help." He lowered his head. "I gotta plan." He scratched his head and looked helpless to Frankie. "Come back later. I… You…"

"Great. Thanks, Ace. You don't know how much this means to me. I'll stop by later." Frankie opened one saddlebag and fished out a small rock, a nugget. "Here, this is payment for taking me." Frankie rushed out the door before he could change his mind. She heard steps on the stairs, so she hid herself around a corner, hoping the steps would go up more stairs and not to Ace's room. It didn't sound like a pair, so not the women following her. That man, Shep, maybe? Relief swept through her when the footsteps continued up to the third floor of the hotel. Now, to hide herself on the scow.

Frankie had seen her chance when Nell and the nurse both worked on the windshield and wipers at the front of the auto. First, she needed to make it look as if she were still in the back seat. Not hard—clothes, the blanket, the tripod Nell had left on the floor. Then she slipped out the back door with as little noise as possible. The boot was open. There were her saddlebags. She could buy her way someplace else. She grabbed them up and tiptoed to the trees close at hand. Janie's and Nellie's voices continued on without a break, sweeping and crunching snow off the front of the auto and the windows. She wore a light jacket. She would have to hurry back to Riggins before she froze.

After a quarter-mile or so, Frankie moved back to the road. It still snowed so hard, her tracks would disappear in no time. So might she if she didn't get below the snow line in a hurry. Shivers overcame her, so she paused to think. The cold in her hands and feet overwhelmed her. She would have to go back to Nellie and hope she had not turned around and driven off to find Charlie. Too bad Charlie hadn't decided to take her to McCall along with James.

As if in answer to a prayer, not that Frankie ever prayed, two weak headlights came toward her. She managed to stand and wave her arms. It wasn't Nell, a surprise. A man climbed out and came to her. "What're you doing out here? You'll freeze yourself in this storm, see. Get in and warm up."

Frankie hurried into the auto. She shivered so hard, she could barely move.

"That woman photographer, Nell Burns, dumped me back there a ways."

"No! No one could be so cruel. The heater don't work so well, see, but it's still warmer than out there. Were you trying to get to Riggins?"

"Yes, sir, I am." Frankie's teeth rattled. "I have a… f-f-friend who will help me out. You are s-s-so… k-kind."

The man rubbed her hands until she had feeling back in them.

"Do you have a blanket? My feet are so cold."

"My gawd. Only a criminal would leave you to die in this storm. We should go back and find her."

"No, no. She'll be coming this way, I'm sure. Maybe you could walk back and stop her. Explain what a terrible thing she did. She's no animal. It was all a misunderstanding, I'm sure."

"All right. You stay here and warm up. I'll leave the motor running. Try to stop shivering."

He closed the door, went back to the driver's side and slung on a heavy jacket. "I got a flashlight in back. I'll get that. You just stay warm and cozy."

Frankie sat so she could see the man walking back up the road. As soon as he was out of sight, she slid over to the driver's seat. She had driven automobiles quite a few times. This one was different, but soon, she had the brake, gas pedal, and clutch figured out, and she drove off.

Frankie found the scow tied up to the town dock. The boat floated light in the water without all the mining gear Ace had transported to the mines along the river. She looked in the tin box with blankets and found it full. They smelled of mildew, so she pulled them out and spread them around. The sun had breached the mountainsides and brought warmth to the deep valley of the town. With the cleanest blanket, she found a rope and tied it tarp-like to one of the sweep poles and to a floorboard. When the others dried, she could pile them up for a cozy sleeping place. She needed a warm jacket, rain gear, and a sleeping bag, with nights beginning to turn cold. That storm hadn't reached Riggins yet but farther north, downriver, might be a different story.

Chapter 28

NELL WATCHED SHEP MOTOR AWAY onto Riggins's main and almost only street. "Janie, where did you leave Ace?" She reached her hand to pet Moonshine, still cozy in the well by Janie's legs. He had moved to the front again.

"At the hotel. He knew the innkeeper who gave him a room for a few days. He's probably still there. We better get rooms, too, just in case we don't find Frankie right away."

A deep sigh filled Nellie. The boat trip and now the racing back and forth on snowy roads had worn her out. She had hoped to ride with Charlie and talk with him about her feelings about when he took James and left her along the river, and about where the two of them were heading in their marriage. Now that all had to wait. Of course, she could hardly have discussed such personal subjects with James in the auto. And Rosy was hurt. Charlie would have to take care of him after he secured James in a jail cell in McCall or Boise. "We can ask after Ace there, too."

Before Nell and Janie made two reservations, the innkeeper told them Ace had a room on the second floor. They were the third people to ask about him—a woman and Shep Hayward had come calling first. The two women climbed to Ace's room, where they knocked. They had left Moonshine in the auto.

"Come in." In an aside, Nell heard Ace say, "I ain't never had so much company!"

In the room, Shep stood at the end of the bed. Ace, fully dressed, struggled to put on his boots. "Hello, Janie. Did you come to look at my backside?" His smile grew. "It's doin' pretty well, thanks to you. Maybe you could re-do the bandage. I'm heading downriver first thing in the morning. I want to get out of here before it snows." He nodded his head at Nellie.

"I'm not sure that's a wise thing to do," Janie said. "You should give your wound a little more time to heal. If Nellie and Shep will step out, I'll check your wound. Roll over and pull down your pants."

Shep roared with laughter. "Now, don't you wish some young dame would say that to you, Ace?" He giggled as he led Nellie out the door.

In the hallway, Nellie asked Shep if he intended to go downriver with Ace. "Is there anyone else going with you?"

"Yup, to both. I'm going to help with the sweep. There's another passenger but Ace didn't say who. The storm that hit us may not get this far north. Hope not. River running in a blizzard sure ain't much fun."

Janie opened the door. "The wound is healing well. With Shep's help, Ace should be able to operate the scow. If they leave in the morning, they might make it to the Snake River near Lewiston. He can see a doc there."

"Shep said there's another passenger." Nell raised her eyebrows at Janie.

"Oh," Shep said and talked to them both. "You know I found my automobile as we came into Riggins. That woman who 'borrowed' it is still around, according to Ace. He didn't know where she was, see."

"Why do you want Frankie?" Ace asked.

"She was on her way to be charged with assault and thievery. She stole from Bull Brady on the Salmon River upstream. Do you know Bull? He suffered injuries as well. I'm sure you don't want her to go free." Nell placed her hand on Ace's shoulder. "Why don't you wait another day or two to make sure you are up to the trip? Who else is going with you?"

Ace squeezed his face. "I hate to wait much longer. I got a contract to take a load of mineral with me and another contract to sell my scow for wood in Lewiston. I can't keep piling up charges at this here hotel." He patted Nell's hand. "Don't you worry about me, Miss Nellie."

"Let's get rooms for one night, Janie," Nell said. "We can see you men off in the morning. Maybe I can even take a photograph of you, primed for battling the river again."

She herded Janie out of the room and shut the door behind her.

"I got news for you," Janie whispered. "When Ace took his pants down, a rock fell out of his pocket. I'm betting that's a nugget, and Frankie was here and bought her way onto the scow. If we don't find her today, we can catch up at the dock in the morning."

Janie and Nell, this time with Moonshine at their side, stopped at the mercantile and asked about Frankie. A clerk told them a woman had bought heavy clothes and paid with gold. No, he said, he didn't know where she was staying or going. Pretty lady, though. In answer to a question about a telephone, the clerk told them the hotel had one they could use if they were staying there. The only other place was the saloon up the road.

"Let's go to the saloon. I'll go in. Who do you want to telephone?" Janie asked.

"I thought I'd try to see if there is a sheriff's department in

McCall. I want to tell Charlie what we're doing." Really, she just wanted to hear his voice.

"There aren't many places to look for Frankie around here. Let's find some food and decide what to do next."

Further searching found nothing. Nell retrieved her camera from the auto boot and set up to take a few photographs of Riggins's main street, as well as the front of the saloon. Janie went in and tried with a telephone operator to look for a police or sheriff's department in McCall. They couldn't find one. There was a doctor's office, so Janie tried that. The receptionist said a Rosy Kipling had visited but was no longer there. Janie told Nell that when she identified herself as a nurse who had treated Rosy, the person on the telephone was a little more forthcoming. The doctor had bandaged Mr. Kipling, and he was to come back the next day. No, he was alone.

"That makes sense. Charlie couldn't leave James in the auto alone. So, either he found a jail to put James in, or Charlie left to go to Boise." Nellie knew she sounded discouraged. "How far is it from McCall to Boise? Do you know?" She glanced around for a place to sit down. Weariness swept over her from the events of the day.

"Maybe a three- to four-hour stint in an automobile, longer if it's still snowing." She placed her arm around Nellie's waist. "Now, don't you worry, Charlie will be back here tomorrow, I bet. He's gotta bring the forest service automobile back to the ranger."

Nell took Janie's arm. "Let's find a place to get something to eat. Maybe back at the hotel." A carriage headed past them and turned to go over the bridge. Dust stirred by the wheels caused Nell to lower her head. "And then the four of us can take Rosy's auto to get to Boise, assuming we find Frankie."

"You don't look so happy about that." Janie hugged Nell.

"No. That's all right, as long as he gets here." Even the thought of Charlie coming back from Boise raised Nell's spirits.

Nellie crawled into bed as soon as she could after a brief dinner at a café and a walk with Moonie. He circled the rug beside her and curled into sleep, too. As much as she liked Janie's company, she was happy to have her own room. She told the clerk that her husband might come along and to give him a key. Before going into her own room, she had looked into Ace's. He wasn't there, but his things were, so he hadn't left already. Just in case, Nell sneaked her dog upstairs.

She was so tired it took a while to fall asleep. The next thing she knew, a key scratched in the lock. Moonshine roused and made his funny sound: "*Arp, arp.*" Nell awoke, too. "Charlie?" He answered, "I am here." Before long, he slipped into bed beside her. For a moment, she thought she was at Last Chance Ranch.

"Go back to sleep."

Nellie rolled into her husband. "You're here." She held back tears and wrapped her arm across his bare chest. He spooned around her.

* * * * *

As soon as the room's window held even a sliver of light, Nell sidled out of bed, dressed, kissed Charlie's forehead, and left the room. He was so tired, he didn't stir. Moonie padded out with her before she could stop him. She was not going to miss Frankie. She took her camera pack so she could pretend she wanted the photograph of the scow.

Scooting down the stairs of the bank to the dock in the dark required careful attention. She found the scow where Ace had left it. Boot steps and people getting on and off a boat from the dock led her to it. Shep and Frankie loaded crates onto the middle of the craft. The seat at the back sweep that Frankie and Nellie had fashioned for Ace still held. Ace directed the other two people from there. All of them talked in whispers.

"Good morning," Nell said in a normal tone.

Everyone looked up. "Out a little early, ain't you, Miss Burns?"

"Yes, I wanted to meet up with Frankie, although she has been determined not to meet up with me." Moonshine stood beside Nellie. "We need to talk."

"Come aboard," Ace said. "You can talk with her here."

"She might not want you and Shep to hear our conversation." She directed her stare to Frankie. "Come on, Moonshine. Let's climb aboard. You remember how, I'm sure."

Once on the scow, Nell and Moonshine settled down near the front sweep to stay out of the way of the crates. "All right, Frankie. I want you to come with me. Charlie is here and we'll finish the trip to McCall. Janie, too." Nell gave a brief thought to four of them in the auto.

The other woman sat on the floorboards. She lowered her head. When she raised it, tears streaked her cheeks. "Please just let me go, Nell. I didn't hurt anyone. I can give the saddlebags back, although I've spent a few nuggets. I made a godawful mistake going with James. Norman, too. I didn't know they were real criminals." Frankie lifted the saddlebags as if to give them to Nellie. "I just need a little money or gold to get by until I can find work." She glanced back at Ace. "I told Ace I wanted to learn to be a river guide. He said maybe he would teach me, but it would have to wait for spring until he could get another boat lined up near Stanley."

Nellie remained silent. Frankie's request appealed to her. Without Frankie, she might not have survived. But what would Charlie say? He was so bound to the letter of the law. Nell was relieved not to be a real deputy, just a helper.

"We're ready to go, Miss Burns. You gotta leave the scow." Ace stood above the two women. "You and your nice dog." He leaned over to pet Moonshine.

Nell studied Frankie. She couldn't leave Charlie just as he returned, could she? Frankie had moved away from Nell along the bench. Nell wasn't certain she could get the other woman to go with her. She wasn't certain, either, that it was best anyway. She turned her head to glance at the road going north out of town. Maybe she could go with the boat and return before Charlie was even up and about.

"Go," Nell said. One way or another, she could get back to Charlie. "Moonshine and I will accompany you for a while."

"There ain't no good landing place north of here. How will you get back to Riggins?"

"I don't know. I just know I am not getting off here." Nell still carried her camera pack. She fastened it to the bench where it had been earlier during their river trip. "Wouldn't you like a photo or two?"

"I sure would," Shep called. "Ridin' in a scow is a dangerous trip. I want to prove I did it."

Moonshine roamed the boat and settled near the rear sweep where he had once rested next to the sheriff. He seemed ready to further the river trip. Nell watched him. "I'll come. Push off." It struck her that in a way, she was now abandoning Charlie. If she could only leave a note or message, but all the people up this early were on the scow. She noticed her life preserver corks still attached to the bench. That decided her. Abandon away.

"Nell, don't leave Charlie. You'll never find another man as good as he is and as strong and smart." Frankie stood. "You are lucky. Don't dash the luck."

"I am not leaving him. I'm just taking a short trip away from him for the time being. He'll understand." Nell doubted he would. Rosy would, but he wasn't there to defend her.

The river at Riggins ran wide and flat. Circular shapes reflected the movement of water under the surface. No whitewater appeared at all near the dock. Shep jumped off and unloosed the rope. He gave a huge push and jumped on again, almost straddling the boat's edge. "Whew! Made it."

"Frankie, you must tell me exactly what happened at Bull's ranch before I even consider letting you go. If you were involved in any of the shootings, you have to go with me back to Riggins and McCall, or even Boise. The law can decide if you should go free."

"All right, Nellie. I'll try. It will take a while, so you better sit down again. It's a long story." Frankie scooted closer to Nell and dropped to her knees on the floor of the boat. Nell joined her. Both women sat near the bench where they had ridden the boat most of the way.

"James said I could earn a bunch of money if I would help him with a cattle deal he said would happen at Salmon. I'd never been to Salmon and said I'd go along. We found a riverboat at Stanley and paid the boatman to take us to Bull's ranch. James said he had a partner waiting for him there. Bull and he had been friends for years. It turned out the boatman disappeared, so James borrowed a small scow, much smaller than this one, and we towed it to a place below that silly dam." Frankie gestured all around the scow. "Maybe half the size. When we neared Bull's place, James lost control, wanted me to jump onshore—maybe ten feet away—and I just couldn't. He finally tipped me off and I went straight to the bottom. I nearly died of drowning. James pulled me out and shoved me to shore. From then on, I didn't trust him at all."

"Was Norman the other person?" Nell moved her legs to a more comfortable position.

"Yup. Left me in a touchy situation as I'd been stepping out with Norman, too. He took me to nice places." Frankie looked as if she were seeing the nice places in her mind. Maybe she was regretting what happened to Norman.

"Go on."

"Norman didn't expect me to arrive on that scow. By the way, the scow broke up and floated down the river. I'm surprised we didn't see it on our way to Challis or Salmon." Frankie leaned her head on her left hand. "Anyway, from the house, we saw this big scow pull into the landing. James sent me to the shed where horses were kept. Did I mention that Bull had not greeted us? I saw the horses and recognized Norman's. I figured I could leave those two ne'er-do-wells right then and there, so I saddled Norm's horse.

"I heard a couple gunshots outside. Just then, Bull came from one of the stalls. He'd been hit on the head so hard, blood spilled down to his shoulders. He carried a gun and was fighting mad. He headed right for the window on the shed. No glass in it. He stuck the gun out the window sill. Norman trotted toward our shed. Bull yelled, 'That man stole my gold, and now he aims to get me.'" Frankie waved her arms around, maybe to demonstrate her next description.

"I couldn't let Bull kill Norman, so I grabbed his gun and we fought over it. I tried to jerk it away. Bull tried to shake me loose. In that scramble, the gun went off. I looked out the window and there was Norm, lying on the ground. He tried to get up. James ran to help him, I think. Anyway, James ran to him.

"A big man jumped off the arriving scow with his revolver drawn." Frankie leaned closer to Nellie. "Sounds like a Western movie, don't it?"

Nellie nodded. She looked back and saw that the town of Riggins had disappeared around a river bend. Too late to change her mind.

"Norman still lived. He crawled toward the house, and James helped him. I figured James could take care of him, one way or another. I wanted out of there. I didn't have many things, but I had brought my small pack with me. Just before I mounted the horse, I looked around for the gold." Frankie rose to her knees, as if she were going to mount a horse and leave the boat. "Bull had just keeled over. I covered him with some hay. I heard a couple more gunshots as I rode the horse away towards Challis." Frankie's shoulders slumped.

Nellie wondered how much Frankie had made up and how much was the truth.

"And that's the truth, Nell Burns. Too bad you can't take a picture of what I just described. I bet you could sell that to one of those fancy Eastern newspapers!" Frankie sat down again and wrung her hands. "Then I met up with you and your sheriff not long after in Challis. You know the rest of the story. I was just the victim here. Please, let me go."

"What about James? How did he get away?"

"He and Norm had a dory boat in the shed. They carried it to the shore when James and I arrived. All three of us were supposed to ride in it. I wasn't going to go with them in that dinky boat. That's why I took off on Norm's horse. I thought James was looking after Norman, so I didn't worry much about him. Bull's gun was a shotgun. I don't even know if it actually hit Norm or not, but he did go down."

Charlie had arrested James when Charlie was on the way to find her and left to take him to Salmon. Clearly, Charlie wanted the criminals, or he would have let James go. He thought James was a murderer, and maybe he was. Charlie had kept a close watch on Frankie all the way to Riggins. He wanted her, too.

Nellie interrupted. "Who shot the sheriff? He had two wounds. Was it Norman or James?"

Frankie frowned. "I don't know." She lifted her hands toward Nell. "I didn't know the sheriff was wounded until I helped Janie on the boat. I heard gunshots as I was hurrying away on Norman's horse. There were a couple shots earlier, too. It could have been either Norman or James. I'm sure it wasn't Bull or me." She shook her head.

Nell didn't want to talk about the wounds. It would not help to have Frankie speculate about which gun shot Charlie. Nell couldn't remember if Charlie had located the bullets. That would tell them something, she assumed. Both wounds had gone clean through him. The wounds on Norman would tell them something, too.

Moonshine scrambled to Nellie as the boat bounced through white water. Nell held onto him and the rope holding the bench and camera pack. What in the world was she doing here? She was not a deputy.

As soon as the water calmed down again, Nellie crawled back to Ace. "You are right. I want off." They had already passed farmhouses and mining sheds as they swept north. "Surely we can stop along here somewhere, and I can walk back to Riggins with Moonshine." She added: "And Frankie."

"There's a little town at Slate Creek. At least there's a post office. I can pull in there." Ace scratched his head. "Let her go, Miss Burns... uh, Nell. You take the saddlebags. I'll see that she gets along all right." He handled the sweep and watched Shep for a minute or two. "If she owes money, I can help with that, too." Ace blushed and turned his gaze back to Nellie. "I'd take your dog, too, but I don't suppose you'd let go of him. Whatever the circumstances." He grinned at her and patted her shoulder. "You're a good trooper."

"All right, Ace. I can wait for Slate Creek. I'll think about the other. And no, you can't have Moonshine." She smiled back and touched his arm, wet from splashes from the river.

When Nellie returned to Frankie's side, she sat down. "I'm getting off at Slate Creek. I understand it is a while, yet." She studied her camera pack. "Do you want to help me get up my tripod and put my camera on it? Maybe I can take a photo or two. No harm in trying, unless we hit whitewater again." She turned and called to Ace. "When are the next rapids? I want to try and take a photograph."

"Wait until after the next series, and then it will be quiet for a while."

Soon, Frankie and Nellie unwrapped the camera and tripod. Nellie whispered to Frankie, "I thought the tripod was your leg in the backseat of the auto. You sure did fool Janie and me." Both of them giggled.

Frankie held onto the legs of the tripod while Nellie affixed the camera and covered her head with the black cloth. She pointed the camera at Shep on the front sweep and focused. The scow moved up and down a little, so she would have to take a quick photo. She took off the cloth, pulled out the black slide, and pressed the shutter. "Done. Now let's try one out the side, then Ace."

All together Nell and Frankie took five photographs. Once the film was safely stowed in the carrier, and the camera in the pack, the two women returned to sitting on the floor of the scow. By then, it was late morning and warming up in the canyon. Rather than rock cliffs, the steep slopes were filled with evergreen trees, so crowded together, Nell thought even a deer couldn't get through. When the water passed river bars, more farms dotted the landscape. Late fall only yielded harvested fields. From time to time, though, they saw people along the way who waved. Nell and Frankie waved back. This part of the trip felt more like an excursion.

Tired from all the activity and getting up so early, Nellie wanted to nap. The water was just bumpy enough and cool enough when it splashed, she stayed awake, worrying. She sensed Frankie would come with her if she insisted. Charlie certainly wanted Frankie back to let the law decide if she was guilty of a crime—murder, most likely—or not. He had left Nellie to get James. She had left Charlie to get Frankie.

"Tell me the honest-to-god truth, Frankie. Who killed Norman? You, Bull, James?" Nell had been sitting quietly. She needed to know.

Frankie squared up her shoulders. "I told you. Either Bull or I did. It was an accident. We fought over the shotgun. James was right. He didn't do it." She turned her face away and then back. "Why don't you believe me?"

"Because James protested too much, and I think you and he cooked up this story between you." And Norman isn't around to say anything about it, Nellie thought. "James and you spent time together at that gold mine site. That was when he found the gun, he said, and then shot Ace with it. Why are you protecting him?" Nell wondered, too, why James seemed to be protecting Frankie. They had been at odds and now were not, as near as Nell could tell.

Frankie sat down with her legs crossed. Her Levi's had been torn in more than one place. She said no more.

Nellie crawled again to Ace. "Ace, Frankie says she and Bull fought over the shotgun and it went off and probably killed Norman. Would you believe that?"

Ace thought a moment. "Yes, maybe. I saw that shotgun when we loaded Bull. Only one trigger had been pulled on the double-barreled gun. I can't remember which trigger, though." He held the sweep steady in the current. "It can't go off by itself, that's for sure. Norman had shotgun pellets in his back. I saw those." He frowned at Frankie. "When you get back to Salmon, see if he has another wound in front. That will tell you something, too."

Chapter 29

ACE MANEUVERED HIS SCOW TO the shore at Slate Creek. A few men walked down from the tiny town with a post office. "All right, Miss Burns. Maybe one of these gents can give you a ride back to Riggins, although I didn't see any horseless carriages as we landed."

Nell stood at the rim of the boat. She glanced at Frankie who avoided her look and kept her chin lowered and her arms hugging herself. Moonshine sat next to Nellie, waiting for her to do something. Her camera pack shifted on her back. It was so much heavier than her Premo camera.

"Do you want to come with me, Frankie? Get this sorted out once and for all?"

Frankie shook her head. "No," she whispered. "Leave me be."

Nell's chest lifted with a huge sigh. "Frankie, I hope you learn to be a river guide. Being independent is important, so important. And stop attaching yourself to bad men. Ace might be the best choice for you, if you have a mind to be attached to someone." Nellie knew her words would probably be ignored. She gestured toward the boatman, then picked up the saddlebags, still heavy and badly scuffed.

"Ace, thank you for all you have done for Charlie and for me.

I hope we meet again, maybe in Stanley when you are lining up another scow. You make a great boatman."

Ace grinned from ear to ear, whether from Nellie's compliment or her decision to let Frankie stay on the boat. "Thank you, Miss Burns. Goodbye."

A man on shore assisted Nell off the boat with her two burdens. Moonie followed her. He stopped on shore, turned around, and barked once.

"Thank you, sir. Can you direct me to the road to Riggins?"

"Ain't much of a road, but it's up thataway." The man, dressed in rag-tag clothing, and a dusty cowboy hat, pointed to the south. "Mighty long way to Riggins. Sure you don't want to stay the night here in Slate Creek? There's a kind of rooming house up by the post office."

"Does anyone have a carriage or an automobile?" Nell had not seen any conveyance either as Ace maneuvered the scow to shore.

"Most everyone is bringing in the last of their harvests. The town is gol-darned empty."

More sky showed above them than Nellie had seen in days. Her helper looked up. "Probably a storm is coming, moving up from the south."

"I believe an automobile will be coming for me eventually, sir. Thank you for your help. Come along, Moonshine."

The man chuckled. "That your dog's name?"

"Yes, it is. He's a very good dog."

"With that name, he should be."

Nellie found the road. She wished she had a walking stick. The sun was becoming hazed over and she spotted a sun-dog. She couldn't remember what that was supposed to signal. Probably a storm or rain or snow. The day was not cold. She strode with strong steps so no one in the little town would think she had no sense. It was a dirt road, narrow and rocky. She watched her step. Did she do the right thing, letting Frankie leave with Ace? Did she do the wrong thing letting Frankie leave with Ace? In her head, she went back and forth with her own arguments and with Charlie's undoubted responses.

She didn't remember pellets in Norman's back. Charlie didn't mention any wounds in his back. Was there blood on his chest? It seemed there had been blood all round, but some of it was probably Charlie's. It could be days before Charlie would get back to Salmon, she supposed. The thought of a day or so in Boise appealed to her—being in a real city. Perhaps her friend, Sammy Ah Kee, would be there. A hotel, a fine meal, a dress and clothing shop—all those things would help her forget the trauma of the last week. Had it only been a week from Stanley to Slate Creek?

Stopping to rest on a rock, Nell shed her pack and the saddlebags. Janie would have insisted that the sheriff drive north along the river, she was certain. The scow had left in early morning. Surely, Charlie and Janie could have reached Slate Creek by now. What was keeping them?

Moonshine lazed at her side. Then he stood up and barked. Nell looked around, hoping it wasn't a coyote or bear. She did indeed need a stick or rock. Her camera would be no defense. She put her hand on Moonie's neck. Her dog was her best defense. He growled, long and low.

Before long, an automobile pulled up with Janie behind the wheel. She stepped out. "Charlie is as sick as a dog, Nellie. I will take you back with me."

"Oh no! What's wrong with him?" Nellie hurried to the

passenger door and called Moonshine to her. He jumped in first. "What else bad can happen on this trip?" She slid her pack into the back seat. "I shouldn't have left him."

"I think it was his broken heart when you did leave." Janie laughed heartily. "That and a bad meal at some roadside diner. He'll probably be fine by the time we get back to him. He said to take this forest service automobile. We can turn it in and take Rosy's automobile south. At least that road will be better than this one!"

Nell fell asleep almost as soon as she sat down. Janie patted her leg. When she woke up, Nell looked around. The forest was familiar. "Are we there yet?"

"Two shakes of a lamb's tale." Janie had it right. Three more curves and there were the buildings of Riggins. It looked like home.

"Where is Charlie?"

"He's at the hotel. I'll drop off this auto with the forest ranger and come join you. We probably don't want to start for Boise this late. You find your husband and I'll meet you both in the foyer. He should take a good walk, get a ginger ale at the saloon. I could use one, too."

Nell talked the key out of the clerk and hurried to the room on the second floor. She unlocked the door and swooped in. No Charlie. Her heart dropped. She hadn't seen Rosy's auto where she had parked it. Maybe he left without her. Ready to cry, she eased onto the bed. Then she noticed something peeking from under the pillow and lifted it. His gun in a holster was there. He had not left.

She heard a key in the door and in walked Charlie. The happy grin on his face fixed everything. He swooped her up and hugged her to him. "You're back!" He twirled her around, he in a bathrobe and she in mostly dirty clothes. He eased her onto her feet.

"You left your revolver!" Nellie said.

"I could hardly use it in the state I was in."

"And where did you get a bathrobe?" Nellie grinned. Charlie had never worn a bathrobe around her.

"Janie rousted one up for me from the clerk. Going back and forth to the bathroom half-naked didn't seem like a good idea."

"Oh, my Charlie. Are you all right now? I have so missed being with you. I am sorry I left so early, but I knew you would object to my getting on the scow again." Nellie leaned her head onto the sheriff's chest. "One night—it was last night, wasn't it?—was not enough."

Charlie sat next to her, his bare legs loosed from the bathrobe. "I could have gone with you."

"No. This I needed to do alone. You will be so upset with me, I'm afraid." Nell patted his leg.

"Why? Did you fall in the river again?"

"No. Worse. I let Frankie go." Nell hung her head. Inside, she was happy and calm about her decision. It had been the right thing to do. "You'll understand why when I tell you her story. It was the only decent thing to do."

Charlie studied Nell without saying anything. His face, earlier wreathed in smiles, grew solemn.

"I do have the saddlebags of gold. I left them with Janie." She waited. "Say something."

Charlie put his arm around Nell. "The decent thing is all I can ask of you as my non-deputy."

A knock on the door and Janie stepped in. "My, aren't you two cozy. Charlie, how do you feel? We can get started now, maybe get to McCall, or leave in the morning. I would prefer the morning. The snow might clear by then. It looks like you both would, too." She gazed at Nellie and lifted both her hands. "Now, you are in the best place."

Nellie nodded. She couldn't think of a better place to be. "Tomorrow will be just fine."

"What happened to James?" Janie asked.

"James is safe and sound in the Boise jail," Charlie said. "I telephoned to Salmon to find out what I could about Norman's wounds. He had shotgun pellets in his back and a revolver wound in his chest, close and in the front. When I confronted James with that information, he caved and admitted to shooting him so he, James, could leave alone."

"Sakes alive. What a bad man." Janie turned and headed out the door, calling back. "See you both for breakfast in the morning." Moonshine watched her go, then slipped out of the hotel room to follow her, perhaps hoping for a morsel to eat.

Nellie shut the door behind Janie and Moonie. She and Charlie looked at each other. "Let's take a nap before we find a place for dinner, if you even feel like eating." Nell wrapped her arm around Charlie's waist. She pulled the holster out from under the pillow and laid it on the floor. They would not need a gun.

Author's Note

IDAHO FLOWS WITH FRESH WATER in the best of times. The state is known for two main rivers—the Snake and the Salmon, the latter also known as The River of No Return. Smaller rivers wind through the deserts, mountains, and forests, including the Big Wood, the Lochsa and Selway, the Boise, the Imnaha, the Middle Fork, and the Coeur d'Alene. We have been lucky enough to flyfish all of them and to raft the larger ones. Their names evoke clear streams, the scent of evergreens, falls over and around rocks, and the continuous sound of rushing water.

The main Salmon and the Middle Fork of the Salmon garner magical reputations in the worlds of fishing and rafting. The Salmon is the longest free-flowing river in the country all in one state. It flows wild and free as a Wild and Scenic River designated in 1968.

My husband and I have floated the Middle Fork several times, both before and after we married, with the Sevy Brothers and Pat and Jean Ridle of the Middle Fork River Expeditions. We also rafted the Rogue River in Oregon, the Green River in Utah, and the White Salmon in Washington. I used my experiences on all of these rivers to inform Nellie's and Frankie's times on the main Salmon.

The *River of No Return*, a book by Johnny Carrey and Cort Conley, served as my guide to the main Salmon. *The Middle Fork of the Salmon River: A Comprehensive Guide – 5th Edition* by Matt Leidecker and *Guide to the Middle Fork and Main Salmon Rivers, Idaho: Boundary Creek to Carey Creek – 4th Edition* by Duwain Whitis and Barbara Vinson, both focused on the Middle fork, helped with background information on the main Salmon as well. *Idaho's Salmon River Chronicles: Reflections of a River Guide* by Gary Lane also helped with a river guide's perspective and knowledge.

Escapades and flora and fauna in these sources and our own experiences expanded my imagination in the writing of this novel. The Sunbeam Dam not far from Stanley was blown up in the 1930s, as Janie suggested it might be. The controversy continues as to whether fishermen or state authorities planted the dynamite.

Acknowledgments

RECREATION ON THE RIVERS OF Idaho bloomed since the days of the 1920s, assisted by the development of rubber rafts, outboard motors, and ease of travel from outside the state. The backcountry of the forests and mountains has been the aim of outdoor recreationists all over the state, but particularly the area of central Idaho.

I grew up in northern Idaho in the mining town of Kellogg and began visiting central Idaho in the 1950s with my parents. I began skiing in Sun Valley in the early 1960s to the present day, added river rafting in the 1970s, and learned to flyfish in the 1980s. By then, my husband and I lived part-time in the Big Wood River watershed, and we moved here permanently in 2012. Because my great-great grandparents arrived in Idaho in the 1870s, and my grandmother and mother were born in the state, I was immersed in its history from my earliest days. Their love of Idaho became my own love, and I hope it shows in my writing.

As with my past novels, I thank my writing colleagues—Belinda Anderson, Mary Murfin Bayley, Charlene Finn, and John Rember—for reading my manuscript and providing in-depth comments and critiques to improve my efforts at telling another Idaho story. As always, the Center for Regional History at the Ketchum Community Library helped with my research of the rivers, times, and people of Idaho in the 1920s. I have mentioned other sources of assistance in my Author's Note, and I thank those writers. Any errors in logistics and river and travel details are my own.

Encircle Publications provides assistance in many ways, the most important of which is publishing my Nellie Burns and Moonshine mysteries. Both Ed Vincent and Deirdre Wait support the Encircle authors and help all of us to succeed. Thank you.

My husband, Gerry Morrison, not only provides photographic expertise, he is my first reader and wields a red pen with comments and advice. His ongoing support remains vital to my writing life, and I love and appreciate him every day.

About the Author

JULIE WESTON GREW UP IN Idaho and practiced law for many years in Seattle, Washington. Her short stories and essays have been published in *IDAHO Magazine*, *The Threepenny Review*, *River Styx*, and *Rocky Mountain Game & Fish*, among other journals and magazines, and in the anthology *Our Working Lives*. Her book, *The Good Times Are All Gone Now: Life, Death and Rebirth in an Idaho Mining Town* (University of Oklahoma Press, 2009) won Honorable Mention in the 2009 Idaho Book of the Year Award. She appeared on a C-Span2/Book TV interview in December 2013. Both an essay and a short story were nominated for Pushcart Prizes. She is the author of the Nellie Burns and Moonshine Mysteries: *Moonshadows*, a Finalist in the Mary Sarton Literary Awards; *Basque Moon*, winner of the 2017 WILLA Award in Historical Fiction; *Moonscape*, Bronze winner of the INDIE Foreword Awards; *Miners' Moon*, Bronze winner in the Will Rogers Medallion Awards for Mystery; *Moon Bones,* published by Encircle Publications in October 2022, and Book 6, *Salmon Moon,* published in November 2024.

Julie and her husband, Gerry Morrison, now live in south-central Idaho where they ski, write, photograph, and enjoy the outdoors. You can learn more by visiting www.julieweston.com.

Milton Keynes UK
Ingram Content Group UK Ltd.
UKHW042042111124
451073UK00006B/100